THE SPRING BEFORE OBERGEFELL

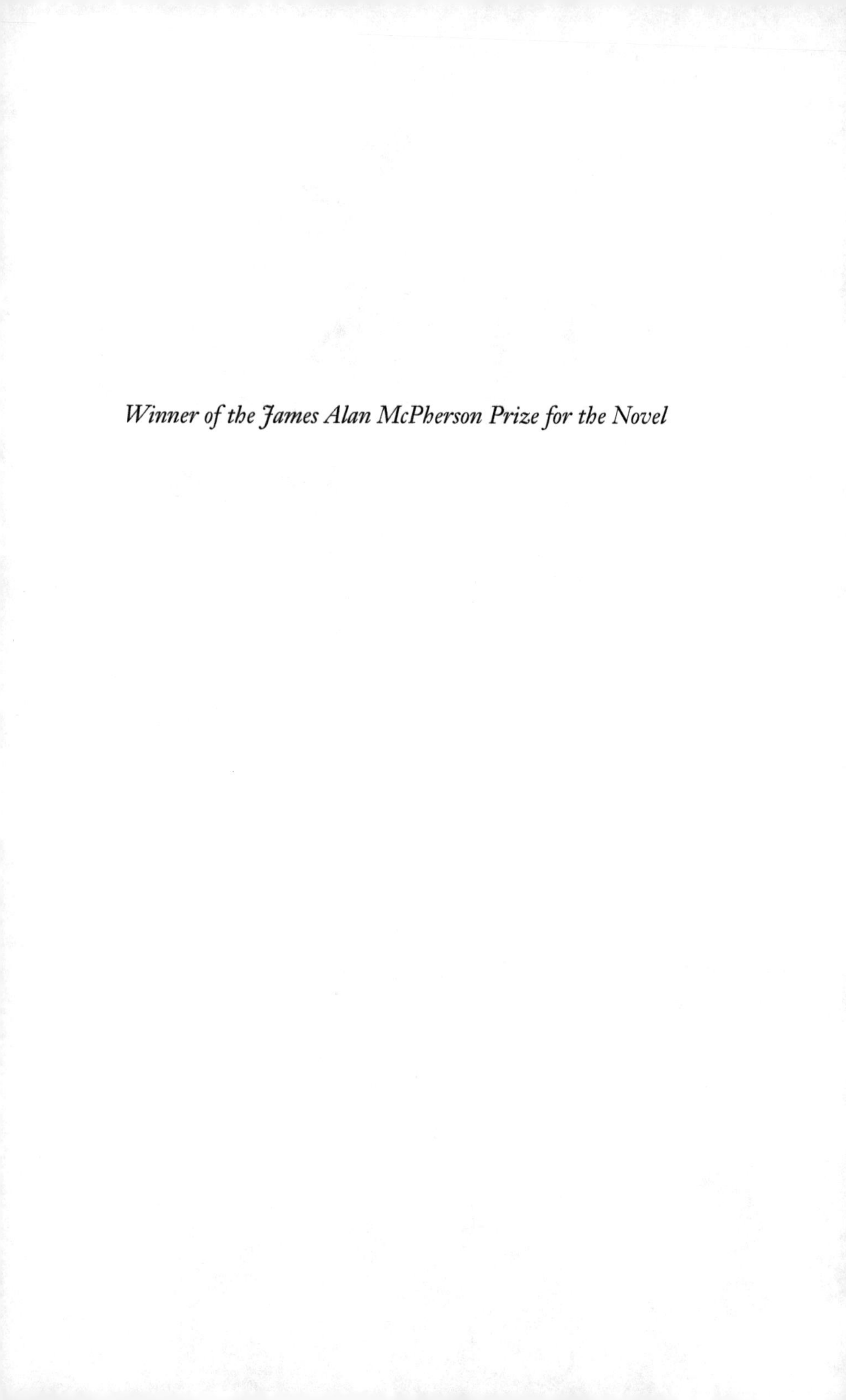

Winner of the James Alan McPherson Prize for the Novel

THE SPRING BEFORE OBERGEFELL

A Novel

Ben Grossberg

UNIVERSITY OF NEBRASKA PRESS
Lincoln

The University of Nebraska Press is part of a land-grant institution with campuses and programs on the past, present, and future homelands of the Pawnee, Ponca, Otoe-Missouria, Omaha, Dakota, Lakota, Kaw, Cheyenne, and Arapaho Peoples, as well as those of the relocated Ho-Chunk, Sac and Fox, and Iowa Peoples.

Library of Congress Control Number: 2024939691

Designed and set in Janson Text by N. Putens.

For my father, Samuel,
who put us first.

THE SPRING BEFORE OBERGEFELL

1

IF I WERE straight, or if I lived in one of a handful of cities—really, a handful of neighborhoods—it could happen at a coffee shop. Failing that, it could happen at work. It wouldn't be a "meet cute." I'm too uptight for that. But a hello, a recognition that we were connecting in a space of romantic possibility, rather than the usual space between men who don't know each other, which is more about measuring distance, maintaining boundaries.

Sometimes people just start talking to strangers. That's how it would happen. He starts talking to me. Complaining. Maybe about the weather because it's early February in the Midwest. Let's say we're in line at the post office, and he says, "Line's long but at least it's warm in here," clapping his gloved hands together, a padded envelope between them. He shows a little bit of tooth, a smile under his beard.

Then I'd have to say something, and I'd want to say something because he's got a kind, wide face. A little grizzled, wrinkled around the eyes, but bright eyes. I'd want to continue the conversation.

But I wouldn't be able to think of anything fast enough, and the moment would pass.

No, not this time. That's the second thing that's different. Not only are we free from the assumption that we're both straight, but the moment doesn't pass. He puts out his hand and says his first name: maybe it's Sandro or Chris or Jake.

I say my name, shake his hand, and ask how he's holding up with the snow. I mention that I heard on the news they're up to eight feet total accumulation this winter in CMH. (The airport code for Columbus. He'd be local; he'd recognize it.) And he says that must be why his back has been sore for the last week, shoveling that much. "That shit weighs a ton." And I say that it's my left rotator cuff, that I fucked it up with decades of bad form at the gym, and I really feel it shoveling. The line dwindles as we talk, and soon he's at the front. He nods at me, then goes up to the counter. While I'm waiting—at the head of the line now—I scribble my phone number on a Priority Mail label and step up to leave it beside him as he watches the clerk weigh his envelope. "Hey," I say as I place the square of paper, "say hello sometime."

The Castro. PTown. Parts of New York City. Neighborhoods where that kind of interaction would be possible. They are as foreign to me as if they existed in some other epoch: a Roaring Twenties, a Summer of Love. I don't live in those neighborhoods, and those neighborhoods don't live in me.

THOUGH THERE ARE gay men around here. Most are out, too; though we are scattered, living on streets we don't define. We're not invisible because we're out, but we're not quite visible either. On Thursday night, I have one of these men over. He has a partner, and he lives with the guy. He's a repeat, so he knows to knock softly, to keep his voice down. It's after 10:00, and my widowed father is in his room. My father's not asleep; at least I don't think he is. His light is on. He doesn't sleep much anymore. It's not a secret that I have guys over, and what I have them over for, but there's no reason to make the kind of commotion that would bring him out of his room for awkward introductions. Awkward and unsexy. So when I hear Josh's car roll up the gravel driveway, I crack the door and wait there for him to walk up. I've pulled on a wifebeater and jeans, a getup which I know he likes. And I like wearing it. Josh is a lawyer, thirty-four (if his profile is to be believed), with brown hair and moony eyes—though he's very much a type A personality. The kind of guy who has all the items on his desk arranged at right angles. He has soft hairless skin, which is not my first choice, but not my last, either.

I open the door wide enough for him to slip in. "Hey," I say, stepping back so he can enter.

"Hi, sexy." His voice is hushed. Josh is conscientious, polite.

"Give me your coat."

He pulls off his gloves, unzips and removes his puffy jacket. Then steps toward me and puts a hand on my chest. Usually we have a little small talk; I find it makes the sex easier. But as I lean in to kiss him hello, another car pulls into the driveway. The headlights are coming straight in the front windows because it's an SUV and the lights are higher. The blue intensity shines right into the foyer, which is really a screened porch that some previous owner converted into a room. Josh turns his head toward the window, looks out for a moment, and says "fuck." He says it twice, the second time louder. Then the SUV door opens and slams, and Josh freezes. Someone is walking toward the door, loud steps on the gravel. There's a sharp series of knocks.

"Gary," Josh says.

Gary. The guy bangs at the door. Of course he does. He can see us through the windows standing less than a foot apart.

"Do we need to call the police?"

"No, no, just let me talk to him." Josh goes to the door and opens it, blocking it with his body as he steps out, the screen door smacking against the frame behind him. In a minute, they are screaming. Then I hear my father's door open.

"What the hell is going on," my father says, tying the knot of his terrycloth robe as he comes toward me. "It's almost midnight."

My father is just a few years shy of eighty, but he gets around well. A little stooped, but plenty capable of raising a fuss. "Who's out there?" he asks. He goes over to the window and looks out. I assume he sees Josh and some guy screaming at each other.

"Don't worry about it, Dad, just go back to bed," I say, waving him off. He doesn't move from the window. I grab my coat and go outside.

GARY IS A good fifteen years older than Josh, salt-and-pepper hair, glasses, thin, and a lot taller than either of us. A good-looking guy.

"Look," I say, "you guys have got to take this home." I turn to Gary. "I don't know what's going on here. I didn't realize Josh was breaking any rules, but I have neighbors. You guys have to take this home."

This is half true. About the rules Josh might have been breaking. I didn't ask. I pointedly didn't ask.

Then Gary is moving toward me. I haven't been in a fight since middle school, when Eric Glickman told me he'd beat me up when we got off the bus at our stop and then proceeded to do just that. That fight was a pretty one-sided affair, with Eric on all fours on top of me, pinning me down, laughing in my face.

Gary throws a fist at me. It lands on my chin, sending a jolt of pain through my jaw and thudding in my skull. I reel back onto the small concrete patio outside the front door, and then he jumps forward, his body rushing against me. I am knocked against the side of the house, but I steady myself and put my hands up. Then Josh grabs Gary, pulling him back, and my father comes flying out of the house. My dad is an NRA Republican. He has a shot gun in his hand.

Gary pushes Josh away from him, and Josh falls back on his ass, right to the ground. Then Gary stalks back to his car. He shouts "Fuck you, Josh" before getting in. I glance around the street, looking for neighbors' lights that are on, or are just going on.

"Please Dad, get back in the house," I say.

"What's going on here?" he says. "What are you involved in?" Then he turns to Josh. "What's your business here?"

"Look Dad, Josh is a friend, okay. Just get back in the house."

"Oh my God," says Josh. He's still on the ground, a hand on his forehead.

"Please Dad, please, it's okay, let me talk to Josh."

My father walks down the driveway, out to the street. I go over to Josh.

"Are you okay?"

"I'll deal with this," he says. "I just need to think a minute." Josh walks over to the steps leading up to the front door and sits. My father comes back up the driveway.

"It looks like he's gone," my father says. "We're going to talk about this tomorrow." Then he heads back into the house. I consider sitting next to Josh, but I don't want him to stay any longer than he has to.

"Okay," I say to no one in particular.

"I am so sorry. Gary knows what I'm doing. He knew about this. I don't know what—"

"I have to go talk to my dad."

"We've been living together for nine years," Josh says. And now I can see that Josh is crying, so I sit down beside him on the stoop. Then the porch light goes on, which means my father is waiting for me, or worse, watching through the front windows.

"Nine years is a long time," I say.

It is a long time. I'm struck by that when I say it. It's more than four times as long as I've been with anyone, and I'm fifty.

"I fucked it up," Josh says. "Totally fucked it up."

He's really crying now.

"This happened before, you know. Once before. I told him then that it was just sex, that it didn't matter. He got it. He seemed to get it. I've never seen him do this before, get like this. Gary is a really sweet guy."

I rub a hand along my throbbing jaw.

"Gay men do this all the time," Josh says. "I just need to go over this with him again. It means nothing to me. It's just bodies. This is just bodies. That's all you and I are right now." He is pointing his finger at himself and then at me, moving back and forth between us as if we were specimens. "I'll tell him again, and it will be all right. Gary and I have been together for over a decade."

"You want a cup of coffee?" I say. I try not to sound grudging.

We're silent for a moment, and I'm suddenly aware that it's very cold.

"I'm going to go home," he says.

"Yeah," I say, putting a hand on his shoulder. "That's good. Go talk to him."

He gets up and heads toward his car. "I'll text you tomorrow."

"Just give him a few days to calm down."

"Yeah, okay. Probably a good idea."

Then Josh is in his car, and I'm back in the house. There are two wicker chairs in the foyer, and my father is seated in one of them.

He looks up at me, scowling.

"What was that about?"

"Just drama," I say, shaking my head. "It's late. I'll explain in the morning."

"What kinds of things have you been doing? Is this about drugs?"

"No, Dad, no drugs. The only drug I do is ibuprofen. I'm going to go take some of them right now and go to bed, okay? This hurts." I touch my jaw.

"Put some ice on it," he says. "Put a steak on it. We'll talk about this in the morning."

2

WE DON'T TALK about it in the morning. I'm up early to grout a tile floor, then do a half shift at Lowe's.

My father is awake when I get up, as usual. He's sitting at the kitchen table in pajamas and a bathrobe when I walk in. He's got his glasses on, but he's holding a piece of paper two inches from his nose to read it, perhaps some fine print.

"Hey, Dad, you sleep all right?" I walk over to the counter and undo the tie on a loaf of bread.

He puts down the form. "I'm going to renew your mother's driver's license," he says. "It's twenty-four dollars."

"They sent a renewal form?" I put three slices of bread in the toaster, then go to the table to look over my father's shoulder.

He has my mother's last driver's license beside him and taps his finger on it. The license is from early 2011, the final year of her life.

"She looks good in that picture," he says. "She was a little tired that day, but she was doing well. Going to rehab, walking every day. We were planning to go to Las Vegas. Well, I wanted to go. She wanted to wait until she was better. That's where she had the attack of stenosis, walking at the airport. I think she was afraid to go back."

I study the license, picking it up. She doesn't look like herself in the picture. Her face is puffy, so her eyes look small and mean. Her lips are pressed tight.

"They don't require a new picture?"

"It's one last thing I can do for her." It's a phrase he uses a lot. "Look, I have all her licenses going back forty years." He takes one of the licenses from a pile to the left of him and brings it to his face. "This is from 1988, so she would have been fifty-one. Look how young she looks there." He holds it up for me.

My folks were married fifty-eight years. People say "we were kids when we got married." My folks weren't even kids. They were whatever comes before kids. He was seventeen. She was sixteen and pregnant. It's hard to imagine what they were thinking—besides sex. They must have been thinking that. I'm not sure if it was a good marriage. In some ways, children are both too highly qualified and completely disqualified from having an opinion about their folks' marriage: ringside, but maybe too close to the action to see it clearly. In any case, my parents certainly had a *long* marriage. Maybe after a while the distinction between good and long becomes less important. Most people find their lives precious, whether it's a particularly good life or not. And their marriage had been, for both of them, essentially their whole lives.

My toast dings. I head back to the toaster without looking at the license my father is holding up. I've seen it before: my mom with a bleached perm. She does look good in that picture; you wouldn't guess she was fifty-one. I take out the toast and yank a paper towel off the roll hanging under the cabinets to serve as a plate. "You have a lot to do today, Dad?" I ask, then take a bite of toast. I eat the three pieces in quick succession as he explains the purpose of each of the six drugs he needs to pick up at the pharmacy.

I'VE GOT THREE JOBS: adjunct professor at a local college, sales associate, and handyman. And one of these, "handyman," is a catch-all, so maybe I have about twenty jobs. This employment is equally a function of what I like to do or have some aptitude for, and what I just don't seem to be able to do—which is forty hours a week of any one thing. After college, I stayed on to get a master's in English, thinking I might teach high school. The problem was that I hadn't given any thought as to what that actually entailed. Once I started looking into the requirements for certification, I realized I couldn't see myself doing it. I'm not sure if it was the set curriculum or heavy oversight, or just the thought of trying to keep hold of the attention of a room full of hormonal kids. It's important work, no question. I can imagine a bright, animated guy in khakis and a button-down spreading his arms wide for emphasis, or posing challenging and profound questions about *A Separate Peace* or *The Great Gatsby* or whatever is on the curriculum these days. I wish I was that guy. My life might be better if I were. Maybe I could have been with more discipline.

I drove a van for a while, through the second half of my twenties. I enjoyed it. But it's a different thing, doing that kind of work when you're young. Possibility is on your side. The work was no different than it would be if I did it now—but at twenty-seven, twenty-eight, twenty-nine years old, it felt like I was playing at it, like I was killing time before the great stuff of my life began. I drove for DHL for a while and then as a kind of mini-school-bus driver for a church out in Jersey, which ended when a few of the parents found out I was gay. I was also an HVAC tech for a couple of years, and I did a stint in sales with a textbook company. I have always supplemented my income with side jobs. At some point, the idea of a "main job" just fell away. I stopped thinking about what I was going to do for a living and started thinking about what work I had lined up for that day.

It helps that it's cheap to live out here. I have a house, which I got with no down payment. The place was a mess. After eleven years of living here, parts are still a mess. I haven't replaced the siding, and at some point soon the roof is going to go. But the kitchen is in pretty good shape now. I finished the bathroom last year. All the interior walls have been repainted. Also, there's room for my father.

MARIA GRECO DOESN'T like the grout. I'm kneeling on her bathroom floor, float in hand, smearing it into the space between tiles. She's standing over me, puffing on a cigarette, watching.

"I do not think this is the right color. We will see how it dries, yes? But I do not think so. It is too bright. It is *pink*. Not 'dusty rose,' no, *pink*. No one would like grout in this color. I do not know why they would even make grout in this color because no one would buy it." She holds her cigarette up to punctuate her point.

I put down the float, take the sponge from the pail, and wring it out a few times. Then I wipe it across the tile, clearing the white hexagons. What can I tell her? Hell, I can offer to dig out the grout right now. That would be a lot easier than trying to remove it tomorrow morning if she still doesn't like it then. But I've done work for Maria before. If she wants me to stop, she'll say so.

She walks out of the bathroom, over to the kitchen counter. I glance up and see her ash her cigarette in a teacup.

"I want you to talk to my brother," she says. She is eyeing me in a way that makes me conscious of my body. I swing around so I'm facing her.

"You have a brother?" I ask.

"I have a brother. His name is Matt. Matteo, but he is usually called Matt. Or Matteo. I think you will like him. He is a graphic designer."

I pick the float back up, load it with grout. It really is almost the color of bubblegum.

"I'd be glad to talk to your brother," I say.

Maria's husband comes into the kitchen. James is a large man, and he walks heavily. His footsteps rumble the floor I'm kneeling on. He's probably in his late thirties, about ten years younger than Maria. She goes over and kisses him on the lips, a quick smacking, then says good morning and turns toward the bathroom. "Pink!" she says. "Did I make the wrong choice?" He turns his head toward me, too, but she doesn't allow him a moment to answer. "I do not know, but in the store they had these models, like plastic toys for children, little plastic lines. Almost like the snapping toys—we used to call them Minitalia. Legos. Almost like Legos, and the dusty-rose Lego did not look like that."

James raises one hand in greeting when he catches my eye, then he looks back toward Maria.

"It will be all right, maybe?" she says. "We will see tomorrow morning."

He goes to the counter and begins shuffling around with a coffee pot. I go back to grouting.

"Yes, I want you to talk to my brother, and if you are okay with it, I will give him your number," Maria says.

"Is he looking for a guy to do some work?" I am using my fingers now, pushing grout into the tile right by the tub, along the side where the float won't reach. Then I look for other places that seem insufficiently filled, all along the whole floor.

Maria doesn't answer. I don't look up again until I'm finished with my fingers and need to prepare a towel to remove as much of the pink haze from the tile surface as possible. When I do look for her, Maria is gone. James is at the table drinking coffee, gazing into his laptop.

"Where's Maria?"

He doesn't look over. "She went to work. She left you a check."

MY FATHER AND I don't usually eat together. When we do, it's an accident of timing. But it works out that night. Maybe he waited to eat until I came back. Sometimes he cooks, making the things my mother used to make for him when she was alive. He never cooked before she died, but now he tries to recreate those simple dishes. Today it's fried chicken breasts bright with paprika, and mac and cheese. Also a salad, a concession to his bowels.

"What kind of business was that last night," he says as soon as I step in the kitchen.

I scoop mac and cheese onto my plate and sit across from him. *Business*. Is he still thinking drug deal or does he mean "monkey business"?

"A friend of mine was having a fight with his boyfriend." That's the plan for this conversation: *their* fight. Me only tangentially involved. Conveniently, my plan is also the truth.

"You're sleeping with your friend, what's his name, Josh?"

"Yeah," I say.

He's silent for a minute. I don't stop eating.

"It's not smart, you know, these things you're doing."

"Boundaries, Dad."

He and I have talked about boundaries before. Him living here is a little precarious. But there aren't a lot of options for either of us. He gets around too well to go into a facility, and he'd be miserable there. He's actually kind of miserable here, but he'd be infinitely more miserable there. I'd be miserable, too—with guilt. I can't imagine him in a place like that, in some dayroom with linoleum tile and fluorescent lighting squares on the ceiling, surrounded by people who are sicker, less clear in their thinking than he is, drawing him downward. My father also gives me a couple of hundred dollars a month to help with bills. Money I need.

There's another silence. Then he puts down his fork. "People get killed for doing what you're doing, running around with other people's—with the people they are involved with."

"I'm not running around, Dad. It's not like that for gay men. It's usually okay. Josh's partner was just having some problems."

"Yeah, someone is sleeping with his guy. That's a problem."

I don't say anything.

"You don't treat people very well, Mike," he says. "You never have." Then he starts eating again. I know I shouldn't respond, I know I'm going to regret it, but now I can't help myself. It's too hard to take this from a man whose only mode of conversation for the first twenty years of my life was shouting, who could unleash a seemingly unending chain of profanity over the smallest offense. My father was the kind of guy who would roll down his window to tell another driver to fuck off. It still makes my shoulders tense when I think about it. His epithet of choice was "cocksucker," and him shouting that word out a car window. That word was always the finishing touch.

I try to calm myself. I take a breath. Then I make the damn mistake, anyway.

"Who don't I treat very well, Dad?" I ask, jaw set.

"That guy from England. You know I went and talked to him before he went back, to apologize for how you behaved. He traveled across the Atlantic, and you ignored him. He was sitting out on the patio alone, so I went out there and sat with him. He was a nice guy, and he liked you. You could be with him now."

"I was twenty-three." I'm stunned. Has my father really been thinking about this for the last twenty-seven years?

"Why did you treat him like that?"

I had met this guy on junior-year abroad. I was fresh out of the closet. He and I spent a few months together; we bought each other rings. But then I just lost interest. I guess I didn't treat him very well. I was a kid. It's ancient history.

"I don't know, Dad," I say. "But probably you and I have both been guilty of some bad behavior over the years that isn't worth bringing up right now." There is an edge to my voice, an unkindness, and I hope he hears it.

Again, he's silent for a moment, and I think he has let the subject drop.

"I don't understand how you live your life," he finally says, his tone softer. "You have part-time jobs, you can barely afford to keep this place up—" He gestures to the far wall of the kitchen, where the studs are exposed. I took off the knotty pine paneling there a month back, thinking I'd roll in some insulation. It doesn't look great.

"It's just the one wall," I say, letting the anger drain out of me.

"I don't know, Mike." He's shaking his head. "Why are you running around? Do you like this guy Josh?"

Is it possible to explain this? He has no context for it.

"It's not running around. It's just a little . . . company. Josh and I just keep each other company now and then."

My father looks disgusted.

"In this house?" he says.

"Yeah, Dad, in my house."

"I met your mother when I was seventeen. She was my first, and I was faithful to her for fifty-eight years. I am still faithful to her. I've only been with one woman, and that was your mother. I will die faithful to her."

Safer territory. "I know."

"I still can't believe she's gone. She's not gone to me."

"She's not gone to me, either," I say. And this is true, though not in the same way. My mother is buried four hours from here, near the town where they had a house for over thirty years, and my father still makes the drive out there once every few months, more than three years after her death. *I'm going to see your mother*, he says, or *I'm going to visit your mother*. But I know he has corresponded with women on the computer in the years since her passing, that he has thought about dating—though so far as I know he has never met anyone in person. A little company would do him good, too.

"She was my life, Mike," he says. "But she's gone now, that's just the reality, and I have to face it."

If the conversation continues down this road, it's going to be a grim night. But as it turns out, it doesn't. My father doesn't say anything after that, and I don't either. After dinner, he heads to his room to watch television or sit at his computer. I hear the television through the walls, as I do just about every night.

I suppose I do more or less the same thing. I waste a lot of time on social media, though sometimes I still have the wherewithal to read—some fiction, some nonfiction, history or politics. I'm reading Hersey's *Hiroshima* tonight, which is a brutal account of the days immediately following the dropping of the bomb as related in six real-life accounts.

I'm lying on my bed reading about a missionary's experiences when Josh texts. It's after ten. On most nights, I'd have gotten myself washed up for bed by now, but the book is compelling. He and Gary are working it out, Josh says. Gary is deeply sorry and ashamed. He wants to meet to apologize.

I put down my book. A meeting like that sounds fantastically awkward, and it's not clear to me how it would benefit anyone involved. Also, I don't need an apology. Gary got pissed off. We all get pissed off.

No need, I text back. And return to my book.

A minute later, another text. *He really wants to*, Josh says. *And I want him to. He hit you. It's important.*

As if I didn't know he hit me.

Okay, I text back. And nothing else, indicating, I hope, that this seems like a pain.

Josh's reply comes instantly: *When can we come by?*

They are not coming back here. I'm thinking about how to reply when my phone vibrates again. Josh is relentless. He's like this when he wants to hook up, too. He will text again and again until I agree to a time—always a few days in advance. When he texts, it can feel like a chore, but I'm usually glad once he's here. Josh is a known quantity, so there's no stress or risk. And the contact is good.

I turn the phone over and see a number I don't recognize.

The text reads: *Hello, Mike. I'm Matt. My sister Maria gave me your number.*

It takes me a minute to recall who Matt is, and while I'm thinking about how to reply, a Scruff notification comes up. Some guy whose chat name is just an asterisk has messaged me. In the thumbnail picture, he looks like he might be someone I'd like to play around with. I open Scruff and say hello to this guy, which quickly becomes exchanging compliments and then more pictures. I simultaneously get drawn into two other conversations. The closest of these men is 541 miles away, in Philadelphia, the city of brotherly love. People I Will Never Meet. That's the genus. The species varies. After another half hour on Scruff, I begin to feel like I'm wasting my night and go back to reading *Hiroshima*. I don't reply to either Josh or Matt, and—like most nights—am asleep by 11:00.

3

ON WEDNESDAY, a couple of days later, my phone buzzes at exactly 7:00 a.m. Maria Greco's name flashes on the screen.

Grout.

I'm at the kitchen table eating cold sweet potatoes from the night before. I've mashed them up with a scoop of protein powder, and it's making for a surprisingly good breakfast. My father is eating shredded wheat. He eats quickly, almost violently, splashing milk on the table when he brings his spoon down to the bowl. He doesn't look up when the phone goes off.

"Maria," I say, picking up. "How's the floor? Have you bought sealer yet?"

"Hello, Mike," she says. "How are you, Mike? How is your father?"

I assure her that all is well and then return to the subject of the floor. It's way too early for chitchat.

"The floor is beautiful, Mike. You did a beautiful job—as always. You always do a beautiful job."

"And the grout—"

"I love the grout. It is dusty rose, just as the label promised. Well, it's still a little pink—but eh, pink is okay. A little pink a person can learn to live with. Maybe." I start to say "good," but Maria continues. "So I'm calling to talk to you about my brother, Matteo. You said I could give you his number, but you didn't text him back. He told me he has not heard from you. You were just being polite about the number?"

"No, Maria, no. I will text him back today; it's just been a busy week." Actually, it hasn't been especially busy. I'd just forgotten about Matt.

"Good. Then you will text him today? You need to have a drink with him. This is important: you need to meet in person and you need to have wine."

Then I understand. Probably I ought to have realized this earlier, but it's never happened to me before—someone trying to fix me up, much less with their brother. But I'm game. Why not? What else do I have to do most nights? I wonder if it would be rude to ask if she could send me a picture of him. It's been years, maybe a decade, since I've been on a date with a guy I haven't seen a picture of beforehand—usually naked, or mostly naked for the modest guys. Suddenly there's novelty in the prospect.

"I will text him today, Maria. I'll begin with an apology for not getting back to him sooner."

"Good, good," she says. "As you should. I will let him know. And Mike, Mike, I will be calling after you meet, to find out the details." Maria's voice gets a little low and sultry, and it sounds like she's joking, but I think she fully intends to call.

"Okay," I say. Then I remind her to buy grout sealer.

A FEW HOURS LATER, I'm grading comp essays arguing for and against language censorship. The arguments are bland, but it doesn't matter. I'm reading to see if the students have learned to write a paragraph, to make *any* argument. So I'm glad to take a break when the phone vibrates. CVS. Prescription filled. I'm on PrEP and a statin. While I've got the phone out, I decide to text Matt. A short apology for the delay and a quip about Maria insisting that we meet over wine. I put the phone down, and it starts buzzing immediately. I pick it up, and it's a text from Josh. Shit. I ought to have texted him days ago, too. I started to at one point but stopped because I really don't want to meet up with him and Gary.

So you're just not going to respond?

I text back right away. *Sorry. It's been a tough week.*

Gary wants to apologize. It would be good for him to meet you.

Before I can reply, Josh texts again. *Have a drink with us.*

I pause. The invitation is starting to feel loaded. Maybe too loaded. Getting mixed up with a married couple has drama written all over it. But despite myself, I'm interested; I feel it in my gut and groin. I'm not generally adventurous, but Josh is a known quantity, which makes the prospect feel a little safer. I hedge my bets. I say I'll meet them at the Starbucks in town. We agree for Saturday afternoon.

I FINISH GRADING, get dressed, and check in with my father. He's heading to the gym, a whole-day activity for him. It's a "Silver Sneakers" center. As near as I can tell, he walks on a treadmill, does a few stretches, and then spends hours in the coffee shop in the lobby. He's got acquaintances who gather there. Then I teach my classes, handing back papers, going over them, and setting the students up to write another draft. Pretty much an average day.

But on the way home, coming out of the Kroger—I stopped for a few essentials—I immediately notice something strange. A guy by my car in the parking lot. I see him as I'm heading over with my cart, and I tense up right away. He's much too close to my Celica. Kneeling by the passenger door, studying it. I walk faster.

"Hey," I say loudly, a little too far away to be natural. I breathe in, get closer, then say it again.

He stands when I approach. He's a few inches taller than I am. Mostly bald. What little brown hair he has is shaved to stubble. Square jaw, big nose. Thick mustache. Eyes pale blue. Blue-collar sexy. I feel a catch in my gut and turn it right off. I now see what he was looking at. There's a dent in the passenger-side door. It wasn't there before.

"What happened here?" I say. I sound like a cop.

"Shit," he says. "I knocked your car. With a cart. I hit the cart and the cart hit you." He bends down, puts his hand on the car and then runs his thumb back and forth over the damage.

I exhale, looking down. He has nice shoulders. Square, broad. Then I look at the car. The metal is slightly pressed in, the area scuffed. A puzzle piece of black paint has flaked off.

"You have insurance?"

"For this?"

"This needs to get fixed."

He straightens and looks over the car, trunk to hood. "Man, it's not like it's a new car." He winces as he says it, as if trying to soften the comment. "I can give you a hundred bucks."

I don't want a hundred bucks. I want my Celica without a dent in it. He's right; it is an old car. A '96. But it's beautiful. I got it ten years ago with really low miles. It's one of the few nice things I own.

"A hundred bucks won't cover this," I say. "I want to get my car fixed."

He puts his right hand on his forehead, then bends down again.

"Look," he says. "My brother has a body shop. He'll take care of this."

He looks right at me, serious, even a little plaintive, and I glance briefly at his face, his lips, the way his mustache curls over top of them. I turn my head aside to think.

Brother has a body shop. It sounds shifty.

"Let's just trade insurance," I say.

He pauses. "I don't have insurance right now. It just lapsed. I've been meaning to get to it."

I look at this guy again. Jeans, sweater, gray wool jacket unzipped. The sweater looks worn out, the jacket frayed at the cuffs. Lines on his face, too, now that I look close, around his eyes. I don't need this guy's money.

"Don't worry about it," I say. "It's not a big deal. Like you said, it's an old car."

I go around to the hatchback and start loading my groceries. There's no point in drawing this out.

"No, really, my brother can fix this, no problem. I can make it so that he doesn't charge either of us."

"Don't worry about it, things happen," I say.

"Hey, you have a pen?" He's fumbling around in his pockets, then he pulls out a scrap of paper—a receipt—and rips it in half.

I pause. I'm skeptical about the car fix, but I want his number. Not that he's given me any indication that he's gay, much less that he's interested, but it doesn't matter. On a gut level, I want it.

"Yeah," I say, "in the car." I unlock the door, kneel into the driver's seat, and fish one out of the glove box. Then I walk back around to the passenger side and hand it to him. He scribbles for a minute.

"There's my brother's email." He hands me the paper, along with my pen. "I'm going to call him now. Just tell him you're the guy Dave dinged in the parking lot. He'll set it up." Dave is nodding his head and smiling, his eyes brightening and squinting up as he does. There's something both boyish and rugged about his smile. Even though the talk about his brother's body shop seems like nonsense, I can't help but smile back. For a moment, we're both nodding and smiling.

"Okay," I say. "Thanks, Dave. I'll email."

"What's your name?" he asks. "So I can tell my brother."

"I'm Mike."

"Okay, Mike. Good. You're going to email, right? Here," he says, holding out his hand, "give me the paper."

I hand it back to him, and he gestures for the pen, so I give him that, too. He writes two additional words: *MacAllister Collision*.

"Look them up. They're a good shop."

I look down at the name. "Thanks; I'll email." Then I head back around to the driver's side, and Dave raises a hand to say goodbye, before turning to walk away. I shove the paper in my pocket.

When I get home, my father is in his room. I can hear the television. He doesn't usually come out when I get back. He may not have his hearing aid in. I unpack the groceries and my bag from school, leaving my laptop on the kitchen table so I can tool around online while I eat. I place the slip of paper with the body shop information on the keyboard. Then I promptly go to my bedroom and get myself off thinking about Dave. Like most people, I guess, my fantasies flip around, back and forth between vignettes. But this time I focus on Dave, imagining him telling me that he needs a lift somewhere, then putting his hand on my knee once I start the car, feeling upward along my thigh. I don't get much further than that, his large hand cupping my crotch. Don't need to. Afterwards, I google *MacAllister Collision*, half surprised to discover it's a real place. The email address on the website matches the one Dave scribbled. It's a half hour from here, deep in corn/soybean country.

Can't hurt to see, right?

THE NEXT MORNING at breakfast, I get back to Matt before heading to Lowe's. Matt and I text back and forth while my father frets about his latest blood work results, which show, apparently, high cholesterol. He debates the pros and cons of cutting eggs from his diet.

It turns out that Matt came here from Italy decades ago to go to school. Maria didn't come over until years later, after their mother died. Maria ended up in the Midwest. He was down in Texas for a while, working for a product-design start-up. He's just moved to Ohio. We agree to meet that afternoon at the local green, a strip with benches between a couple of store-lined streets. It's a warm day for February, and we've both got the time. I'm scheduled for a half shift, and Matt doesn't have a job here yet.

I look up from the phone when my father asks who I've been sending messages to.

"The brother of one of the people I do work for," I say. "Maria Greco's brother. Do you remember her? She's just a few blocks down. She came to the house last spring to drop off a check. She brought us a ham."

My father remembers the ham. "I didn't know she had a brother."

"Me neither," I say. It's getting late; I need to get going.

"Did she put you in touch with him?"

"Yeah." I stand and carry my bowl to the sink. "He's new in town. I guess she wants him to make some friends. So I said I'd meet him out for a walk." I can see the question forming on my father's face; he's sputtering a bit. I quickly run the tap and do my best to short circuit the conversation on my way out of the kitchen. "Yes, Dad, he's gay. I think she's trying to set us up."

AT 2:30 p.m., I'm waiting for Matt. I've come right from Lowe's. My red work vest is stuffed in my trunk, along with a couple of rolls of insulation. I don't have any handyman jobs this week, so I've decided I'm going to put the kitchen wall back together.

It's in the upper forties and sunny. People are out, strolling around. The town green is only a few blocks, but there's a coffee shop, a dozen stores, and a couple of restaurants that put tables outside during summer. It's not an old town center. The whole thing was built from scratch less than ten years ago—all of it recently cornfield—so there's a uniformity to it. It's charming, but it feels like a movie set. Still, it's a good place to meet and talk. I figure Matt and I can get coffee.

At 2:45, I'm starting to get fidgety and a little annoyed. It helps marginally when Matt texts to say he's parking, that he'll be there in five minutes. I tell myself I'm being generous, helping someone who has just arrived in town. Framed that way, as an act of generosity, it feels more palatable to wait for a stranger.

A few minutes later, Matt approaches. He walks right toward the bench where I'm sitting. Maybe Maria has shown him a picture of me. He's a sprightly guy. Curly hair, slightly rounded nose, big beard, impish grin. He sits down on the bench beside me and says "Hello!" brightly.

He's cute. He's got a playful busyness about him.

He turns to me, thrusting out his right hand. "Mike. I am Matteo. Or Matt. Whichever you like."

I smile. "Good to meet you, Matt."

He looks around. "This is nice. Prefabricated, suburban, and heterosexual, but nice."

"It is, yeah. I think you've hit on the big three themes."

"This town needs a few gay Italian boys to liven things up," he says.

"At least one," I say. "It might be a good idea to see if we can handle one first."

Matt springs off the bench onto his feet. "Come on, let's walk."

As soon as I get up, Matt starts off. We head toward the shops, and he's interested in all of them, even the dry cleaners. He peers into the window of the Yankee Candle and asks if I like candles.

"During a blackout," I say.

He rolls his eyes. "I don't like candles at all," he says. "Like training wheels for people who don't know how to create mood." But then he opens the door, the bell atop it ringing, and he's in. There's a long wall of scented candles, bin after bin. He picks up and smells each, generally making a face and putting the candle back down, but occasionally handing one over to me.

"Cinnamon vanilla," he says. He grabs my hand and places the candle in it. I'm a little startled by the touch, by how public it is.

The candle smells like a cinnamon vanilla candle.

"Nice," I say.

"Acceptable," he says, and moves on. He hands me some half dozen others, and after a little back and forth we agree that "Peach Cobbler" is the winner, so he buys one.

Then we visit the toy store. Here, Matt is drawn to the back, the aisle of stuffed animals. There's a range of creatures—bears, certainly, and dogs and cats, but also the kind of wildlife you see in zoos: giraffe, elephant, rhino, big cats. Matt looks around until he finds an otter with plastic whiskers and a white patch on its belly. He puts his nose to the otter's leather nose. "We otters have to stick together," he says.

"Are you an otter?"

"I am," he says. "If you pick up a gay dictionary and look under O, you will find a picture of me. You're an otter, too. But not as much of an otter as I am."

I see some hand puppets at the end of the aisle and grab one. I stick my hand inside it and press my fingers to my thumb, to practice moving its jaws. Once I've got it down, I make the panther chomp all over the otter in Matt's hand.

"What are you doing?" he says, pretending to be horrified. He pulls the otter against his chest and turns away.

"Panthers have got to eat," I say.

Then he turns back toward me, jabbing the otter forward, so its butt lands squarely on my puppet-panther's head. "Well, some otters fight back."

EVENTUALLY WE MAKE it to Starbucks, where he tells me about his life. There was a guy in Houston. They were together five years, cohabitating for most of that time. After the relationship ended, it didn't seem like Matt had any real connection to the city.

A few friends, a job he could do reasonably well. But no compelling reason to hang around. So Maria told him to come up here. She said that in Ohio he had family, and family was the center of gravity for a life. That was her phrase, "center of gravity." Matt wasn't sure he'd ever get laid again—wasn't sure, in fact, that people in Ohio actually got laid. But he figured he'd try it for a while.

He kicks my foot under the table. "So how about you. You have a center of gravity keeping you in Ohio?"

I tell him that I have a small house on a couple of acres about fifteen miles outside of town, and my father lives here.

"A house is just a thing. Is your father a center of gravity?"

I swallow the last of my coffee and mull over that for a minute. I like the fact that Matt is silent, waiting for my answer. "No," I say. "He's definitely not. Maybe I just haven't found one yet. It would be nice to."

"Or maybe it wouldn't be," he says. "Gravity is overrated. Asteroids shine brighter, zipping out past the planets." He makes a whirling motion with his forefinger.

I consider pointing out that asteroids are pulled by gravity, too, just in a much wider orbit. But I get what he's saying: there's something to be said for freedom, for a ranging path. "Well, some people are held to their lives by more gravity than others," I say, thinking it through. "Like their lives have the gravity of the sun. My life is more like the moon, sort of in between."

I wonder about Matt—about anyone who travels that lightly, or says they do. Is it really possible? Is it something they want?

"Hey," I say, "do you know The Police song, 'Walking on the Moon'?"

"We didn't have singing police in Italy." I'm not sure if he's making a joke. There's barely a beat before he adds, "Do you want to go back to your place?" and flashes his impish grin.

I pause. Sure, I do. I guess. But my father's going to be out of his room now. It's about 4:30 p.m. He's going to be eating dinner or reading the paper in the foyer. If the thing with Josh and Gary hadn't happened a few weeks ago, I might have gone for it, but it's just too soon.

"I live with my father," I say. "It's a little awkward bringing a guy back until he goes to bed."

Then Matt asks when my father goes to bed.

WHEN I GET home my father is seething about something Obama proposed—free community college, I think. My father assumes (correctly) that I voted for Obama (twice) and has therefore concluded that I'm personally responsible for our country sliding into socialism. Not a bad idea, if you ask me. It's an affront to him that I get health insurance through the ACA.

"Do you want to live in a socialist country, Mike?" he says as soon as I step through the front door. He's in the living room with his laptop open in front of him. It's like I've walked in on an argument between two people, and both are hellbent on dragging me into it.

"Making sure people have health insurance isn't socialism," I say. So much for hello.

"No, but this is how it starts," he says. And then he's talking about community college. I know where this is going: him reminding me that Nazi is a contraction of "national socialist." In the past, I've reminded him that the Nazis were allied with big-business interests in Germany, but somehow that fact never sticks.

"I won't be around to deal with this. You and the kids you teach will have to deal with it."

I go into the kitchen. There are a few pots on the stove. He yells after me that he made rice. I lift the lids. One pot has rice, the other limp broccoli. He must have finished the chicken. Good enough. I set up my laptop, grab a plate, and sit at the kitchen table. Among a number of spam-like notifications (all of which I delete except one advertising a car show next month) is a reply from MacAllister Collision. *Dave mentioned it. Can you bring the car in Monday morning?* No sign off. I game it out. I can do that—and then Uber over to school, I suppose. Maybe my father will drive me. I've got a truck, an old F150 I use for contracting work, big jobs. I'll drive that until I get the Celica back. I start writing a reply.

My father walks into the kitchen and sits down at the table while I'm typing.

"A woman at the gym wants to have dinner with me," he says.

I will be there around 8:00 AM Monday. Thanks. I hit send.

"I think she means this as a date."

I look up. My father is staring into the distance like he's trying to total up numbers in his head.

"I'm going to tell her no," he says.

"Why not go to dinner? Just to get out of the house. What's her name?"

"Beth. Beth Weiss. She's a widow. Her husband had a heart attack ten years ago. We started talking on the treadmill. She was walking on the one next to me, so we started talking. But I'm going to tell her no. I said yes when she asked, but I don't think it's a good idea."

I lower the screen of my laptop. I'm not sure what the best line of attack is here, but I know that a direct attempt at persuasion is likely the worst.

"How's she doing without her husband? She have any kids?"

"In Tucson!" he says, brightening. "She's got a kid out in Tucson. Her brother lives in Des Moines."

"It's got to be hard," I say, "not having family local. She's retired?"

"She worked in Human Resources."

"She sounds like a nice woman, Dad. Maybe just meet her for coffee one morning, get a donut. It's got to be tough for her, being alone out here."

He hesitates.

"I miss your mother, Mike. There was only one woman for me and that was your mother."

"I'm not sure having a cup of coffee and a donut changes that," I say, but he's already standing, indicating that the conversation is over.

4

MATT TEXTS *HERE*, which I knew because I heard his car pull up. He's at the door with a bottle of red wine. I let him in, take his coat and the bottle. "Classy," I say after reading the label aloud.

"I'm from Italy. We're civilized. We drink a little wine before we fuck."

"It sounds like a better country."

I need to watch it. My father is in the house. He went to his room an hour ago, but if he heard us talking, he'd go ballistic: both over the better country part and the fucking part. Matt follows me into the kitchen.

"No wine glasses. We got juice glasses or water glasses."

"Juice glasses," he says. "Also more civilized."

I start toward the table with the glasses, and Matt comes over and presses himself into me. "It's even more civilized," he says, "to drink the wine after." He puts his hand on my back and pulls my chest to him, then he presses his mouth on mine. We're about the same height, so this is an easy fit. It feels good—his body, his mouth against mine—and I relax into it. But only for a minute. My father could come out at any time. I break away from Matt and put the glasses down on the counter. "Let's go to my room."

Once we get in there, I close the door and turn to him, and we kiss standing up again. He draws his head back to ask if I'm on PrEP, and when I say I am, asks if I "fuck raw." Then he takes off his shirt and lies on my bed with his hands behind his head. Matt has a skinny torso, paler skin than I expected, and he's covered in curly hair. I take off my shirt and pull myself on top of him so our chests fit together. "Fuck," he says, making eye contact with me. I now see his eyes are hazel. "Fuck that feels good. Rub yourself on me."

"Yes, sir," I say, brushing my beard against the side of his neck. I rock my body on his. He puts his hands on my back, and we make out for a while. Then I sit up on my knees to gaze at him. Matt's a really sexy guy splayed out like that. Relaxed, uneven smile. Not shy at all, looking right at me. "Woof," he says, reaching up to lay a palm on my chest. Woof: the Scruff equivalent of a Facebook "like," but completely sexual. I laugh and run my palm down the front of his jeans.

He undoes the button, then unzips them for me. Soon I've got them off, and my own jeans and underwear are down past my hips. I'm pressing my hard dick right against his, and we're chest to chest again. He's moaning.

"I could come just doing this," I say.

Eyes closed, he says, "Don't. I want you to fuck me."

"Good, I want to fuck you."

I kick off my jeans and get on my knees between his legs. He bends his knees up, and I spit on my forefinger and massage it into him, at the same time, lowering my head to take a good long suck on his dick.

"You're gonna need lube."

I've got a few bottles in the night stand. I lean over him to get one, then squeeze some into my palm and grab Matt's dick. He shivers when I do. I stop and put a little on my finger, other hand, and slide it into him while jerking him off.

"Don't make me come," he says. I ease off his dick and concentrate on working my finger inside him.

"What's your favorite part of sex?" he asks, looking up at the ceiling as I'm gently massaging him back there.

"I guess it's the questions people ask while they're getting penetrated."

He smiles but doesn't look at me.

"Smart-ass. Answer. And don't stop doing that while you answer."

My finger is moving easily in and out of him now. He's warm and tight. I reach up with my left hand and grab onto his dick again, jerking it just a little. He closes his eyes.

"My favorite part is coming," I say. "Or maybe the moments just before I come, when I know I'm about to, but it's still building."

"Of course you say that," he says. And then, "Put your dick in me now."

"What's your favorite part?" I slide my finger out of him, root around for the lube and then squeeze more on my palm. I slather it up and down on my own dick, too. This is a practical measure, but it feels good, so I do it a few times.

"When the rhythms match," he says. "When you are both in the same rhythm."

I put my dick against Matt's hole, making my fist into an extension of him, then slowly start fucking my fist and going just a bit inside him, to relax him fully. He does seem relaxed, but his face tightens once a lot of me is in there.

"Okay?"

"Keep going," he says.

The Spring Before Obergefell

I COME IN Matt and stay inside him after, slowly fucking him to keep myself hard as long as I can while he jerks off. Thankfully this doesn't take long because it's tough to keep that up. After he comes, I lie on my back beside him. We're silent for a few minutes, and I begin to worry that he's falling asleep. There are half a dozen reasons why he can't spend the night.

"Hey," I ask, "did the rhythms match?" I nudge my shoulder against his.

He responds without opening his eyes. "No. If they matched we would have come at the same time."

This jolts me. It seemed pretty obvious that he'd enjoyed himself. And in fact, I came when he told me to. "It's a hell of a time for honesty."

I feel him shrug. "Doesn't mean it wasn't good sex. We'll work on the rhythms next time."

"Do you usually critique your partner's performance afterwards, like a post-game show?"

"You asked," Matt says. "I don't lie; when I'm asked, I answer." He raises himself on his elbow and looks over at me. "Kiss me and let's drink some wine."

"Okay," I say, trying to shrug it off. I kiss him and sit up.

The truth is that I'm not sure I want company right now—Matt or anyone. It's been a long day. But a glass of wine can't hurt. So we do, we have a glass. Matt asks about the house and living here with my father. I tell him I got the place in 2004, when all you needed to qualify for a mortgage was a pulse and a smile. I had the pulse, I tell him, and they gave me a pass on the rest. Then Matt talks about his father, who he last saw seventeen years ago, when he left Italy to go to school in America. By the time Christmas break rolled around, his father was dead. Lung cancer. The man had trouble walking, put off going to a doctor, and finally went to an orthopedist who x-rayed the area and told him there was a mass in his hip. The cancer had already metastasized that far. It took a few weeks for his father to get in to see an oncologist, and by then the cancer was in his brain. He died four days later, only intermittently aware of his surroundings, on increasingly high doses of morphine. Matt's parents hadn't told him—hadn't wanted to until there was a diagnosis. Why worry him unnecessarily? But when there was a diagnosis, the man was just about dead. Matt barely arrived in Italy in time for the funeral.

Matt heads out forty minutes later. As I'm falling asleep, I think about him. About his honesty, his directness, all the different places that he's lived. And how alive he seems. Matt is someone I want to know.

AFTER BREAKFAST ON SATURDAY, I make progress on the kitchen wall. There's no drywall in there, just knotty pine, so it's easy. The project will still leave three quarters of the house's exterior walls without insulation, but it's something. I finish removing the rest of the paneling and begin fitting the pink fiberglass between the studs, then cutting the sheets at the top. I get four studs done before I see that I'm going to need another roll. Plus it's almost noon, and I want to get to the gym before meeting Josh and Gary at the green. I'm working at Lowe's tonight, too, from four to close, so it's going to be a full day.

My father is drinking coffee and watching me work, giving me tips. He was a site manager for forty years, so he knows a lot. When anything isn't up to code in the house, he gets agitated and gives me a long explanation of what can go wrong, sometimes even a history of the relevant safety codes. This morning he's in rare form about the house's balloon framing, describing how quickly a fire in the kitchen could move through the walls, up to the second floor, the whole structure going up in minutes. This isn't really something I want to imagine—neither he and I burning to death nor the time and expense involved in opening the walls to install fire blocking between the levels. But he's still talking about it as I'm getting my shoes on to go and stops only when I ask him his plans for the day.

He says he's just going to "hang out here." I suspect this involves a lot of time in front of his computer, responding to blogs, with FOX News on. My father needs a hobby.

I get to the Starbucks late. Josh and Gary are already at a table in the back. The store is long, with the counter up front, so the back feels isolated, almost private. I have to look around a bit before I find them. They are sipping tall, foamy drinks, having a quiet conversation as I approach. Josh sees me and raises a hand.

"Thanks for coming, Mike," he says.

"Thanks," Gary says, but he's not smiling. Without the fury on his face, Gary looks different. Quiet, gentlemanly in his wire rims. Even refined. Like the kind of lawyer you'd refer to as a barrister. He's wearing a plaid button-down and a sports coat, which seems overdressed. I see at once, by his body language, that I misjudged the reason for this invitation. There's no sexual energy. Gary is closed off, his lanky form curled around a latte. He doesn't want to be here.

We're silent a moment so I ask what they've been up to this morning. Grocery shopping, apparently. They spend Saturdays doing chores. Walking around the supermarket, filling their cart, maybe razzing each other about what they like to eat. Gary says that this afternoon they'll do laundry and work in the yard. I picture them clearing brush or kneeling side by side, preparing landscaping beds. That's how my folks used to live—weekends doing chores together—except they were freighted with kids. I wonder if Josh and Gary enjoy that life, even feel lucky to have it. I tell them about balloon framing and my father, which lightens the mood. Josh asks if I'm going to have something to drink, so I go up and order a decaf. When I sit back down, he immediately starts speaking.

"So, Mike, I just wanted Gary to meet you. To see that you're nothing to be scared of, to see that there's nothing here."

"I'm sorry I hit you," Gary says. He's sheepish, running his right hand over the top of his head, looking down.

"It's okay," I say. "Given, well, what was happening, I probably deserved to be hit."

"Josh says you didn't even know he was in a relationship."

Josh never directly told me, but given how cagey he was about meeting, at least at first, his situation seemed obvious.

"A lot of guys are okay with it," I say. "I guess I just figured it was okay." My head still tells me that I haven't done anything wrong, playing around with Josh, but now my gut isn't so sure.

Josh reaches over and touches the back of Gary's hand. "I should have talked to you about it," he tells him.

"Just don't do it again, okay?" Gary says. He looks at Josh and then over at me, and I notice his eyes through his glasses. Gary was hurt—and still is. It shows there, the vulnerability. The sweetness. It's clear why Josh loves him, why anyone might.

THE NEXT MORNING, my father follows me to MacAllister Collision. We have no trouble finding the place; it's the only building along that stretch of Route 48, just a few miles north of Covington. An old brick garage with four bays. The exterior was probably once painted white, but now it looks gray. There's a small office attached to one side, a one-story cube. Thankfully my father wants to wait in his car.

The office isn't messy, but everything seems covered by a patina of motor oil. There are three chairs and a television on a side table, plus a coffee table covered with magazines from the aughts. At the back is a counter with an open door behind it, and I can hear conversation coming from a room in there. No one is behind the counter, but I wait a few minutes before I say "hey" and then "hello" loud enough to carry to the back room. Eventually two guys come out.

One of them is a little guy, wiry, shaggy brown hair, in oil-stained dark blue coveralls. His name is written on the left pocket in black sharpie: Hansen. I look at the other guy only a moment before recognizing him: mostly bald, stache, square shoulders. Not wearing coveralls. I realize I'm staring, so I look away. Dave comes out from behind the counter and walks up, smiling, to shake my hand as if we're old friends.

"Hey Mike, I'm glad you got down here," he says. We shake. "This is my brother Hansen. Hansen, this is Mike." Hansen stays behind the counter. I lift my hand in greeting.

"Hansen's going to fix you up," Dave says.

"It's a Toyota?" Hansen asks.

"A Celica. A '96."

Hansen fills out a few items on a clipboard, and then the three of us walk out to the parking lot. I'm noticing Dave's body, the fit of his jeans, his hoodie, which looks soft, like something I want to press my face against.

Hansen kneels by the passenger-side door and examines the dent, then circles the Celica, stopping to take the VIN off the windshield. I want to ask Dave something, anything, just to get him talking. Where to start? "You guys grow up around here?"

"Yeah," he says. "There was nothing out here in the seventies." He looks around. I do, too. There's not much out here now. A few strip malls farther down and the occasional farmhouse from back when this was a dirt road. There's an old gas station on the corner by the stoplight, and then there's this body shop.

"It must have been a pretty dull place to be a teenager," I say.

Hansen has me open the car so he can take the mileage off the odometer. "Press it out, paint it. Easy," he says. "Let's go back in, we'll get the paperwork started."

I glance over at my father, sitting in his car. He sees me and lifts his head. I hold up one finger, to indicate one more minute. I'm not sure he understands, so I shake my head and hold up both palms, to indicate that he should stay put. Then I turn back to Dave and Hansen. Hansen's walking back to the shop; Dave has been watching me.

"That your dad?"

"Yeah, he lives with me."

As we walk to the office, I wonder if I can push this. How I can. Just a little. An opening. I've picked at this knot dozens of times over the years. Probably all gay people have. How to communicate that you're gay to someone who is, or who might be. You can just announce it, I guess. But it's not usually comfortable to dive into personal information, and some people—homophobic assholes, no question—will react badly. And you may need to deal with those people in the future. Like here, with my car. So I usually just choke it off in these situations. Just pack away the impulse or desire or whatever it is that I'm feeling. But standing next to Dave right now, I just can't. Everything about him makes me want to touch him.

"It can be a pain in the ass," I say. "But I was living alone before, so this is good. I have the space, anyway. Your dad still around?"

"He's in Florida," Dave says. "He'll never come back here."

We reenter the shop. Hansen is over at the counter, so we end up there, too.

I pause.

"I guess it's better to live with just the wife and kids, huh?" I study Dave's face as I wait for him to answer.

Then Hansen slides the clipboard across to me, so I have to glance down. I examine the details about my car: year, make, model, VIN, a two-sentence description of the damage and the repair to be conducted, and an estimate for $495. I start. Hansen notices and says, "Don't worry, Dave's going to work it off."

"I'm going to fix his deck." Dave smiles. That big smile again.

"At this rate, the deck might be ready for Labor Day," Hansen says.

"Thanksgiving," says Dave. "We'll grill a couple of turkeys out there."

"You guys sure?" I ask. Hansen reaches over to the clipboard and crosses out the $495 and writes a big zero by it. I sign.

"Should be ready by Thursday," Hansen says. "Repainting the panel is the slow part. I'll text."

I don't want to leave, but I can't figure out a reason to stay. Plus my father is waiting. But there's time for one last shot.

"Hey," I say to Dave. "Thanks again for taking care of this. I was a little skeptical."

"Yeah, strange guys offering body work," he says. "Probably warranted." He smiles again, and we both laugh.

"Who doesn't need a little body work, now and then?" I say. There's an awkward pause. Dave laughs a little, but it feels like he's being polite.

For once in your life, I think, take the goddamn risk. But what? How? I could just blurt out that I'm gay. Hey Dave, I could say, just to be clear, I'm available for whatever you want: coffee, fucking, dinner, fucking, a weekend somewhere that includes fucking, whatever. Hell, I'll get down with you right now, if you're into it. On this greasy tile floor. Hansen can watch. I feel a jolt of anger and envy: straight people, all the information they can take for granted—even when they shouldn't take it for granted. They even have wedding bands to further telegraph the status of availability. I glance down at Dave's hand. No band.

"Hey," I say. "I do some contracting. If you guys need a hand with the deck, you should give me a call."

Hansen calls from behind the counter a little too loudly, "My brother's going to do the deck."

I smile, then Dave smiles. Another pause. We lock eyes a moment before I walk out.

MY FATHER DROPS me off at school, and I spend the rest of the day gaming out strategies. Well, that's not entirely true. I also spend three hours teaching logical fallacies. Fallacies and strategies, that's my Monday. I have the students work in groups, writing bad arguments then exchanging with another group to ferret out the weaknesses. The paragraphs are pretty funny. One group argues for nationalized health care for house cats. Another for lowering the legal drinking age to twelve. But even then, while the students are puttering, I'm strategizing. My first idea is to wear a Pride T-shirt to pick up my car. But what are the odds that Dave will be there? Plus, I don't have a Pride T-shirt. I do have an old sweatshirt from an AIDS walk back in the mid-'90s, but it's got paint on it from half a dozen jobs so the writing isn't totally legible. Another possibility is just to email Hansen and ask for Dave's number. What excuse could I give for needing it? Because I want to thank him? By the time I'm out on the curb waiting for my father to pick me up, I'm angry and ready to throw in the towel. Dave's probably straight anyway. I felt something—a pull between us—but that's probably wishful thinking, interpreting a straight guy's friendliness as possibility. I've been down that road. That's the logic that tells me to give up. I could write this out for my students, see if they'd find any fallacies in it.

I'm pretty down by the time my father pulls up in his old Elantra. It was my mother's car. She didn't drive for the last fifteen years of her life, so the car's got low miles, but it's covered with dents. Pock marked. That's not from her driving, but from his. My father is always backing into things: mailboxes, medians, shopping carts, other cars. It's nothing new. Even when I was a kid, he was always off in his head, wrestling with some work situation, at best half aware of his surroundings.

And, of course, he did all the driving. They were a couple from the 1950s in a lot of ways. Met on the beach in Coney Island. Did people exchange numbers back then? Who said hello first? It's a little disconcerting for me to imagine how sexualized that initial encounter must have been. Both teenagers. My mother in a bathing suit—could it have been a two-piece?—with a friend. My father with his shirt off. Apparently the four of them—my father had a friend there, too—got ice cream cones. I can picture that, four half-naked teens licking ice cream, walking the boardwalk, glancing up at the rides, hearing the roller coaster rumble past on its wooden trestle. Flirting. They must have been doing that. And what you'd expect to come from that did. Less than a year later, my mother was pregnant with my older sister, and it was just assumed they'd get married. Somehow the story got revised after the fact: love at first sight, the only woman for me. My father uses those phrases now. But facts are stubborn. My parents wanted to fuck, and they didn't use contraception. My mother was pregnant when he proposed.

But maybe it was love at first sight, too. Maybe both things can be true.

When I see the green Elantra pull into the campus lot, I stand. "Campus" isn't the right word. The community college where I teach is located in a shopping mall. We've got one of the anchor-store spaces, the former home of a Sears, and a few offices in the mall itself, old slots where there used to be retail. There's still a Jo-Ann's Nut House, a Barnes & Noble, and a few other stores.

The Elantra stops, and my father leans over and manually unlocks the passenger door. He asks how class went, and I tell him it was okay, that the kids had a good time today. He pulls onto the highway, clearly not listening. It's all right; there's not much else to say about it. It pops into my head that maybe Dave is on Grindr, so I think about that. I'm not on Grindr. Just Scruff. It's not a bad way to kill time, but one of those apps seems like plenty. If he's gay and single, he must be on one of them, too. Though there are still old-school ways to hook up—places guys park, a few public restrooms. And even if he is on, it's possible that his profile picture might not show his face, or that he might not have a picture at all, in which case it would be impossible to find him. I really am too old to be doing this kind of calculus. Something undignified about it. The guy is interested in guys or he isn't. Would it be so strange to email Hansen and ask? "Hey, I'm into your brother. You know if he's attracted to guys?" I can almost imagine a world where that could happen. Hansen writing back with the full truth, say, "Yeah, but he's into darker-skinned dudes. You could give it a shot," or "No, he's hetero, but if you get him drunk, he'll probably let you blow him." We'd all be much happier in that world. We'd get laid more.

"I am going to have coffee with Beth," my father says, breaking the silence when we're about halfway home.

I look over.

"The widow I told you about, who asked me to have coffee. I told her I would have coffee with her. She wanted to go to dinner and see a movie, but I didn't want to do that. But on Wednesday morning we're going to have coffee. Are you going to need my car?"

"I've got the truck," I say. If I appear glad about this coffee date, it will seem too big, too important—and my father might well cancel. The way to reassure him is to minimize it. I nod. "That's nice. What can a cup of coffee hurt? It will get you out of the house."

"I told Beth I wanted to show her a picture of your mother. That was my condition for saying yes. So she knows I was married for fifty-eight years."

Beth must be a patient woman.

"That's good, Dad. I'm glad you're going to show her a picture of Mom."

"Nothing is going to happen," my father says. "It's just a cup of coffee."

My father goes silent again, so I check my phone and find that Matt texted—a short note: *Dinner? Wed? Thurs?* I also have a text from an unknown number about hanging some light fixtures. I respond to the latter right away.

My father doesn't speak again until we pull into the driveway. "Don't tell anybody," he says.

For a moment, I'm not sure what he's referring to. "About Beth? Who would I tell?"

He doesn't answer; he just gets out and heads into the house. I text Matt a quick *Thursday*, and then I get out, too. As I cross the threshold, I can hear that my father has already turned on the television.

OVER DINNER, I decide on a course of action. I comb through my laptop and put together a few files, things I downloaded a while back, the one time I built a deck. Basic specs, a cost-benefit analysis of various types of wood. I also find a picture of me building it. I'm a little younger in the picture—maybe forty-five. Only five years ago, but back before working out wasn't constantly negotiating one injury or another. It's a good picture. Drill in hand, tightening screws on the railing. Sweaty. I'm not sure who took it.

Then I go about composing an email to Hansen. It's short, but I fuss with it for half an hour. I want it to sound—what?—neutral, I guess. I want to convey interest, but I also want plausible deniability.

I settle on: *Hey Hansen, can you forward these files to Dave? From the last time I built a deck. Might be useful. He can text me if he has any questions.*

I include my number.

At the last moment, I decide not to attach the picture.

It's not much, but it's an opening. At least I did something. If Dave wants to write back, he will.

5

THE LONGEST I'VE been with a guy is a couple of years, and for most of that second year, we limped along. I was in my late twenties. These days I wonder what I've been waiting for or looking for over the last twenty years—what I'm waiting for or looking for now. In retrospect, it seems like I passed up some decent opportunities. Maybe a guy came on too strong or we didn't seem to be into the same things. It's possible that it was a numbers game. There just aren't many gay guys out there, not many chances to meet them unless you live in a city. It's also possible that the problem is gay-male culture. The apps, the websites that preceded them. They maximize your chances of meeting someone, but they also create a false buyer's mindset: as if the shelves are loaded with choices and you're sure to find something better in the next aisle over. It doesn't exactly promote human connection. But the problem could just be something about me. At some point in your life, you begin to see yourself differently, not only as a sort of ahistorical consciousness, but also as a pattern of actions. You might be your consciousness, sure. But an equally good case can be made that you're the pattern, that you can characterize a ship by describing the wake it leaves in the water.

It's not really how I think of myself, but my wake has been pretty closed off to other people.

By the time I'm finishing up at Lowe's on Tuesday night, I'm feeling listless. I spent half the day checking my email, so much so that my supervisor Rob barked at me. "We don't pay you to check your phone." I was at the end of an aisle, standing in front of a pallet I was supposed to be unloading. I flashed him my middle finger, but then quickly slid the phone into my back pocket. Rob said, "Good boy, Breck," shook his head, and walked out of Flooring. I went back to moving tile. There was no email for me anyway.

I check my phone one last time before heading home. This time I've got a text, but it's CVS. I still haven't picked up that prescription.

I spend the night chatting with strangers on Scruff in front of the television in the living room, which pretty much shuts off my head. I hate nights like that, but sometimes I don't seem to be able to manage much else, especially when something is bothering me. I text Matt again too. He hasn't responded to my last text, suggesting Thursday. *Hey, are we having dinner this week?*

He replies instantly. *We are. Thursday. With wine and dessert.*

Good. And where are we having said dinner?

Again, his text appears instantly: *I have to think of everything?*

I do a Google search and eventually decide on a Mexican restaurant, a new place in the strip mall that contains the one large supermarket in the area. This takes a little while, as I'm also chatting with two guys on Scruff, one of whom is a buff thirty-year-old in Amsterdam. We are at the stage in the conversation where he's asking if I ever get to Europe. This comes after the You're So Hot stage but before the What Do You Get Into? stage. One of these days, someone should do an endorphin study on this kind of chat—what it does to the brain, how it conditions us. The apps have made us all lab rats.

Los Cabos? 7:00?

Matt responds while I'm chatting with a local guy who hits me up whenever I get on. This guy wants a specific thing: an older man wearing a button-down, tie, and leather belt to tell him what to do, to fuck him, to control every aspect of the encounter. I've hooked up with him a couple of times in the last few years. The encounters aren't bad; everyone needs touch. But they are mechanical, even a little stale.

Matt texts, *I'll be the one in a montera and cape*, which I smile at.

I check to see if Josh is on Scruff tonight. He's not. I wonder if he and Gary talked about the apps. Josh's picture is—maybe was—anonymous. Just a shot of his chest. I never start conversations with profiles like that. I figure if you're choosing to hide your face, you're taking on the burden of initiating contact.

I respond to Matt: *And nothing else?*

Only a smile.

Over the next few hours, I chat with some half dozen other guys and watch three episodes of *Chicago PD*. It's almost eleven by the time I drag myself off the couch.

THURSDAY MORNING, my father and I drive out to MacAllister. Hansen is there, and this time the shop is busier. There's a couple waiting in the office and cars in all four bays. Mechanics buzzing over them. I look around while I'm waiting at the counter. I even walk out to the bays where the guys are working, careful not to get too close. No Dave. He isn't in the office, either—or if he is, he doesn't come out of the back room. But my Celica looks good. Dent is gone. Door has been repainted.

Hansen is true to his word about not charging me. As he's sliding the keys across the counter, I say, "I guess you're getting a deck for it." And then, "Hey, were those files useful for Dave?"

"The files?" he says, not looking up. "Oh, I didn't forward your email yet." He scribbles on my printout. "Here's Dave's email, you can send them yourself."

I look down and see "Nursedave@aol.com" in squat blue print.

I nod, trying to act cool, but I can't help myself: I snatch up the paper like a winning scratch-off ticket.

I SPEND MOST of that afternoon wrestling with a leaky sill cock. A guy called that morning, asking if I could install a frost-free one, and by the end of the day, that's what he's got. We settle on $85, which is good—more than enough for dinner with Matt.

When I get home, my first order of business is to email Dave. I send the same note as before, but I add a couple of sentences explaining that Hansen gave me his email address and telling him the car looks great.

And this time, I do attach the picture with the drill.

My father comes home while I'm still at the kitchen table. He takes off his coat and walks into the room talking, then starts unpacking a sack of groceries. "I had coffee with Beth," he says. "We had a cup of coffee and talked for an hour. We shared a donut." He takes the last few items out of the sack and sits across from me.

I'm feeling jazzed. "Nursedave." Lots of straight guys are nurses. But lots of gay guys are nurses, too.

"Did you have a good time?"

"She told me about her husband," he says. "They were married thirty-one years."

My father describes the guy. A fighter pilot. His reflex times set an Air Force record when he was first starting out. The base commander saw fit to call him into his office to let him know.

"He flew a lot of missions overseas. He bombed people."

I nod.

"I told her about your mother. I showed her a picture." He reaches into his back pocket and slides out a picture of my mother and him from about thirty-five years ago, from a trip they took to Palm Springs. She's in her early forties, done up. A close-up in a restaurant. This was before the advent of cell phones, so someone with a camera must have come around to all the tables.

"That's a nice picture of you and Mom," I say.

"We were married fifty-eight years. I told Beth we could go to a movie. I'm cheating on your mother."

"Dad, Mom would want you to go out and see a movie," I say. But actually I'm not so sure. In some moods, that's what she would have wanted. In others, she would have wanted him to weep over her grave until the day of his death. She was a complicated woman.

"I got a roasted chicken," my father says. There's a clear plastic dome on the counter. Beside it are a couple of Styrofoam tubs. I imagine one of them contains mashed potatoes. "You want some dinner?"

My computer chimes, indicating I've got an email. I look down and hastily bring up Gmail. Not Dave. My father goes to the counter to dish out food. "Do you want a plate?"

"No, Dad. I'm having dinner out tonight."

"Are you going on a date?"

I tell him that I am, and with whom, and he asks what kind of work Matt does. After I say that Matt's still looking for a job—he's just moved here—my father starts talking about Obama and the slow pace of the economic recovery. He starts to get ranty, so I say I've got to shower and jet off to my bedroom with my laptop.

MATT IS AT the restaurant when I get there. He's wearing a pale blue button-down with a blazer, jeans, and a belt. And boots. He looks good. I'm dressed more casually—no jacket, no belt. Cross trainers.

"Hey," I say, raising my hand. He's in the small lobby, waiting on a carved wooden bench against the wall. He stands when he sees me. "You look nice."

"I usually look nice," he says. "You look nice, too."

"I'm usually a mess," I say. "If you judge relative to our usual appearances, I've actually taken way more trouble to clean myself up than you have."

"Let me smell you." Matt leans in toward my shoulder and inhales audibly through his nose. "You smell reasonably clean."

"When it comes to evenings out, I make olfactory hygiene a top priority."

I hold up two fingers at the host, who has asked how many there are for dinner, and he picks up a few menus, telling us to follow him. The host looks like a high school student, in no obvious way remarkable, but sweetly handsome like most eighteen-year-olds. I'm curious if Matt will make some comment about him, but to my surprise he doesn't. A lot of gay guys would.

Over dinner, Matt and I talk about medical procedures. He's recently had one, hernia repair a few months back. I've never had surgery.

"So you're a surgery virgin?" he says, filling a flour tortilla with meat and roasted peppers. We both ordered fajitas.

"It is my last remaining citadel of virginity."

Matt nods and takes a bite of fajita.

"And I'm in no hurry to lose it," I say. "I prefer to think of my body as a kind of black box. I don't want to know what's going on inside it; I just want it to function."

"That gets harder at your age," Matt says.

I tense. It must show on my face. I hadn't thought of Matt and I as being different ages. Are we different ages? I study him. No gray in his beard. But lines around the eyes and mouth when he smiles. He's not a kid.

"How old do you think I am?"

"Daddy age," he says. He takes another bite of the tortilla wrap he's just assembled.

"Does that make you twink age or a b-o-i?" I spell out the last word.

"No," he says, "it makes me thirty-six. A singularly uninteresting age in the gay world. Maybe we can invent some designation. How about 'prime rib'? You can say you like twink, daddy, or juicy prime rib."

I'm not that much older than Matt. That said, I was starting high school when he was born. It isn't that I care about age difference, just that it hits me, looking at Matt, that what I'm seeing is not the age I am. That what I'm seeing is not how I am seen.

After dinner, we go to Matt's apartment, a small place above a detached garage in a subdivision east of the green. The houses in that part of town are a little newer, a little more homogeneous. I've done jobs in them.

"Be warned, I like it sparse," he says, turning the key and pushing the door open. "Well, either that or I sold all my furniture when I left Houston, and I haven't gotten any more yet. Except a mattress." He grins. "I've got my priorities. Oh, and a chair."

There's a brocade wingback in the middle of the living room, along with a pyramid of various-sized sealed boxes and a half-unpacked box containing kitchen wares. And that's it. The rest of the apartment is empty.

"The only piece of furniture you brought up was that chair?"

"I didn't bring the chair. Maria wanted it out of her house, she said it was too 'grandma.' So I was happy to oblige. If you want, we could try fucking in it," he says thoughtfully. "It seemed to me it could be a good fucking chair."

"Did you tell Maria that?"

I smile, walk over, and put my hand on one of the wingback edges, rocking it back and forth a little. Sturdy. It would make a good fucking chair.

Matt takes off his blazer and sets it over an arm. I glance around: no closets.

"Want a drink?" He moves to the kitchen counter and holds up a half-finished bottle of white wine. "I had some of this last night. It's surprisingly good."

I nod, he pours.

"We're just going to skip the stage of sipping wine on the couch and go right to bed," he says, walking across the living room, holding the two glasses.

I follow him to the bedroom. It looks like the place is only two rooms, a living room with a kitchen area on one side, and a bedroom. There's a bathroom off the bedroom.

The mattress is on the floor. No box spring, no frame. Matt sits on it, his back against the wall since there's no headboard. I settle in beside him, and he hands me my wine.

"Salud," he says, clinking my glass. "To friendship."

We sip meditatively.

"Tell me something," he says slowly, as if he's rolling the question around in his head. "Tell me something intimate. Tell me about the first time you had sex."

I take another swallow. "You mean, full-on penetration?" I look over. He does. "High school prom. I was drunk. My date and I were sharing a motel room with three other couples. They all must have heard us. My date rolled a condom on my dick and pulled me on top of her. I can't imagine the whole thing lasted more than five minutes. Only thing I remember clearly is her face right next to mine—I could see it even in the dark—with her pointer finger in front of her lips saying, *shhhhh*, after she put the condom on me. Next morning one of our friends called us disgusting. It didn't seem like it had really happened."

"You are disgusting," Matt says, still looking forward.

"Thanks," I reply. "Why? Because we fucked in front of other people?"

"Because you lasted only five minutes. She should have thrown your ass out."

I shrug. "I was eighteen, maybe seventeen. How about you?"

"A schoolmate," he says. "We were thirteen. We would meet in the morning. After school, my mother kept strict track of me. Before school, not so much. One morning we met in the woods behind the school and agreed to try it on each other, since there were no girls around. That's what we said, 'since there were no girls.'"

"Sounds ideal. Pastoral, homosexual . . . no alcohol, no audience."

"Yeah, it was nice. Except that we were pretending to be straight, it was." He finishes his wine. "It went on for a couple of years, too, until he moved to the south. His name was Stefano. He lived down the street, so we'd always walk to school together. Things have gotten more complicated since."

"What has?"

"Sex. More complicated. Then we were just two bodies fucking. Now we are tops, bottoms, subs, masters, otters, bears, single, married, poly, bi. With Stefano and I, we were just bodies. We hadn't given much thought to classifications yet, so we just slathered each other in cum."

Matt leans over and kisses me, so I put down my wine glass, and we make out for a while, which gets us both going. Then he sits up and begins unbuttoning his shirt.

"Do you like to get fucked?" he asks. "I'm in the mood to fuck."

I slide back up against the wall.

How to answer? *Sure, everyone likes to get fucked.* That's one answer. And I think it's the truth. But there's a Part B: *everyone likes to get fucked by the people they want to fuck them.* I could say something more emotional: *sometimes, if it feels safe.* Only I wouldn't use the word "safe," but something like "cool." Or I might say, *if the vibe feels right*, vibe being so dated that it's hip again, and makes the statement okay. Or maybe I could think phenotype. *Certain guys bring that out in me, Matt, certain dynamics, and so far, you just don't.* All these responses are true. The last one, at least, would end the evening real quick. Suddenly, it feels like I'm here, in Matt's bedroom, under false pretenses. As if I were wearing a disguise.

Matt lies back on the mattress now, his clothes off. He comes up beside me and undoes a few buttons on my shirt, then moves his hand in to feel the hair on my chest.

"I'm not sure I'm up for that tonight," I say.

"No?" he asks, moving in to kiss me. He puts his tongue gently in my mouth for a few moments and then draws his face back. "Okay, we'll figure something else out." Then he starts kissing me again.

Matt and I continue to kiss, but I'm stuck in my head now, and even though he's naked and has my shirt open, my dick is not cooperating and not showing any sign that it's going to cooperate. I pull away to take my shirt off and clear my head. "Hey, I'm going to use the bathroom."

"Back there." He points.

I get in, close the door, and spend a few minutes standing over the toilet holding my dick, even though I don't need to piss. Then I wash my hands and breathe.

When I come out, Matt's lying on his back with his arms behind his head. "All good?"

I say that it is.

"Then take off your clothes."

Because I am in his bedroom, because my body has always been reliable, and because I'm not really sure what else to do, I do take off my clothes. I get into bed with Matt, and the friction of our bodies against each other has the effect that such friction usually has. Matt and I make out and jerk each other off. I don't try to fuck him, thinking that might lead him to expect reciprocation, or try to do much of anything else, either. Neither does he. The whole thing is quick, maybe fifteen minutes.

When we finish, I get up quicker than I usually would and head to the bathroom for toilet paper. Matt is silent until I come back. He doesn't get out of bed.

"You want to leave?" he asks.

I do want to leave. I don't want to say that I want to leave.

"No," I say, "I can hang out for a few minutes, but I've got to work tomorrow, so I can't have a late night."

"All right, for a few minutes. Lie down."

I do, and he pulls his comforter over us, inclining his head on my shoulder. There's one light on in the room—the overhead that was switched on when we got in here. He curses under his breath, scampers to shut it off, then lies back down beside me. There's still light coming in from the kitchen and living room side of the apartment, though, so it's bright enough to see. But it's softer now.

"What's it like for you," he says, "after you come?"

He has turned toward me, so he's talking into my neck, and his right hand is running over my body. Not in a sexual way. Closer to how you would stroke a child or a nervous companion animal, soothing it.

"I don't know. I relax."

"I mean, you want to go. Why do you want to go?"

I start to protest that I didn't say that, but then I remember something Matt said the last time we were in bed together, about the rhythms matching. So I talk about that instead. "Maybe it's like gear teeth, when one gear turns another." If they're syncing up and you looked at the face of the gears, it wouldn't be clear which was turning which. But if they weren't correctly timed or aligned, you wouldn't be able to make them interlock. The teeth would grind against each other."

Matt nods; I feel it against my neck.

"Have you ever been with someone where the gears synced perfectly?" I ask.

"Javier, the guy in Houston. We were a good match. A great one."

For the first time, I think I hear a little sadness in Matt's voice. But he continues running his hand slowly from my chest down my stomach over and over.

"You miss him?"

Matt tells me about their life down there. How they went for walks along the bayous, got season tickets to the Alley—the big regional theater—and ate at restaurants where the staff knew them, would bring their drinks as soon as they sat down. Javier was a bank executive, kind of a big shot. He spent a few months out in LA every year, overseeing a branch there, visiting his family. Matt would come out for a week or two, but otherwise they'd just spend a season apart. "In a lot of ways," Matt says, "Javier had his life and I had mine. He's out there permanently now."

Matt's breath is gentle on my collar bone.

"But you guys lived together, right?"

"We had a condo with a view of downtown. Space City. Houston is Neverland-magical in the sunset. Some nights we'd sit on the balcony and sip wine."

I've never seen the Houston skyline, and Matt's at a loss when I ask him to describe it. He just says "Neverland" again and tells me to think of pixies.

I try to picture their condo, too. White furniture, tan carpeting, a lot of takeout food. Floor-to-ceiling mirrors. Maybe Javier coming home late in a business suit, draping his jacket over the back of a dining room chair.

"I've never lived with someone," I say. "Unless my dad counts. And never dated a guy for anything like five years. Not even if you add up all the guys I've dated. But maybe that's how humans are meant to live, paired up like that."

"Sometimes Javier and I didn't see each other for months."

"But you'd talk every day, right?"

Matt shakes his head. "Not always."

That distance is hard for me to wrap my head around. I imagine someone moving into my place. Beginning the day with a quick kiss. Getting in each other's way as we dress for work, enjoying the bustle in the kitchen as we grab breakfast. Seeing each other back home later. Being able to depend on that. It's not something I've let myself imagine in a while, and I get lost in it.

After a long silence, I say, "I don't think I could manage it."

"What?" Matt is still running his hand down my chest, but his voice is sleepy, far away.

I mean the months apart, but maybe the truth is that I couldn't manage any of it, any part of living with a guy—not anymore. If I ever could have. The intimacy, the compromises required. Maybe there's a period in your life when you can adapt to all that, and the period has passed for me.

I keep my eyes closed and let the thought go. "That feels nice," I say.

"I know." His voice is almost a whisper.

When I open my eyes again, it's very late. Matt is asleep, curled facing the other direction, and he stirs only a little bit when I lift myself off the mattress to check my phone, which is with my jeans on the floor. It's after 4:00 a.m. I dress and tiptoe out of the apartment.

6

IT'S A LITTLE before five when I get home. Morning, more or less. My father won't be up for an hour. I decide to make toast and coffee and burn some time on my computer before work. I see I've got half a dozen emails. The first is from Dave, and there's an attachment.

I take a moment to breathe before reading it.

The email is short. *Thanks, buddy. This might come in handy. You want to get a drink?* I click on the attachment. A picture: Dave on a crowded street, summer, leaning against a railing with two other guys. He's smiling, his bright blue eyes squinting, looking into the camera. One of the other guys looks like he's mid-conversation with someone outside the frame. The third guy, next to Dave, is taller, with a shaved head and a few plastic-bead necklaces around his neck. They're all wearing the same T-shirt: *Columbus Pride 2011*, decorated with fireworks and a rainbow flag.

Jackpot.

I write back right away. Normally I'd wait five or six hours in order not to seem too eager. But my fingers fly to the keyboard. *Looks like you and your friends had a great time. I haven't been to Columbus for Pride in a decade. I should head there this summer.* I also say that I'd love to get a drink and ask if he has time this weekend.

Then I read news, eat toast, and chat with a few guys over Scruff, all at the same time. Everything feels light and easy. At 6:00 a.m. I hear my father padding around, and then it's 6:15 and he shuffles into the kitchen.

His bathrobe is hanging open over a sweatshirt, sweatpants, and a pair of pajamas. He looks quilted.

"You were out late last night," he says. He's surprised to see me up. Usually it's me walking in to find him in the kitchen. He walks over to the counter to fiddle with his medications.

I bang out a response to a guy on Scruff. *Thanks, you too.* The guy lives in Canberra. What's the point of chatting with a guy in Canberra?

"Yeah, it was a late night."

"Oh," my father says. "So you had a good time?" He's over at the sink now, filling a glass from the tap.

"I don't know." I reflect for a moment. How could I not know? "I think I did." I tell my father where we went for dinner and that I fell asleep at Matt's place. I gloss over the sex. I say we had a little wine, so I ended up crashing on the couch. My father listens while he's fixing his cereal. He doesn't answer, so I go back to the internet, scrolling through a few left-wing blogs I frequent for news. My father settles in across from me with his bowl.

"Do you think you're going to start going with this guy?" he asks.

"Going with Matt?"

"You got to make a choice sometime, Mike."

I see on my phone that I have a new Scruff notification. The guy is about thirty miles away, which is close by rural Ohio standards.

I open the app and check out his profile. He's too young for me, but he looks kind of grizzled, so maybe it's all right.

"Not making a choice is a choice," my father says. "You want to be an old man, alone in this house? At least I have you, you won't have anybody."

I look up to see my father shoving a spoonful of cereal into his mouth.

"Jesus. Thanks, Dad."

"You think you have all the time in the world. It runs out quick. You're fifty? There's a hell of a lot less time between fifty and eighty than there is between twenty and fifty. It feels like there's a lot less."

"I know I don't have all the time in the world." I put down my phone. Now that I've unlocked my other pictures, the thirty-year-old has started giving one-word responses. Never a good sign. I also scroll over to see if Dave has replied. No dice.

"I'm just not sure if this is the right guy."

"All right. Spend some time with him."

Maybe my father's advice comes from a desire to see me happy. But even if that's true, the trouble is that he understands only one path to happiness: work, marriage, kids. I'm not sure that path worked out so well even for him. His life was fully shaped by it—by the demands it placed on his time and behavior—before he was old enough to imagine other possibilities. Who knows what other things he might have done, where he might have traveled, the human connections he might have made. There's something tragic about that: a life tracked so early, so rigidly.

But I can see the flip side, too. What my life must look like to him. I do just about everything alone. Except for guys coming here at night sometimes. For all the places I might travel and all the connections I might make, I spend a hell of a lot of time sitting on the couch, chatting on Scruff. The food equivalent would be sucking on sugar cubes rather than eating a balanced meal, much less a home-cooked one. Would marriage to the same person for fifty years be a balanced meal? There's just not enough time left for me to find out, but there must be some depth or discovery possible in that kind of life that's very hard for me to imagine.

To change the subject, I ask my father what he has planned for today. He's going to his podiatrist to get his toenails cut. For a moment I feel intensely grateful that it would never occur to him to ask me to help with something like that. Then he's going to get a sandwich at Quiznos. The thought of this peps him up. He has a coupon.

BY THE TIME I'm driving to Lowe's for my 8:00 a.m. shift, I'm already feeling tired. I should have tried to go back to sleep after returning from Matt's. The phone rings in the car, and I glance down to see Maria's number. I do a quick calculation and decide it's a good time to answer. I'm only a few minutes out from work, so she can't keep me on long.

"Mike!" she says as soon as I pick up. "Good morning, Mike! Listen, I want to ask you about my brother. I just spoke to him, and he says you had dinner last night."

"That's right. We went to *Los Cabos*." My car's much too old to have anything like a Bluetooth connection, so I nestle the phone between my shoulder and ear when I shift gears.

"And that this was your second date."

"It was the second time we saw each other, yes."

"So I don't want to pry, it is none of my business, but what do you think, will there be a third?"

For a moment I wonder if Maria has been talking to my father.

There's a set of old jokes about what lesbians and gay men bring to a second date. The punchlines are, respectively, a U-Haul and "What's a second date?" But even beyond the problems with stereotypes, the joke's calculus is off. Gay men often have second dates. If the sex is good on the first date, you have a second. But is there chemistry on that second date, when there's usually no longer much suspense about whether sex is going to happen? The third date's the cliff.

When I don't answer right away, Maria continues. "He's sexy, my brother," she says. "When we were younger, he was the sexy one. Me, not so much. I got a little sexier. Matteo stayed just as sexy."

"He is sexy."

"And fun. He's a fun man, Mike. He can dance."

"Yes," I say, suddenly deciding. "I think we will see each other again."

"Good," Maria says. I picture her somewhere banging the flat of her hand on a tabletop for emphasis. "Good! Then my work here is done."

THE SHIFT AT Lowe's is fine, except Rob tells me he has to cut me back to sixteen hours next week. That's going to make things tight this month. In the course of the morning, I text Matt, thanking him for last night and letting him know that his sister called to remind me that he's sexy. He replies that she does, indeed, know sexy when she sees it. I also check my email half a dozen times to see if there's anything from Dave. I try to be subtle about it, ducking into the bathroom or heading to the scratch-and-dent area behind the kitchen displays. I don't want to get called out again, especially when they're already cutting my hours.

It's almost 2:00 p.m., just before the end of my shift, when Dave replies. He suggests Sunday afternoon, a sports bar just a mile out of town on the interstate. He also includes a phone number and tells me to text him. I feel super energized for the remainder of the shift, randomly smiling at customers, asking if I can help. But I decide to wait until tonight to text back. Especially because I responded right away this morning.

My upcoming date with Dave stays at the front of my mind all that night and Saturday. I do all the things I would normally do, but with an eye toward Sunday afternoon. At the gym after work on Friday,

I push myself hard, thinking about looking especially buff. When I'm doing laundry on Saturday afternoon, I put aside the clothes I'm going to wear. I've got an old, navy blue sweater that looks good on me, fits snug around my arms and chest. I even keep off Scruff for most of the day and finish the Hiroshima book instead. I'm not interested in chatting with other guys.

That's what I'm doing—lying on my bed, reading about radiation sickness—at 4:00 p.m. when my father steps into the doorway of my room and knocks to get my attention. He has shaved and dressed more carefully than usual—jeans, belt, a button-down. My father was a big man in his day, over two hundred pounds, a good four inches taller than I am. He's thin now, narrower, but when he straightens, he still has some of that presence. He seems to fill the doorway.

"I'm going out to see a movie," he says. "I'm going with that woman I told you about. Beth. We're going together."

I nod slowly. He hasn't been to a movie in years, not since my mother died. He must have wrestled with the decision for days.

"What are you going to see?"

"*Everest.* It's a true story about some climbers who get lost or injured or some shit like that. It's what Beth wanted to see. She likes determination."

"I think you'll have a good time," I say.

My father shrugs.

"You'll have a good time, Dad. Are you going to pick her up?"

"No," he says. "We're going to meet there. But we'll get coffee at the donut place afterwards." He pauses. "It's not a date."

"It will be good to get out of the house. I saw a trailer for *Everest.* It looks like it's going to have some great special effects."

"We'll see." He opens his hands, a little resigned.

He turns, and I get up from my bed to walk him through the hall, to the foyer. He sits on one of the wicker chairs in there and begins tying his shoes, something that has recently become a painstaking process.

"Weren't you telling me just this week that it's good to spend time with people?" I ask as he starts on his second shoe.

"It's good for *you* to spend time with people. I've had seventy-eight years with people. That's all the time with people I'm going to have."

"Apparently not," I say, smiling.

He stands and shrugs. "I guess not."

Suddenly it feels like my father is leaving for a very long time, as if he's going overseas to serve in the military. I tell him to have fun and close the door behind him.

7

SUNDAY MORNING, the water heater gives out.

The unit is in the basement, right beside the washer and dryer. I find a puddle when I go down to start the final load of laundry. It looks like a dog peed up against it. The leak is at the bottom seam; when I look close, I see a tiny flow of water bubbling out. The unit must be twenty years old, so I'm not surprised, but the timing isn't great. It will cost every bit of $500 to change it out.

Normally, something like that would ruin my day, but I'm too excited to let it. Neither my father nor I will much enjoy cold showers in late February, but I decide to worry about that later. Maybe I'll even head down to Lowe's tonight to pick up a new unit. I go upstairs to take a shower, then shave my neck and trim my beard. I go the extra mile and tweeze the hair out of my ears, too. And just before heading out, I set the tank to drain into the sump.

Dave is at Bolt's when I get there. I see him as soon as I walk in. Football season is over and baseball hasn't started yet, so the place is dead. Bolt's has a long bar up front and a series of booths along the opposite wall. There are windows along that wall, too, but they've been darkened with some kind of film. So even at 1:00 p.m.—or a little later, I lost a few minutes fussing with the water heater—the place feels dusky. Bolt's is a good place to forget about time.

Dave's in one of the middle booths, facing the door. He's wearing a T-shirt with sleeves that stop just past the elbow, so I can see he's got a faded tattoo on one forearm—a dragon, I think—underneath the dark-brown hair.

He smiles and stands when he sees me. "Hey, you made it."

"Yeah, just a little late."

He waves this off. I reach out to shake his hand, then we sit. On the way over, I ran through subjects I could ask him about: his brother, being a nurse, more about what it was like growing up local. If all else fails, we can talk about being gay in the area, what that's like. It's the one thing we've definitely got in common.

"Thanks for coming out," I say. "And for getting the car fixed up. Your brother did a great job."

"He's not good for much else." Dave laughs.

The waiter comes over, and Dave orders coffee, which is unfortunate because I was thinking beer would make this easier. I get coffee, too, and one of their desserts, what the menu describes as "hot caramel apple cake."

"So you're a nurse?" I fumble with my silverware, trying to unwrap it. Eventually I just set it down with half the paper band torn off.

"A nurse? I wanted to be. How'd you know that?"

"The Gmail addy."

"That's old," he says. "In my next life, maybe. I *am* good at the care-taking part; I like that. But I washed out in Biochem. I'm a nurse's aide at Cardio Med, north of Dayton. I still get to wear scrubs, though."

"It's all about the scrubs." I poke the top of my chest with a few fingers. "As long as you can show a little fur."

The waiter brings our mugs to the table, and I try to think of something else to say as Dave opens a packet of sugar into his.

"You help with surgery?"

"No. Way above my pay grade. There are perioperative nurses for that. I give a lot of meds." He takes a sip of coffee. "Empty a lot of bed pans. I'm good at bed pans. I'm almost a specialist."

"My own job has an aspect of that." I take a swallow of coffee, too, and will myself to relax. This is what I want, isn't it? To hang out with a beautiful gay guy? I lean back against the seat. "I teach a few classes at Northeast. Grading papers is pretty similar to emptying bed pans, except that you assign letter grades at the end of it."

He nods. "And make comments, right? No comments on bed pans, though if things don't look right, I tell the nurses about it. They make the comments." Dave pauses. "You're a college professor?"

"Professor is the best-case scenario. I'm the other scenario. What happens when you can't get a real job as a professor. I just teach a few classes. I have a couple of other part-time jobs, too."

I tell him about Lowe's, and then explain what I teach, and he apologizes for any grammatical errors he's made so far. I let him know that I'm not the grammar police. Then the cake arrives—a brown hunk of it covered in steaming caramel sauce.

"That's a brick," Dave says as the waiter sets it down. It really is almost the size of a brick. "You could club someone to death with that."

He's gay, right? And we're on a date? I gesture to the cake with my fork. "I hope you're going to eat some of this."

Dave looks skeptical—either about the cake or my offer. But he takes the spoon out of his mug, wipes it on a napkin, and carves a bit of cake off the opposite end. He slips it in his mouth and mulls for a minute.

Again, I try to think of something to say. "You out?" I ask.

"You mean as in gay-out?"

I say I do, and then he starts talking. He came out in his late twenties, though he was having sex with guys since he was fifteen. He would do it at a rest stop out on I-70, a few miles past Hebron. An hour's drive from where he lived. That was the point. A good hour between his life and the sex he was having.

"I was with a woman for a while," he says. "I think I've got a kid running around somewhere. She split." I raise my eyebrows. He looks up at me but starts speaking again before I can say anything. "Hey, how did you know I was gay? Did I set off your gaydar in the parking lot?"

"Too hot to be straight. I hoped you were."

He smiles, his eyes brightening. "And here I thought you were wanting to take a swing at me because I hit your car."

"Yeah," I grin. "Both things."

He laughs.

"So hey," I say. "You've got a kid?"

Dave shrugs and says again that he thinks he might. She must have put it together, his ex, that he was getting off with guys on the side. One day he came back to their apartment, and all her stuff was gone. A few weeks before that, she'd been worried that she was pregnant. She was late, fretting about what kind of life she could make for a baby. I ask if he looked for her, and he makes a pained face. "Not very hard."

He takes another spoonful of cake. A larger one this time.

The conversation starts to feel easier now. I tell him that I came out to my folks when I was a teenager. Well, to my mother. In the cereal aisle of the local Meijer. I'd been trying to do it all morning, and that's where I was finally able to get the words out. My father was off in search of paper towels. I don't remember what words I actually said, but she just hushed me with a harsh whisper. "Don't talk about that" or "Don't talk about that here." Something like that. And it never really came up again. Though she stopped asking about girlfriends after that, and a few years later, out of the blue, told me that she always knew I was gay, even when I was a kid. I figured that meant that she'd always feared. I never officially came out to my father. I guess my mother eventually told him.

Dave asks if my mother is still alive. I tell him she passed a few years back, and that's when my father moved in. Then I mention the water heater, that it just went bad, and that the old man's getting a cold shower tomorrow. Though I suppose he can shower at the Silver Sneakers gym if he wants to.

Dave takes another bite of the apple cake, which is half gone now, more so from his end, and the waiter comes around, coffee pot in hand. I hold up my hand, palm out. I'm feeling jittery enough as it is, sitting here with Dave. Another cup and I'll be a mess. We didn't talk about doing anything other than getting a drink. Part of me wants to continue to hang out, but it's been about an hour, and the truth is that I'm still not quite relaxed enough to enjoy this. Also, the conversation has felt heavy, serious. What I'd really like is to have sex with him. But not out of lust—or not only that. It would just feel good to be with him in a physical way, not having to think and talk so much. Sex or a good workout, anything like that.

"Hey," I say. "I'm thinking about going for a walk in the reservoir after this. Get some of this cake digesting. You want to come?"

He puts down his spoon and pushes the plate away. The cake is dense as a brick, too. "I was thinking we should do your water heater," he says.

My heart starts to pound. Getting him back to my place? It doesn't seem likely that we'd spend much time on the water heater, but I'm down. "You want to do that?"

"You think a gay guy is going to pass up an opportunity to handle some pipe? It's Sunday. I've got nothing going on. No reason for your dad to have a cold shower."

"I've still got to buy one. A water heater, I mean."

"Okay. We've got a few things to do. We'll pick one up first."

"We'd have to stop back at my place to get my truck," I say, testing him. "You sure you have time for this?"

"Sure." He smiles. "Besides, you're going to help me fix that deck."

I put a couple of bills on the table, and we head to my place, which is only a ten-minute drive. We don't go inside, just switch out vehicles, both of us parking in the street so I can get the truck out. I feel a little self-conscious. It's from the late '80s, with rust flaking around the wheel wells and a big crack in the dashboard from an accident when I first got it. Most of the time I keep it parked against the garage, covered by a tarp.

As we're pulling out, Dave pokes at the radio, moving to another preset. He turns up the volume. It's Adele belting about being on the telephone with an ex-lover. He jabs another preset.

"I'm checking out your stations," he says. "This is like rifling through your underwear drawer or looking in your wallet. I'm getting the skinny on you."

A classic rock station comes on. Clapton's "Cocaine." Dave moves his finger away.

"Can you imagine a song like this nowadays?" I ask. "With a funky baseline celebrating the virtues of crystal meth."

"She don't lie, she don't lie, she don't lie, meth," Dave says—really, half-sings. "It needs another syllable. Do you ever do that stuff?"

There's a lot of drug use out here, especially among gay men.

I did ecstasy once in my twenties. I tell Dave about it, about a night in a dance club with a guy I never saw again. "The thing I remember more than anything else is how easy it was to talk. Talking to strangers, to people I was interested in and to people I wasn't. It felt automatic, like the words were just flowing out of me." Usually the words only trickle out. I don't mention that.

"I did meth for a few months," he says. "Out in LA. I went dancing a lot out there."

Dave is a gruff-looking guy. He's got that big nose, square jaw, leathery skin along his neck. I try to picture him younger, thinner, with smooth skin. At a circuit party? Maybe.

"You lived out in LA?"

"For a year in my early twenties. Had to get out of the fucking Midwest sometime. I went down in flames, and my dad came out and brought me back."

"Was this before or after you were with that woman?"

He says it was after. A couple of years after. Going down in flames wasn't due to drugs, but it wasn't *not* due to drugs, either. It was about not finding work. About finding too much sex. Burning through all the money he'd saved to bring with him. By the time he met his father at the airport, everything he owned fit in a single duffel bag. He'd been crashing on people's couches, had spent a few weeks staying with some older rich guy he met at a bar. He and his father sat there for four hours, not talking, watching people come and go through the concourse until it was time for the return flight.

"All of LA that my father has ever seen is LAX terminal 7," he says. "I came back here and stayed in the closet for a while. Went to school. Flunked out. Went back to school. I didn't come out till he moved south."

I'm feeling a little jealous, listening to this talk. Even if Dave did get burned by a dragon or two, at least he ventured out of the Shire. I did X that one time. I liked it, but I never did it again. Or any other drug. I had sporadic sex back then, just like I do now. But that's about it for my wild youth. It occurs to me that if you're going to feel out the boundaries of your life, you're bound to stumble a bit.

We get to Lowe's and head behind the kitchen displays. Karen from Flooring is back there, and she asks why I don't have my vest on. I explain that I'm there as a civilian and introduce Dave. No scratched or dented water heaters. Dave suggests we go to the water heater aisle and dent one ourselves, then claim it should be marked down. I remind him that people get fired for that kind of stuff. "Only if they get caught," he says. We make our way to the water heaters, and since

Lowe's carries only one brand, choosing is easy. I find an associate—it helps that I work here, I know where we hang out—and tell her which one I want. The insulation area is right by there, so I grab a roll of that, too, for the kitchen wall. I might as well do all the spending at once—rip off the Band Aid quick. Then we head to Plumbing for couplings, and I introduce Dave to the wonders of Shark Bite technology. He examines a coupling then jams his finger in and out, testing it.

"You wanted to handle some pipe," I say, "that's where we'll be sticking it."

"Woof," he says and claps his hand against my shoulder. The touch is brief and muffled by my jacket, but it feels electric.

IT'S ALMOST 7:00 p.m. by the time we get the new water heater in the basement and cut the old one out. My left pant leg is soaked, and tools are everywhere. But working with Dave is good. We don't talk much, just a comment or joke here and there, and it starts feeling comfortable and easy, like we're a team. It makes me forget about sex, or the possibility of it now that I'm alone with him. We remove and measure the old pipe, cut new lengths, and I show him how the couplings lock into place. When we lift out the old water heater, we're almost on top of each other, bear-hugging the cylinder from opposite sides, arms touching. By the time we put it down, well out of the way, the physical distance between us feels completely disarmed. I place my hand on his shoulder and start to say good job. And for a moment—just a moment—it feels like we're going to kiss, like it would be the most natural thing in the world for us to fall against each other. But we stay a foot apart, my hand on his shoulder. We spend a few seconds like that, then he laughs, sheepish, and the moment passes.

"Okay," he says, clapping his hands together. "Let's get the new unit in place."

Soon all that's left to do is hook up a few wires at the top. Dave is sitting on the floor, leaning against the dryer, while I'm securing connections. I've got the directions open in front of me, consulting them step by step.

I glance back. Dave hasn't spoken for a while. He looks pensive.

"Hey," I say. "The joys of home ownership."

He nods.

"You having a good time?" I continue tightening screws, but suddenly I'm not so sure he's enjoying this.

"I am," he says, brightening. Then he pauses. "I don't usually mention that—earlier, what I was saying about my ex. Not when I first meet somebody."

"It's okay. No judgment here." Does he mean the woman? "Were you guys married?"

I glance behind me again. He's shaking his head.

"This was like thirty years ago, right?" I'm wondering if I have the timeline straight. The woman, LA, back to Ohio, nursing school, failing out of nursing school. Then . . . what? Nothing for twenty years? It seems top heavy. Or bottom heavy. Like all the big stuff happened early on.

I turn back to the water heater to finish with the screws.

"Almost thirty years," he says. "It doesn't seem like that long ago. But I guess it was pretty much my whole life. Twenty to fifty, or thereabouts. That's pretty much the heart of your life. Those are the years when you build whatever it is you're going to build."

I hear him stand, so I put down the screwdriver and turn around. I'm just about done, anyway.

He puts his hand on my shoulder, then lifts it and places it on my chest, briefly cupping my pectoral muscle, smiling. "You ready to heat some water?" he says, but he steps back before I can get up the nerve to kiss him.

LATER THAT NIGHT, lying in bed, I fixate on that exchange by the water heater, what Dave was saying about those thirty years being the heart of a life. I think about how the prospects of a life change between twenty and fifty. What's still in front, what's left behind. Maybe he's right: those are the bookend years, the years before then just getting up to speed and the years after slowing down to a stop. Is that what he meant?

I also think about him stepping back.

In my experience, guys go all in on the first round of betting. The evening ended well. We got the unit working, then chatted over Pop-Tarts in the kitchen. I even considered introducing him to my father, who was watching television in his room. Dave hugged me goodnight and said we should get dinner later in the week. He suggested it. That seems important. But we didn't have sex. We didn't even kiss. Pretty far from going all in. I did text a few hours later, to thank him for helping out, and he texted back right away. But he didn't mention hanging out again.

8

"I CAN'T SEE her anymore."

I'm at the counter, eating a couple of pieces of toast. I'm already late for school so I'm shoving them down fast. My father is sitting at the table.

"But you liked the movie," I say. "You were telling me about the challenges faced by each of the climbers. You said Beth had a good time, too."

"Yes," he says. "She said the climbers were good role models."

"So what's the harm in that?"

"There are a lot of lonely people in the world, Mike. The harm is that they attach meaning to things. If I keep spending time with Beth, she's going to think I am dating her."

It occurs to me that people in their seventies and eighties date essentially the same way high school kids do. Maybe the same way middle-aged men do, too.

"I don't know, Dad. Beth could be lonely. But you spend a lot of time alone, too, right? I just don't see what the problem is if you see a movie with her every now and then."

"She wants to meet you," he says. "I told her you were a liberal. Beth is a liberal."

"We're surrounding you, Dad. Us liberals. I want to meet Beth, too." This last part isn't really true.

I pick up my book bag, get myself into the foyer, and begin putting on my shoes. My father follows me with his mug of coffee. He stands, watching me tie my laces, and starts telling me about Beth's sister, who died of a stroke almost twenty years ago.

As I'm about to walk through the door, he launches into a whole new subject. "So that guy who was here helping you with the water heater last night, he is. . . ."

I look back. I can see my father reaching for the word.

"Gay, Dad. Yeah, he is."

My father starts nodding slowly, registering the information. I pause in the door frame, waiting to see if he has anything else to say. Then I tell him I'll see him later and head out.

IN CLASS WE analyze a series of editorials looking for logical fallacies. A few of the editorials are national pundit columns, but most are local, things I've clipped from the town paper. A few years back, there was a controversy about bringing city water to a street at the edge of town, where they still used wells. There was no controversy over the need to do it; the wells had biological contaminants. The controversy was over how to pay for it and whether those dozen or so houses should face additional assessment. I like the locality of the issue and the questions it raises about collective welfare. Also, some of the vitriol in the editorials is pretty funny.

While I'm teaching, I get a text from Matt. He wants to go for a hike. He has recently learned that all gay men go on hiking dates, and he's afraid he might be missing out.

I text back that I'm teaching logical fallacies and that he's just committed a bandwagon fallacy.

He replies that he doesn't care, and when are we going hiking?

We agree to Wednesday afternoon, after my classes, at John Bryan State Park on the edge of Yellow Springs.

For a moment, I think about what my father said this morning, that there might be some inherent promise made simply by spending time with someone, by continuing to spend time with them. Am I making a promise to Matt? But you have to spend enough time with a person to know what you want with them, don't you? I've never dated two guys at once before. But then, I'm not really dating either of these guys. Coffee with Dave. A little playtime with Matt. Dating suggests something more sustained. Getting off with Josh certainly doesn't count. But with both Matt and Dave, the stakes have felt far higher than that. So I'm not quite sure.

THAT NIGHT AFTER DINNER, my father comes into the living room where I'm sitting on the couch watching the news and tooling around on my computer, and he starts talking about Beth again. She went out to Tucson to see her son last year. The son and his wife are in excellent health and love living out there, in the Sunbelt. They go for long walks every morning, just as the sun comes up. Beth and my father were imagining how nice it would be, being able to do that year-round, while they were walking on the treadmills.

"Do you think you would enjoy living down there?" my father asks.

I shrug. "This is my home."

"You could be home down there, too."

I look up from my laptop. "Are *you* thinking you'd like to live down there?"

"No," my father says, coming around to sit on the lounge chair beside the couch. "But it's nice to imagine, the warmth all year. I'm sick of winter. They have coffee on the deck in the morning. That's what Beth said, her son and his wife come back from their walk and sit out with coffee. I wanted a few years like that with your mother. I thought we were going to have a few years like that."

"I know, Dad. I wish you could have."

My father worked until he was seventy-four. My mother died just a few months after his retirement. He retired only because she became ill. I suppose he always imagined a kind of buffer—an extended period between his working life and his death. Or hers. Retirement as a semi-mythical state when the texture of life would be completely different. And better. The ultimate delayed gratification. Beth's son and his wife having coffee on their deck in a place without winter: I can see how that might seem like Valhalla to him.

My father is silent, his face downcast, sullen.

"You think you'd prefer Tucson or Florida?" I ask. "I guess you've got hurricanes in Florida."

"It would be the same," he says, shrugging.

Then he picks himself up and starts walking toward his room, but he turns back before he gets too far. "That guy who was here yesterday, he was the guy from the auto body place, wasn't he? Where you had your car repaired?"

My dad must have been watching when we came out to inspect the car. I'm a little jolted that he made the connection.

"He is like you?" my father asks.

I know what he means, of course, but I'm struck by the question. I do think he's like me. In some way that I can't formulate but that feels important.

"Yeah, he's gay, Dad." My father nods. I thought we'd covered this, this morning. Maybe my father saw us coming up from the basement, my pants soaked. "He was only helping with the water heater," I say.

"Oh," my father says. "Oh."

"IT'S FUCK INFLATION."

Matt and I are walking through John Bryan, and I'm not exactly sure how we got on this topic, though I think it might be because he dragged us here. It's a beautiful afternoon—high in the fifties, bright. One of those late February days that can fool you into thinking it's already spring. Matt's donned a backpack and hiking boots, which he may well have purchased for the occasion.

He continues, "If you fuck anyone but only get fucked when it feels safe or when you feel some special intensity, then fucking has become a debased currency, and getting fucked is where the value is. Getting fucked is legal tender. For you, fucking is like paper money during the Great Depression. You need a wheelbarrow of it to buy a tub of lard or a sack of flour."

"I don't think that really happened," I say, looking around. Matt is talking loud. "And it's not fuck inflation. It's still fucking for me, there are just levels of it. If what you're saying is right, then people who fuck and get fucked casually aren't capable of any kind of fucking at all."

Matt stops. "For some of those people," he says sententiously—pausing at the critical moment—"a kiss on the lips might be the whole act of fucking."

I continue on, walking quickly past him. "Absurd," I say. There's a kind of outdoor theater or classroom up ahead. It's not clear to me how it got here, unless this area was once a park or campground. "So for it to be fucking it's got to . . . what? Make you uncomfortable?"

"No," he says. "But you have to offer a bit of your soul. Just a little cutting of soul, like you might take from a plant to give to someone else, so they can make their own plant. Real fucking takes a cutting from your soul."

"So I guess that means I haven't had sex in years."

Matt comes up alongside me again. "I think you might still be a virgin," he says. "In all the ways that count."

"You know, you can't argue your way into my ass, Matt, even if it is a good argument."

"Maybe I can," he says. Then he reaches down and grabs my hand.

"There it is," I say, pointing, and Matt springs forward, running up to it. There's a clearing ahead, carved out of the forest. In the clearing sits a diamond-shaped stage made of two-by-fours, well weathered now, and in front are lengths of log arranged as seats, five rows of them. Matt jumps up on the stage.

"Ladies and gentleman," he says, "For my first number, I'd like to share a song I wrote after meeting a little girl at one of my shows. She had this beautiful red hair, and she said her name was Jolene. Sing along if you know this one." Matt speaks into his fist as if it were a mic. I glance around. There's no one else out here, so I sit on one of the logs in the last row.

Then he starts singing. He really starts singing. "Jolene, Jolene, Jolene, Joleeeene. Please don't take my man." He sways his shoulders and his hips and gets halfway through the first verse before stopping. "And that's all the words I know," he says, bowing before popping down to sit on the edge of the stage.

"Damn. You do a pretty good Dolly. You even have the vibrato down."

"I practice. In the shower, I practice. Dolly is one of my gods." He pats the stage next to him. "Come here, sing something."

I'm not going to sing something.

But I get up and sit next to him on the stage. Not close enough, apparently, because he pats the side of the stage right next to him and then points to it with his finger. I slide over.

"Choose a song," he says.

"I'm not a singing guy."

"Everyone is a singing guy when they are in the shower. So let's just pretend we're taking a shower together. Which is a good idea, by the way. What's a song you like to sing in the shower?"

I hesitate.

"If I answer," I say, "you're going to make me sing it."

"No shit," he says. "Now tell me a song or we're going to be here all day."

"Okay. Otis Redding. 'Dock of the Bay.'"

"Excellent. Teach it to me."

"You don't know Otis? What kind of a person—"

"Calm down. I'm about to know Otis."

I speak the words. "Sitting in the morning sun. I'll be sitting when the evening comes."

"Okay," Matt says. "Can you see my eyes are closed?" He points up to his face, and I can see his eyes are indeed closed. "Now close yours and sing the first few lines for me." I look around again and there is no one at all, so I do it. I close my eyes and sing the first few lines. I'm a little off key on the first notes, but I sort of catch it as I continue. I'm singing low and gentle, not just to avoid making too much noise, but also because the song demands it.

"A little more," Matt says.

I go on for a bit. I get to "wasting time," and it becomes easy, like it would be in the shower, even though I feel Matt beside me, his shoulder up against mine. Toward the end, I am singing as I would at home—drawing out those last few notes, putting a little soul into it. Then I open my eyes, and I see Matt is looking at me. He kisses me quickly on the lips. "I knew you weren't as uptight as you pretend to be," he says.

"Maybe no one could be."

"No, no. Lots of people are. But I knew you weren't."

There's silence between us for a moment, sitting there with Matt's hand on my leg, and it's nice, but it also starts to feel uncomfortable—just too intimate—so I begin talking about the outdoor stage. Imagining what it might have been used for. "Summer camp, I'm thinking. Or maybe the park used to do nature hikes and lectures out here. Can you see it? Campers sitting on these logs. Some guy in a brown uniform talking about the life of the forest."

Matt turns his face toward me and kisses me again, his beard against my cheek this time, and then the side of his hand turns my face toward his until we are kissing on the lips.

"Maybe we could do a presentation on men making out," I say.

"Okay, kids," Matt says. "This is how guys get down."

"It's all fun and games until one of them asks which of us is the woman."

"Kids these days don't think like that," Matt says. "Adults don't think like that anymore, either."

I'm pretty sure my father thinks like that, but he's almost eighty, so maybe that just proves Matt's point.

"Do you think like that?" he asks.

I pause. Maybe, on some level, I do. "No," I say.

Matt jumps to his feet and walks in front of me so I can reach into his backpack. "Granola bars. Just rifle around until you find them."

I unzip and fish around until I locate an unopened box of Nature Valley bars, which I set down beside me.

Matt doesn't move. "I hope you plan on at least feeling me up while we're positioned like this."

I run my hands over his shoulders, then down his sides. He has a compact, toned body. For a moment I admire it, my hands below his waist, settled on the curve of his hips. It occurs to me in a slower, fuller way than it has before that Matt really is a beautiful man.

IT'S ABOUT 4:30 by the time we get back to the cars.

"So now I have experienced that hallowed gay ritual of 'The Hike,'" Matt says, leaning against his Hyundai. "Was it good for you?"

"It was," I say. "Though for the full experience, we'd have had to jerk each other off behind a tree."

"We still could."

I look around for people. He's right.

"But I need to go," Matt says, getting up off his car. "I have a job interview tomorrow morning, and if I don't get a job soon I will have to move in with my sister." Then he tells me that the job is at a local print shop. They have a one-person design department to work with clients. He kicks at my foot with the toe of his sneaker. "I want to spend the night with you again. Maybe you could even stay until I wake up."

This makes me nervous. Last time was a fluke. I wouldn't sleep at all if we tried it again. Aside from last time, it's been more than a decade since I tried to sleep next to anyone.

"Okay," I say. "We can figure out a time to do that."

He seems to be studying my face. "Not going to happen, is it?" he says. "At least come by one night this week so we can fuck."

9

THE NEXT DAY at work, customers go off on me. A guy with a four-by-eight sheet of plywood balanced precariously atop his cart comes up to me while I'm telling another customer about epoxy grout. I'm explaining all the benefits and drawbacks, and she's nodding along. Then this guy bumps me in the hip with the edge of his plywood. It's sharp, and it pisses me off. He doesn't seem to notice; just starts talking as soon as I turn to him, asking if I can cut the wood. I say very politely that I'm sorry, I'm not certified to use that machine, but if he'll wait until I'm done talking to this customer, I will call someone who is. The guy doesn't quit. He starts going off about how he can never find anyone to help him in this store, that there are never any employees around, and before I know it, Rob comes over. I finish telling the woman about the grout, and Rob walks the guy off. But a few minutes later, Rob is back, lecturing me about how I treat customers, saying that my demeanor isn't respectful. Before he stalks away, he says that if I don't like the requirements of the job, I'm free to leave at any time.

The truth is that I need to work here. Or somewhere. I usually clear about twenty-five grand a year, all told, from my various jobs. My place is cheap; my property taxes are dirt cheap. And there's the money from my father every month. But things are tight. Some months I'm in the red—that's going to be the case this month because of the water heater. It's not that I mind working at Lowe's, doing the job. Just that, at fifty, I see it for the scut work that it is—most of the time I'm stocking shelves—and realize I don't have many other options.

And I'm on edge because Dave hasn't texted. I was thinking it would be today. Or yesterday. It's been four days since our date. This feels like a game of chicken, two guys driving toward a cliff, competing to see who can wait longest to slam on the breaks. In this case, the cliff edge is Just Too Long—the point beyond which it's clear that there really isn't any interest or connection between us. That would be the car tumbling into a ravine.

As I'm walking into the parking lot, Lowe's vest in hand, I decide I'm not going to let that happen. I like Dave. No shame in that. I get into the Celica, throw the vest on the seat beside me, and take out my phone.

Best bet is to be casual.

I type, *Hey, you still up for dinner this week?* But I don't send it. Too direct. I try again. *Hey Dave, changing a lot of bed pans today? Ha ha.* No, not funny enough. Maybe just *How's your week?* Then I consider something about the water heater—that it's working great, which it does seem to be—but finally I type in one word, *Hey*, and hit send.

A minute goes by, and the single word begins to seem rude, so I add, *How are you?*

Then I start the car and head out.

Dave still hasn't texted back by the time I get home.

My father's car isn't in the driveway, which is surprising. But I'm glad to have the place to myself. I put music on—Norah Jones because I'm feeling subdued—and decide I'm going to work on the kitchen wall. I know my father doesn't like having it open like that, that he thinks it's low class. Maybe he's right. It's like there's a small jobsite in the middle of the house. The additional roll of insulation is right there, where Dave and I left it on Sunday night, so I kneel down and get to work. First, I check my phone again, but then I turn the ringer off. Scruff notifications, too. I'm going to focus on the job.

By the time my father gets home, it's dark out. I've got the rubber mallet in hand, and I'm gently knocking the tongue-and-groove paneling back into place, lining up a piece and tapping it into the adjacent board. It takes a little wrestling to get the final two pieces situated, but once I do, it's extremely satisfying to knock them flat. I run my hand where the seam was, from the top of the boards all the way down to the floor. You would never know the wall had been opened there. I'm contemplating it, just standing there admiring it, when my father walks in.

"Hi kid," he says from the foyer, taking off his coat. That's how my father used to address me when I was younger, when he was in a good mood. I can see right away, by the energy with which he's taking off his coat, putting it on a hanger, that he's in a good mood now.

"You finished with the kitchen." He walks over to inspect the wall, then puts his palm flat against it. "Did you get the insulation in there?"

"Should be a little warmer now," I say, picking up the mallet and the screwdriver I used to pry the panels apart. The north wind blows hard against that wall.

Then I ask my father where he was, something I try not to do because it's not my business and because I don't want it to become a habit, that we know each other's whereabouts at all times. Not that either of us goes anywhere particularly clandestine, just that a little polite distance seems key to keeping this arrangement stable. He sits at the kitchen table, puts on his glasses, and begins going through the mail, pulling out letters addressed to him.

"We went to the buffet," he says. "Chinese buffet. After the gym. The one on 48. Moon Moon or some shit like that. It was good. I had the egg foo yong and a salad. Beth had fried rice—"

"You went with Beth?" I don't quite manage to keep the surprise out of my voice, which is a mistake because my father immediately gets defensive.

"She said she was hungry after walking. I told her that your mother and I used to go to Chinese, and she said she sometimes goes to the buffet there."

"What else did they have on the buffet, Dad?" It's the least offensive question I can think of on the fly, and it starts him talking until he loosens up again. He describes the plexiglass sneeze guard, the orange wedges and pineapple rings (he says they felt a little soft), and how Beth read their fortunes out loud. Then he starts going on about the restaurant bathrooms, which he felt weren't all that clean.

As he's talking, I finish tidying up, putting small chunks of insulation into the garbage and coiling up the one larger chunk to store in the basement. It will probably be in there for the next owner of the house—and maybe the owner after that—but I still can't bring myself to throw it out. My father stays in the kitchen for another twenty minutes, watching me finish and telling me what he and Beth talked about, before heading to his room. And it's only then, when the kitchen is clean and I'm sitting down with four pieces of toast and a bowl of chili I scooped out of a can, that I check my phone.

A text from Matt. *Tonight?*

And nothing from Dave. I scroll through my messages twice. Nothing.

It's been hours.

I text Matt a quick note, asking if the offer is still good. A little company sounds nice right now.

MATT OPENS HIS door just a crack. “How does it feel to be reduced to a booty call?” he says, peering through. He’s in his underwear.

“I thought this was the second part of our date.”

He closes the door to undo the latch before opening it wide. “Whatever you need to tell yourself to maintain your self-respect.”

As we’re walking back to the bedroom, I notice a new item, a standing lamp beside the brocade chair. I point this out.

“I needed more light to read,” he says. And then, “Ask me how my interview went.”

I might have texted to do that. I was so busy *not* texting Dave most of the day that it slipped my mind.

Matt doesn’t wait for me to answer. “It went fabulously. I got the job.” Once we’re at the bed—well, the mattress—he turns to face me. “I will be the design manager and a department unto myself.” He raises his hands over his head in a pose of victory and then comes close.

“Of course you will,” I say. I smile and run a hand down his back to his backside, gently pulling his crotch against mine. We kiss for a minute before Matt observes that I have way too many clothes on and starts to lift the sweatshirt and T-shirt off me, both items in one go. I raise my arms and close my eyes so he can pull them over my head, but he fumbles halfway up, the sweatshirt stuck covering my face. While I’m trying to get untangled, I hear him laughing. He unbuttons my jeans and pulls them down to my ankles. My underwear, too. By the time I free myself, he’s on his knees, his mouth on the head of my dick.

I exhale; it feels great. “Boy, you really don’t screw around when you’re ready to go, do you?” I run my right hand through his curly hair and bend forward, so I can reach further, all the way down his spine. He continues sucking me and gets a rhythm up, and it starts to feel like I could come if he keeps at it—in fact, it feels like I might—so I step back and pull him up to his feet.

We make out for a while standing up, and then Matt pushes me back toward the mattress. I let myself fall on the edge of it, and he pulls off my jeans, first one leg, then the other, this time without tangling. "Lie back," he says. "I'm going to rub myself on top of you."

In light of our recent conversation, I raise an eyebrow, about to say something—I'm not sure what—but he interrupts me. "Don't worry," he says. "You can fuck me after." He pauses. "Maybe you can. Maybe not, we'll see. But for now, I'm just going to lie on top of you."

"You've decided?"

"There was a vote before you got here." I lean back on my shoulders, and he takes off his underwear and crawls on top of me.

"Democracy dies in darkness," I say.

Matt rubs himself against me, his body hair against mine, our dicks pressing together. I put my hands on his back, closing my eyes. We do this for a while—and I enjoy it—but I don't relax into it, don't lose track of myself. When it seems like it's gone on long enough, I press the weight of my body against him to launch myself up, rolling him onto his back. Then I sit over him and take his dick in my mouth, massaging around his hole with my finger. He arches his back, so I put the tip of my finger inside him. "Lube," he says without opening his eyes. "By the side of the bed." I reach over and find a tube of Glide on the floor. I slather some on my left hand and take hold of his dick at the shaft. Then I slowly move my fist up, over the head, while working my pointer finger inside him. "Fuck," he says. So I keep on going, slowly working my fist up and down on his dick and getting my finger all the way in until my palm is flat against his balls. "Fuck," he says. "I'm going to come." I can see from his body that it's happening right now, how arched and tight he is. I speed up, pumping my fist as he curls, bringing his chest off the bed and inward, until the first burst of cum shoots out of him. It goes high up his body, onto his chest and neck.

"Whoa," he says.

I agree fully. And lean over to give him a good long kiss. Then I lie down next to him, my head against his shoulder.

Suddenly, I'm not so sure I want to get off. Maybe I shouldn't. I think about Dave, wondering if he's texted since I got here. Maybe

I'm at Matt's place under false pretenses. I tell myself that I'm not cheating on anyone, and I know that's true, but it still doesn't feel quite right. All this is so loud in my head that it seems impossible that Matt, lying right beside me, can't hear any of it.

"I think my father has a girlfriend," I say. The words pop out of my mouth.

"Good for him," Matt says. "Only one?"

"Two if you count my mother."

"Your mother died, right?"

"He's still dating her, she's just not participating that much."

Matt nods.

"She hot, the new girlfriend?"

"I imagine she's mid-seventies hot," I say. "I'm guessing the standards evolve."

Matt reaches down with his palm and cups my balls and dick, which is soft now. "I want to make you come."

"Maybe if we keep talking about hot senior citizens it will get me going again."

He begins rubbing me. I don't stop him, and soon we're facing each other, mouths almost touching. He's holding my dick tight, and I'm thrusting against his fist. When I do come, I hear his voice, soothing and quiet. "Yeah," he says, "that's right."

I stay against him for a while, willing myself not to think of anything. Not if I'm here under false pretenses or if Dave might have texted. I won't spend the night, but for a few moments I pretend that I will, that Matt and I can just lie here like this and fall asleep. That must be what it's like for couples, a body beside them they can fully relax with. But I know there are bad relationships out there, too. Sometimes people are disgusted by their partners and hate to be near them.

"Tell me more about the guy you were with down in Texas," I say.

So Matt describes how he and Javier met. At a yuppie bar called JR's. Javier in a white button down, slacks, and a cowboy hat, leaning against a wall. By midnight, they were doing shots. They woke up well after noon in Javier's condo, achy and sore below the belt, with pounding headaches. But, Matt notes, quite contented. Over the next few months, they had half a dozen nights like that and exchanged life stories the next day during bleary afternoon breakfasts at IHOP. Javier had worked his way up at Wells Fargo, getting an MBA in the process. Matt says he was born to manage banks.

"When he let loose, though, he let loose. We had parties in the condo: dinner, Christmas, sex. All varieties of party." At some point, the lease on Matt's apartment ran out, and Javier asked if he wanted to stay with him for a while. And that was that.

I observe that the arrangement doesn't sound especially domestic, and Matt seems a little offended.

"We slept in the same bed. We binge-watched *Downton Abbey*. We had a cat. A shared cat. What's more domestic than co-parenting a cat?"

I ask if they were monogamous—even for a while, maybe at the beginning. It seems like a lot of couples start out that way.

Matt says it never came up. But they did wash and fold each other's laundry. He pauses, looking up at the ceiling, hands behind his head. "Neither of us was uptight about sex, Mike. No assumptions, no promises we weren't going to keep. No promises that would set us up for betrayals later. No talk about what we weren't allowed to do. It wasn't about limits."

Matt didn't come home to find his things in boxes. There was no screaming. No other man. Nothing like that. Eventually they just came unstuck, he says, like glue on an old envelope. Whatever mastic had kept them together dried out. Javier wanted to spend a few additional months in LA that year. Matt was tired of Houston, but he didn't think he could make a home on the West Coast. Something about the pace of life out there seemed wrong. There wasn't a formal break up. Only a phone conversation, Javier saying he was staying out west until after Christmas, Matt saying he was thinking he'd go north for a while. Matt tells me they both knew it was time.

I sit up. I can't help myself. I turn and look directly at Matt, to ask—what? "So you were with him for five years and never acknowledged that you were breaking up? Did you at least tell each other you loved each other?"

"We did," Matt says, unruffled, still looking up at the ceiling. "We said it a lot."

I lie back down against him, a little flummoxed. "I don't understand how you could have done that for five years. It sounds so casual or . . . unmoored. How you could have lived with a guy and all that when he could take off at any moment—"

"Anyone can leave at any moment. Love isn't really a great place to look for security." Matt doesn't say this bitterly, or even sadly. I want to ask where is a better place to look for it, but I keep my mouth shut.

"My years with Javier were good. Very good. But I make it my business not to hold on to things too tightly. Not to expect too much."

I want to object somehow—I feel like I need to—that a person can't live that way, that no one could. But I know that's not true. I'm just not sure I could. So I don't say anything. I just lie there under Matt's words as if they were churning in a cloud above me.

After a few minutes of silence, he asks if I'm hungry, and when I say I am, he hops up to make us each a buttered roll. We eat standing at the kitchen counter, and I head home right after. He doesn't press me to spend the night.

AS SOON AS I'm back in my car, I check my phone.

Three messages. All from Dave.

A lot of verbiage.

The first asks how the water heater is holding up. The second says he's sorry for being out of touch and explains that he had a hard week. A patient died; it was "tough to watch." The last message is an invitation. Do I want to come by his brother's place on Saturday? There's going to be a fire.

All the heaviness of the day—from the fight with the customer to the conversation about Javier—leaves me. Even as it does, I know how unhealthy that is—that a few texts from some guy can change my day. I feel ridiculous that it's true, still true at age fifty. But the bottom line is that it is. Even though it's after midnight, I sit in the car in front of Matt's place, engine running, and text Dave back that the water heater is great, that I'm sorry to hear about the patient. I ask what happened. Then I confirm for Saturday.

I don't write *Hell yes*, but that's what I'm thinking.

10

FRIDAY I WAKE up energized, so I devote the day to an advertising blitz, posting notices on Craigslist and Facebook and emailing people I've done work for in the past, letting them know I'm accepting new jobs. I even make paper signs with rip-off slips at the bottom containing my cell number and put them up on local boards: at the Starbucks, the Kroger, and the library.

I also consider getting a cash advance on my credit card or asking my father for a loan. Neither option is particularly appealing. If I start carrying balances on my credit card, it's only a matter of time before it will sink me. And my father doesn't have much money himself. The truth is that I like him having it—like the independence that it gives him, that it gives both of us. My father has enough money to leave my place if he wants to, and for the dignity of us both, that's best.

After I finish with the signs, I stop by Lowe's to let them know that I'm available to pick up extra hours. They already know, but it can't hurt to remind them.

It's almost three when I get there. I walk up to the store manager on duty, and she sends me back to Rob, who's at the design desk, talking with a customer, probably taking an order. I watch from a distance until the woman nods a few times then gets up from the chair. Rob notices me and gestures me forward with his head, so I come over. He goes back to typing. I wait until he looks up again.

"What's up, Breck?" he says.

"I was at the front desk, asking if we're shorthanded. I'm looking to pick up a few more hours next week."

Rob studies me for a moment. He's a big guy, tall, beer gut, red faced. I'd guess early forties. I think it's important to him to remind me that he's the boss in every interaction.

"Sit down."

I pull out the chair and sit where the customer sat just a few moments before.

"Do you like working here?"

"It's not the job I dreamed about in college," I say, "but I like it." I instantly regret saying anything but yes.

"Not the job you dreamed about in college." He looks back down at his keyboard and hits a few more keys.

"How about this," he says, looking back up. "If, next week, you act like you like working here, we can see about a few more hours the week after." He makes eye contact with me, then starts typing again.

"Okay," I say, standing. I push out a "thanks." He nods without looking up.

WHEN I GET back, my father is in his room watching television. I'm glad. I don't much want to speak with him. I eat, do a half-assed job cleaning up after myself, and end up lying on the couch, surfing Scruff by 8:00 p.m., my laptop open in front of me playing back-to-back episodes of early *NCIS*. For half an hour, I make small talk and exchange pictures with a guy in Fort Worth. He's got a handlebar mustache, and we spend a good ten minutes on that alone. My attention is splintered and splintered again by people sending pictures, or saying hello, or by a few minutes of Jethro pulling out his gun, hunched behind a car, waiting for a wayward marine to exit a suburban house. I don't think about Rob pissing on me earlier; I don't think about money; I don't even think about Matt or Dave. It's almost midnight by the time I feel tired enough for bed.

HANSEN LIVES NORTH of Laura, a town of maybe five hundred people. The house is made of cinder block, long and squat with a clumsy addition jutting out in back. It looks like it's been painted recently—it's butter yellow—but you can still make out the blocks. Behind it sits a large old barn with peeling red paint. There must have been a farmhouse out here at some point. The gravel driveway is filled with cars, and there are a few on the street in front of the place, too. I park on the street. I should have brought a six-pack or a bottle of something.

Earlier, Dave texted, *Just head to the back when you get here.* So I walk around the house. About twenty people are in the backyard, all wearing jackets, sitting on a variety of chairs: fold-out loungers, wood benches at a picnic table, also what look like dining room chairs brought from inside. There are a few people on the deck, too, on one side of it. The other side, which backs up against the addition, is blocked off by sawhorses. A radio is playing some old-school rock that I don't recognize. And, in a small pit lined with fieldstones, a fire's burning a good four-feet high.

Out beyond the yard, there's nothing: a high-tension power line and fields that look like they go on for hundreds of acres.

I don't see Dave right away, so I mill around. I spot Hansen on a lounger, beer in hand, with a couple of guys nearby. Their voices are raised, talking over each other. As I get closer, I hear that they're arguing about generations of Corvettes, the C2 versus the early C3, which was better. It sounds like Hansen has a Stingray in storage somewhere on the property, and the other guys are clamoring to get their hands on it.

"You can look at it," he says. "But we're not starting it up. And no way you guys are driving it—"

I introduce myself as the three of them are getting up. Hansen doesn't seem to recognize me at first, but he jerks his thumb behind him, saying Dave is in the kitchen. I thank him and head to the house. The slider doors are open, and as I step on the deck, Dave comes out. He's wearing a brown canvas field coat, board shorts, and a ball cap, and carrying a bunch of mismatched mugs by the handles, three in one hand, two in the other.

"Whoa guy, hey," he says, smiling. "Can you take a couple of these?" He glances down. The mugs are steaming and smell warm, spiced. I lift the two from his left hand.

"Cider?"

"The good stuff," he says, conspiratorially leaning in.

I follow as Dave distributes the mugs around the yard, introducing me as his buddy, standing close. Then he asks if I want some, and I follow him back to the kitchen. He takes a few mugs down from a cabinet. There's a soup pot on the stove, and he reaches in with a ladle, filling one and handing it to me before filling another for himself.

It's sweet and sharp. I taste whiskey.

Back outside, we pull deck chairs up to the fire. Dave explains that it's really Hansen's bonfire, Hansen's friends from when they were kids. But they're more or less his friends now. I ask if he's out to them, and he shouts, "Hey Alice," without turning his head. Alice is sitting behind us, at the picnic table smoking a cigarette. Dave introduced us earlier, when he handed her a mug. "Anyone here a homo?"

She shouts back: "You. And we're not too sure about Jody." Then a gravelly voice, also from behind us, says, "Bite me, Alice."

Dave says he came out to these guys years back.

We start chatting about the fire, which is mostly old pallets and brush from the yard—then we get onto campfires generally and the best places for camping in the area. He's never been to Red River Gorge, which is a couple of hours to the south. I tell him about a guy I knew who died out there, lost his balance taking a selfie on one of the ledges and tumbled over. Then I remember Dave's text about the patient.

"Yeah," he shrugs. "Car accident. She was conscious when she first came in. I sat with her before they took her up to surgery. Surgery just didn't work.

"I'm good in a crisis. I hone in, focus. Got no problem with blood, my own or other people's. Guts, gore. All good. It's just the body. Medicine is just seeing what's inside of us and fixing it up. But this was different. She was a kid. She was banged up bad. Internal bleeding. I could see she was scared, and then what she was scared of happening happened."

I ask if she knew she was dying, and Dave says we shouldn't talk about it. But after a moment, he continues. He describes her face and what she said. Her boyfriend was driving, and she was adamant that the accident wasn't his fault. That was the last thing she talked about. The boyfriend was already gone. "There just wasn't anything I could do to help." Dave clasps his hands together and looks at the fire. "The whole point of me being there is to help."

I was hundreds of miles west when my mother's cancer played out. In a way, her death still feels like hearsay. One week she was there to answer the phone; the next, she wasn't. I know she's gone, but how—the nature of the transition—happened largely offstage for me. It was hard on my father, though. He did what Dave is talking about, sitting there at the end, sharing the fear. An intense form of witnessing. Clearly there's a psychological cost to that.

"I've seen a lot of people die," he says, bringing his mug to his lips.

I'm chewing over that, thinking about how losses mount as you get older, when there's a roar behind us. At first I think it's a lawnmower, and then I think motorcycle. The sound intensifies—and another one starts up. Then a third.

"Shit," Dave says, turning. "That didn't take long."

I stand and look toward the barn. The doors are wide open, and there's bright light spilling from inside. I can see two squat vehicles silhouetted against it. A third is already speeding toward us. ATVs.

"My brother and his damn Yamahas," Dave says.

The lead ATV rumbles forward, its headlights getting larger and brighter, and the others start moving forward, too. The lead one gets within fifty yards of us before veering left, into the cornfield. Hansen is on it, and he lets out a whoop as he enters the field, which is covered with the stubble of broken corn stalks. I'm wondering how he stays on. The ride can't be smooth. More like being on a mechanical bull.

The other ATVs come even closer. One continues past us and circles around the house, getting up real speed. The other stops, the driver—one of the guys I'd seen earlier arguing with Hansen about Corvette generations—shouting over to Laurie to "get on over here." A woman shouts back, "I'm not getting on that thing again. You get hemorrhoids doing that," and the people around her start laughing. Dave laughs, too. Then the guy on the ATV calls again, and Laurie gets up and walks over, eventually sliding on behind him. The exchange is both public and playfully intimate. I feel a pang of jealousy.

Dave stands to look at Hansen's ATV, far off in the cornfield.

"Doesn't cause hemorrhoids," he says. "Makes them hurt like a motherfucker, though."

There are burgers on a portable round grill set up on the deck, so we go get some. They're dried out because they've been there a while, but we eat and talk about our families. Dave says Hansen was always an "ass clown." His words. But even as a kid he knew about cars. This is in contrast to Dave himself, who was an ass clown only some of the time but didn't know much about anything. I tell him about my sister, who lives in Alabama. Her husband worked for a biotech firm down there, testing pharmaceuticals on animals before he retired. She raised the kids and these days has an eBay store. My sister and I talk maybe twice a year, short conversations about my father. I tell Dave that it's enough, twice a year. He seems to understand that, nodding a gruff assent, his mouth full of burger.

As we're talking, I'm following Hansen's ATV out in the cornfield, the line of his headlights brightening when he comes toward us, disappearing when he turns away, wondering what it's like to be rumbling out there with the cracked ground and corn stubble. Then another of the ATVs pulls up, maybe twenty yards away. Laurie and the driver, whose name I never catch, jump off and come toward us bickering. The third ATV comes back about ten minutes after that, and it pulls way too close, smacking one of the plastic deck chairs as it approaches, which goes flying into the middle of the yard. The driver hops off, laughing.

"You sure taught that chair, Gus," someone says from the deck.

I look over and see that Dave has been watching me stare into the field.

He hops to his feet, setting down his last bite of burger. "Our turn."

I look up at him. I've never been on one of those things. After a pause, I tell him that.

"First time," he says, nodding. "Even better." He reaches down, slapping my shoulder. "Come on, I'll be gentle."

I shake my head, but I'm excited to do it, to ride out there with him. I get up and follow him over to the Yamaha. Dark blue, wheel wells high over the tires, long flat seat. Beaten up. The thing looks at least twenty years old. Dave jumps on, grips the handlebars, then tells me to get on. He starts it up, the engine churning. I hesitate, not quite sure how to mount it, wondering how much touch is appropriate here. I step behind Dave and slowly try to ease one leg over without touching him too much—or too sexually. It just doesn't work. Finally I put my hand on the side of his shoulder to steady myself, and once I fully straddle the machine, fall right against him, my face inches from the back of his neck and his canvas collar, my chest against his back, my thighs on his hips.

He leans back to address me, and I feel the weight of his torso. "You better put your arms around my stomach."

I do, feeling his belly through his coat, and pull myself into him. For a moment, it's a little intoxicating, the cool air, the solidity of his trunk, and just being out here, doing this with him in front of his family and friends. It feels almost too free, like some kind of transgression—like it's something too intimate for guys to be doing in public. I glance around to see if anyone is watching us. Then the ATV charges forward, pushing Dave back hard against me. The engine roars, and we pick up speed.

The going is smooth as we head toward the edge of the lawn, but then we're in the cornfield, and we're bucking. The wind feels bitter cold, but Dave's body is warm and substantial, and the rush of movement is intense. It felt free before, but now it's on another level entirely—electric, alive. Even ecstatic. I let out a whoop, just like Hansen did. I look over Dave's shoulder into the tunnel of light that the headlights make ahead of us, the corn stubble and darkness rushing forward. I whoop again and start laughing.

Dave asks, "You want to go faster?" and before I answer the vehicle seems to jump ahead. I know there must be farmhouses on the far side of this field, but the field seems endless, like we're aloft in an airplane—nothing in any direction, just sky and the roar of an engine. Like a damn turbulent airplane ride. The terrain is throwing us against each other, knocking us up out of the seat and then pulling us back down, maybe like being on a roller coaster and a trampoline at the same time. We head out in a line for a while—I completely lose track of how long—before I feel the vehicle turn in a wide arc and realize we must be heading back toward the yard. And soon we're on grass again, but on the side of the house opposite the barn, far away from the picnic table. There's a single tree there, and Dave stops under it, letting the engine idle.

"You like that?" he asks. I can see he's grinning.

"Damn straight, I do."

I keep my arms around his stomach, pressed into him.

My dick is hard, held down by my jeans, but it's not really sexual. Or not just that. I'm enjoying the contact, the warmth of his body and the engine churning beneath us. I put my face against the back of his head, leaning it there, smelling his buzzed hair and the diesel exhaust. Dave settles both his arms over mine, which are still wrapped around him. We stay like that a moment, and then I feel him pat the back of my hand and say, "Okay, buddy, forward," and he presses the gas again. The ATV roars, this time toward the road. We turn left onto it and pick up speed.

There's not a lot out in this part of Ohio: large tracts of land worked by someone who lives in the next town over—or farther off than that, some of these massive corporate farms—and a few small houses on lots carved out by the road. Sprinkled in among them are the original farmhouses—handsome old structures with large eaves, a kind of grace you don't see in new construction. Three or four porches, complex, gabled roofs.

There aren't any cars on the road. So Dave takes us onto it, and for a few minutes we drive into the quiet with a big Midwestern sky above us. Not much light pollution out here, no tall buildings. Just telephone poles, a few grain silos, and stars. At one point, a car approaches in the opposite lane, and its headlights are blinding. I can't see for a minute and wonder how Dave can. But I don't worry about it. I hold on to him, feeling cold rush against my face.

BY THE TIME we get the ATV stowed and walk back toward the fire, it's embers.

There are half a dozen people at the picnic table, and we join them. As we're sitting down, Alice takes a deck of cards out of her purse and starts shuffling, and Chris, the guy sitting across from her—Dave told me earlier that he was her boyfriend—asks what we're playing.

Hansen's there, too. He slides his wallet out of his back pocket and removes a neatly folded wad of twenties, which he tosses on the table. It could be a couple of hundred bucks. "You ladies up for some real stakes?" he says. He's at least a little drunk.

Alice tells Hansen to watch who he's calling a lady, then pulls out two five-dollar bills. Dave gets his wallet out, too. He shakes it over the table and several bills fall out—I'm sitting beside him so I can see they're mostly singles—along with an assortment of coins he must have shoved in there. "Let's go, brother!" he says.

The rest of us also dig out a few bucks—not much. Then we go back and forth passing around bills, cards, and beers. It doesn't take long for Hansen to clean us out. Alice loses all her cash on the third hand, says "shit," and then rummages in her purse for a pack of cigarettes. The game continues for maybe another half hour. We make it around once, each dealing a hand or two. I'm the dealer for the last hand—I call seven-card—and by the final round of betting, it's just Dave, Hansen, and I. Dave and I are all in. Hansen's puffing on one of Alice's cigarettes.

I've got a couple of jacks showing, and my down cards make it two pair. It doesn't look like Dave has much. Maybe he's banking on a flush or a straight, or his down cards give him three of a kind. Hansen, though, is clearly working on a full house. He's got sevens and threes showing. I deal the last down card.

"Two pair bets," I say.

It's hard to judge Hansen's swagger, whether it's the winning streak, the beer, or just his poker persona. "You guys want to make this interesting?" he says, leaning in. He picks through his pile of money and lifts out the twenties, then drops five of them in the pot. He knows we don't have that kind of cash. The biggest bet of the night so far has been five dollars—made by Laurie earlier, to a chorus of oohs. We all folded.

"What can you guys offer to see that?"

Alice nudges Hansen's shoulder. "You wouldn't be pulling this crap if Eileen were here," she says. "And you sure as hell wouldn't have that cigarette in your mouth."

Dave calls Hansen an asshole—in a mostly lighthearted way—and starts talking about table stakes and being all in. But then Hansen asks if he's really going to pass up a chance to win his money.

Dave says, "I'll wash cars down at the shop for a week."

"Just like you'll fix my deck?" Hansen says. He takes another puff of his cigarette. "Make it two weeks. And you sweep the office."

They lock eyes. It seems pretty clear that this is a contest between them, so I'm thinking I'll fold. Maybe Hansen's trying to boss Dave around, see if he can bluff him. A dominance thing.

Dave says, "Kiss my ass" and turns all his cards face down.

Then Hansen starts reaching in for the pot, and I speak before I know what I'm saying. It's because it pisses me off, seeing Dave bested by his brother. It feels like this is a pattern between them. Something about it—Hansen's manner, his smugness—seems to be well-traveled territory.

"I'll take the bet," I blurt out. "I'll fix your deck. I mean, help Dave do it. I'll make sure it gets done." Hansen stops picking up bills and looks over at me.

Same smug bearing. Without saying a word, he flips over one of his down cards to reveal a third seven, then starts gathering the bills again.

NOT LONG AFTER THAT, people start saying goodbye until there are only a few of us left, and I decide to get going, too. Not because I want to. I love being out here, love being with Dave, his solid presence, his horsing up against me, him slapping the table after he laid down a flush, his one big hand. And I like these people, their ease and laughter, how they seem to accept me, and, I think, accept me as Dave's date. There just haven't been many occasions like this in my life.

But I don't want to overstay my welcome, and it's after 11:00 p.m. I put my hand on Dave's and tell him I should head out, too. He nods and gets up, and we walk around to the front of the house.

As soon as we're around the corner, he puts his arm around my shoulder. "Nice try back there," he says. "It would have been fun to nail his ass."

I laugh. We both do.

"Hey," I say, "you want to make out for a minute before I go?"

Dave glances around, smiles, and starts coming close. But then stops. Something changes in his eyes. He leans in and kisses me quick—a peck—before stepping back. It feels like getting kissed by a European grandmother.

For a moment, we're silent.

I'm a little confused. "Jeeze," I say. "No way that qualifies as making out."

Dave sighs. "Yeah, I know. I—I don't do this, Mike. I mean, I get with guys now and then, but not . . . hanging out like this. I'm thinking I need to tell you that right now." Even in the dark, I can see he looks worried, or half-worried, half-apologetic.

I feel a surge of something—disappointment, maybe hurt, I'm not sure what—but I keep it out of my voice. "It's okay. I don't do this a lot either."

He continues. "There was Lauren, that was the woman I was with, and a guy in LA. I'm not sure what that was. And I sort of dated a guy for a while here when I first got back. A married guy. His wife thought we were hunting buddies. It didn't feel weird at the time, but looking back now, it doesn't make any sense at all—the three of us sitting on the couch, watching *M*A*S*H* reruns. But even that was twenty-five years ago. That's what I got. The high point of my intimacy with guys was sitting on a couch on one side of a guy while his wife was sitting on the other, knitting granny squares. Shit." Dave's laughing but it's not quite a happy laugh. "Makes me kind of a fuck up."

"No," I say. "It's all right." I step closer. I want to do something—maybe touch his face, brush his cheek and under his jaw. Something to show him it's all right. But I lower my hand. "Have you wanted to?" I ask. "Date, I mean."

"Sometimes, yeah. I tried a few times. But looking back it seems like a mess. Just some guys I don't talk to anymore, who I put time into, had plans for. Things we were going to do. Projects, road trips. Maybe get a place together. Seems childish now."

I ask Dave if he's in contact with any of the guys he's dated. He shakes his head. "You see what I mean? That girl in Emergency this week, the one who died, she had all this possibility before her. Seems like I wasted mine."

We're silent for a moment.

"When you hit the john, Hansen's buddies were asking if you and I are dating, they were having a good time with that. But I don't even know how guys date. Or if they do."

Of course guys date. That's what I'm thinking. I know male couples who've built lives together, reasonably good ones. At least they look reasonably good from the outside. I think of Josh and Gary. Even they seem to have made a decent life together. There are problems, sure. Aren't there always problems? But between casual fucking and what they have, cohabitation—something like marriage—lies a lot of territory, and that territory seems very tough to navigate.

I wonder if Dave's trying to tell me something specific. We've had such a good night. I look at his face in the darkness. I should straight out ask if he's saying something about us. Or what he's saying about us. I know I should.

But I don't. I just can't go there. So I tell him I get it, squeeze his shoulder, and start walking to my car.

Dave falls in beside me, not saying anything. But before I get in, he steps in close to kiss me. A longer kiss this time, softer. “Hey,” he says. “I had a good time with you tonight.”

“I had a good time, too.” I put my key in the door and turn it. Then I pause. “You told me what happened with her, that woman you lived with,” I say. “You said you don’t usually tell people that, but you told me. How come?”

Dave shrugs and smiles. “You look like a friend, Mike.” Then he steps back, and I open the car door.

11

I DON'T THINK about Dave the next day. At least I try not to, try not to think about riding into the cornfield with him, or sitting beside him playing cards, our knees touching, or the conversation after, when he might have been telling me to reign in my expectations—or might have been doing just the opposite, trying to let me in. Sense impressions come back to me all day, especially the feel of holding onto him, the smell of his coat and diesel fuel in the cold air, and I wonder what he might have meant by "friend." I seem like a friend.

I have a lot of work to do, so I throw myself into it. I spend most of the day at the kitchen table. First up: grading two sets of essays. The students had to examine the logic of opposing arguments about gun control, deciding which made the stronger case. Not riveting, but I get into a rhythm with it. That takes until early afternoon. Then—since yesterday was the first day of March—I go over bills, tallying up which have to be paid right away and how much money there is to do it. Some of the due dates are non-negotiable, but others have more leeway than you might expect. I'm sitting with a mug of coffee, going over credit card charges, when my father comes home. Again, he's carrying a sack of groceries. He goes to the store a lot.

"Hey kid," he says, taking a bunch of bananas out of the bag, then a package of Oreos and a box of Cream of Wheat. "I got a haircut. I think he took a little too much off the top." He pats the top of his head.

I look up to see that his hair is more orderly than usual. He's got silver hair with a few streaks of black in it. There's not much on top—hasn't been for decades. My dad wears a pretty sad comb over.

"It looks good, Dad."

"What are you working on?" He finishes putting away his groceries, then comes up behind me to look over my shoulder.

I mention that the water heater is making for a tough month, and I regret saying it as soon as I do. He asks how much I need.

"No, it should be all right."

"What was the water heater, a couple of hundred bucks?" he says. "I use it, too. I'll write you a check."

Again I tell him it will be all right.

My father leaves the kitchen, and I go back to my scratch paper, gaming out possible scenarios. Paying half the credit card bill looks like the safest bet, though the interest rate is criminal. Still, if I let it ride only a single month, the charge would be negligible—maybe ten or twelve dollars.

My father comes back, and I look up to see that he has his checkbook in hand. He sits across from me, then fumbles around in the basket on the table, eventually pulling out a pen. "Here's a hundred bucks," he says, starting to fill out a check. "I'm here; it's only right that I help."

"I got it, Dad," I say. "I was just looking at the numbers, making sure."

My father tears the check out of his checkbook. "I've been here almost three years. You don't let me help out."

I remind him that he gives me two hundred dollars each month.

"You don't want to owe me anything. Is that it? I was the same with my old man."

"It's cool, Dad; I can cover it," I say. But he's right. I don't want to owe him anything. If he pays for part of the water heater, or pitches in for a new roof or gravel to fill ruts in the driveway, then this becomes his place, too. Partially his place. It would change the dynamic, and not in a way I can accept.

My father puts the check in the center of the table, smacking it down with his palm. "Sometimes you have to accept help," he says. His voice is suddenly lecturing in a way I've heard from him since I was a child. It sends my hackles up.

"Guys manage on their own," I say. "I'm pretty sure you taught me that."

"My father broke my arm when I was fifteen," he says. "Twisted it behind my back as he shoved me out of the house. I came back. I lived in his house for two more years, but I didn't say one word to him. Not one word. I barely talked to him for the next thirty years."

I know all this, of course. I met my grandfather only once, when I was four or five. A large man—fat and tall—with a long gray beard. He gave me a quarter, his big hand putting it on my palm then closing over mine.

"I never broke your arm," my father says. "But you still don't want anything from me."

"It's just a little late to start thinking about giving me things. There was a time for that, I guess, but it's pretty far in the past."

"What didn't I give you? I worked to give you and your sister food and shelter. That's why I worked for fifty years."

My father worked for fifty years in order to be home with us as little as possible.

"I'll cover the water heater," I say, and now I am thoroughly pissed off, so I say it in a way that sounds like the *back off* I intend it to be.

"There's the check, kid," he says. He gets up and walks out of the kitchen.

I leave the check there for the next three hours, knowing he will see it when he comes in for dinner. But it pisses me off again every time I notice it. Toward the end of the night, it starts to seem especially ugly, sitting out there on the table. So I fold it up and put it in the drawer where I keep receipts and stubs for paid bills. It can stay there until we both forget about it.

MONDAY AFTERNOON I get a text about a small job, repairing a fence in Piqua. I drive up as soon as I finish at school. It's an old house on the north side of town with a privacy fence in the back. A few rotted boards; a couple of places where a section has come away from its post and leans inward. Easy. The homeowner and I agree on $125, and I tell him I can come by tomorrow afternoon. I take measurements. I figure I'll pick up lumber and fencing nails at Lowe's tomorrow morning when I'm there for work. After I finish with the homeowner, I spend a minute in my car, making a list of what I'll need: circular saw, extension cords, pry bar.

I tell my father about the fence job when I get home. We don't mention his check. He can see that it's gone, and I don't have to cash it. A win-win. We even have dinner together. He goes on about veterans waiting months to see a doctor through the VA and some new law to stop veteran suicide, which Obama recently signed. He says Obama had to sign it since his Veteran's Health Administration is such an "unmitigated disaster." That's his phrase—"unmitigated disaster"—and he clearly likes it because he says it a few times. I want to ask what "mitigated disasters" he can think of, but I restrain myself. To get him off Obama, I ask if he's going to see Beth this week, and he says they plan to have coffee at Dunkin' Donuts after the gym tomorrow, then tells me a bit about her working life. She was a secretary at a community college for a decade after her husband died.

After dinner, I burn a few hours on Scruff and surfing the net. I want to text Dave, to ask how his week is starting out. And even more than that, I want him to text me. I've been thinking about it all day. But my instincts tell me I need to give him space to do that—even for the possibility of it. Hell, I could have texted when I got back from Hansen's place on Saturday, to thank him for a great night. And it was a great night; I'm sure it was. But in retrospect, I'm glad I didn't. The next move is his.

I do text Matt, though. I ask how life is among the otters. Matt texts back a half hour later, telling me that it's good, laying out on rocks and grooming himself. Then he says that otters keep their fur meticulous. I text back that if I had such fine fur, I'd keep mine meticulous, too. He responds, *You do*. It occurs to me that I want to see Matt again, but that I'm hesitating to make plans with him because I want to keep my schedule open for Dave. Just in case. Once I lay it out like that, the logic seems pathetic, so I ask Matt if he wants to hang out later in the week. He responds with a thumbs-up emoji.

TUESDAY IS A good day. Working on the fence is satisfying. It's nice out, low fifties, sunny, and the work is easy, just cutting boards and nailing them in, then straightening a few panels. It takes a couple of hours, and the best part: midway through, my phone vibrates. I glance down to see it's Dave. Just two words, *Hey buddy*. But it seems to concede everything. He might as well have texted, *I'm into you*. I don't reply right away. I finish the job, bring out the homeowner, and walk him along the fence, explaining what I did, assuring him that the new boards will turn silver soon enough. He is pleased, shakes my hand, and writes a check for $150—a tip, I figure. People don't forget how much they said they'd pay you.

I wait until I'm back in the truck to text Dave. I ask if he's getting outside since it's such a great day. I figure he's at the hospital, but that seems like a safe thing to say. And I'm feeling flush with the money I just got, so I suggest dinner this week. Somewhere nice. My treat. Dave texts back right away, and we agree to Saturday night in the Oregon District. I drive home feeling pretty damn excited. I'll spend half the money on dinner and put half toward bills.

I remain jazzed the rest of the week. Wednesday I introduce my students to "the research paper"—the project they'll work on through the end of term—with all kinds of solemn statements about its importance, really throwing myself into the drama of it. They seem appropriately awed by the gravity of the undertaking. It's all a little silly, but I want them to take the assignment seriously, to do their best. And the weather continues to be perfect. Sunny, cloudless, mid-fifties. Daffodil spears poking up all over town. At Lowe's on Friday, they have me restocking lumber. The guys down there are fun to work with. There are fewer customers around that part of the store, so they chat more. We rag on the management all day, and I don't see Rob at all.

On my lunch break, I text Dave to confirm, and again he responds right away. We settle on 7:00 p.m. We're going to meet out, which feels less like a date than I'd like, but a date is still a date. We decide on a coffee shop within walking distance of the restaurant. Matt texts, too, and he and I banter back and forth during the afternoon. Apparently being a one-man design department, Matt's new job, involves a significant amount of time working a register and processing printing orders. Not that he doesn't have priority when design jobs come in, just that there aren't all that many of them. He texts me a picture of himself bugging out his eyes, with his hands over his head pulling at his hair. I send him a picture of a stack of lumber with me beneath it, one hand raised as if I were trying to keep it from tumbling on top of me. *Death by lumber*.

But I hesitate when he asks when we're going to hang out.

Maybe Sunday. Can I have dinner with Dave on Saturday night, then see Matt on Sunday? Why not? Gay guys date like that all the time. But it still seems wrong, the proximity of it.

I finally end up dodging all together. I tell him I'll text tomorrow, that we'll figure something out.

12

I'M TWENTY MINUTES EARLY. I've cleaned up. Trimmed my beard, shaved my neck. I'm wearing a burnt-orange plaid button-down, sports coat, jeans, and a tan leather belt. Also matching boots. The kind of getup I wear for my semi-annual teaching observations. I also chose socks without holes and the newest underwear in the drawer, though they're far from the bright white they were in the package. I look good, weathered but good.

The coffee shop has an industrial feel—brick walls, old couches, and a few tables. There's a small stage, too, a semi-circular platform against the back wall. I plop down on one of the couches by the door to wait. It's already pretty busy when I get there, single guys at tables with their laptops (they must offer free WiFi) and also couples, most in their early thirties, but some older. I watch one for a while, maybe mid-thirties. Dressed up, probably planning to check out one of the nicer restaurants hereabouts. She's wearing a black dress and diamond earrings big enough for me to notice from across the room. He's got black slacks and a white button-down open at the collar. They're an attractive couple—or more than that, they're a *sexy* couple. Both of them are sexy. She's sipping white wine. He doesn't have anything in front of him. They look successful, comfortable, confident, the kind of people I associate with a city larger than Dayton. It's strange to think that there may be only a dozen years between them and me. They seem infinitely younger, but also something else, possessed of themselves in a way I've never been. They seem like the center of something of which I am on the far margin.

I'm still looking at them ten minutes later when my phone buzzes, then buzzes again. It's Dave. *Parking* and then *Sorry*.

I fight the urge to stand. But I do straighten, adjust my jacket, and train my eyes on the door. Then I decide that looks too eager, so I read and reread the chalkboard on the wall to the right of the door: some guy named Vinny Sezna and his trio are coming on at 9:00 p.m.

When Dave walks in, I forget about the couple. Or rather, whatever I was feeling about them fades. Dave has cleaned up. He's buzzed his hair, trimmed his mustache, shaved his neck and jaw. He's wearing a dark blue button-down that makes his blue eyes seem electric, like a movie special effect. The shirt fits tight against his chest, and it's open at the collar to show brown hair curling up from his clavicle, onto his neck. I watch him come toward the table and sit across from me as if I were watching a movie, not a man alive in front of me.

"I need a beer," he says, sitting. Then, "You clean up nice." He puts his hand on my knee.

I'd fuck you right here, right now. That's what I want to say, and a lot of gay guys would love to hear it. Probably a lot of people who aren't gay guys would love to hear it, too.

"Damn," I say, smiling, making eye contact. "Damn. I'm going to go get you a beer."

THE PLAN IS to have dinner, but it's after 9:00 p.m. by the time Dave and I are finishing our third round. Vinny and his pals are just setting up. We're still on the couch to the right of the door. The place has filled. The sexy couple and the young guys with laptops left soon after Dave got here. It's a different crowd now—indie, early twenties, stylishly disheveled. The couches are all occupied, and there are people standing. It's louder. The lights were lowered about fifteen minutes ago. The coffee shop has morphed into a bar in real time.

The new atmosphere changes our conversation. Makes it safe to talk about riskier stuff. We started out discussing Dave's hard day. Check engine light went on, tweaked his rotator cuff at the gym last night and it hurt all afternoon, lifting patients, turning them. I told him about my week, my dad pushing the check on me, fixing the fence, tiptoeing around my supervisor. A customer tried to return a half-empty tub of grout that he said was the wrong color. It went from me to Rob, up to the store manager, who finally let him. The guy went from screaming to laughing by the time the manager glad-handed him out. Then Dave and I get onto working with the public and human nature more generally. I always try to avoid becoming too cynical about people, but Dave is all in on our selfishness and depravity.

Somehow from there we move to the topic of venereal disease. Maybe it's because of how Dave is sitting—leaning back against the armrest with one leg up on the cushions, the other hanging off, giving me clear sight of his crotch. I think we may be talking too loudly, but the noisy crowd makes it hard to tell.

We exchange stories that it's probably not a good idea to share on a third date—or on any date. I tell him about a skinhead I hooked up with over Scruff, a guy covered in tattoos who answered the door naked, then sat across from me on his couch, explaining what each tattoo meant. No swastikas—nothing that blatant—but eagles and Gothic lettering and Germanic shields.

"And you didn't get out of there?" he asks, shaking his head. "I would have bailed on his ass."

"He was naked. The guy was sitting there naked at half mast, slowly taking me through every tattoo on his body. And he was built."

Dave diagnoses me correctly as a slut, and we laugh. The point of the story comes back around to STDs. I get punished by the gods for playing around with trash like that.

Dave tells me about a time he got rolled. A guy gave him an address in a dangerous part of Cincinnati. He drove down there, and—like they'd discussed—walked into the house without knocking. Turns out there were three guys waiting for him, not one. They roughed him up and took his wallet and his car. But they left him his phone. He took a cab all the way back, north of Dayton.

"Much better to get syphilis," he says, taking a swallow of beer.

"It's a biological mandate, people will do stupid things for sex," I say. "At least some of us." But even as I'm saying it, I realize that Dave and I lead a very particular kind of existence: gay middle-aged men, largely solitary, but with active sex lives. It's a strange thing, to have your physical needs met in a way that takes up such a large space in your life, and not have your emotional needs much addressed at all. Dave and I spend a good half hour sharing hook up stories, and part of the fun is definitely salacious. I love hearing about him pulling down his jeans behind a supermarket at 2:00 a.m. or blowing some guy in an SUV. But it's not just salacious. We don't have family stories to share, no stories about our kids. Maybe it's tawdry stuff, but these are the stories we've got. It feels good, honest to share them with him. There's no one in my life who could hear these things without judging me. Or maybe I just think they'd judge—but the net effect is the same.

Then I say, "What do you do for Christmas?"

The question comes out of left field. Even for me, and I asked it. I'm relaxed, not policing my speech. It's partially the beer.

Dave makes me repeat the question. Then he sets down his drink and leans farther back against the couch.

"Well, always lots of guys coming into town during Christmas. Sometimes I do one or two of them." He laughs.

During Thanksgiving, Christmas, Memorial Day weekend—all the holidays—the Scruff grid is thick with new faces, guys who want to sneak away from family gatherings to "have a drink with some buddies who still live around here," which is code for run over to your place and get their rocks off.

I pause. What am I trying to ask? My head's a little cloudy. "I mean, holidays generally. Do you spend them with Hansen and Eileen?"

"Oh hell no, they don't want my ass there. They go over to her family's place up in Lima for Sunday dinner every week. They're religious. I wouldn't feel comfortable celebrating with them, anyway. Usually it's just me and the can opener. Sometimes I travel. I went to Palm Springs in 2012. I've got a few buddies that rented a house there. No Christmas tree, but we carved a turkey and went out for drinks."

People sometimes talk about being gay as a lifestyle—which is silly, even demeaning in a way. Minimizing. But being gay does shape a guy's choices. I wonder if Dave could have been a family man in a different context. Or if he still could be. Maybe he senses my question because he begins talking again.

"I imagine it's a different experience when you're with someone. Long term, your own family. Christmas becomes a bigger thing. That woman I told you about, Lauren, she and I celebrated together one year. We made a ham at her place, just the two of us, sat across from each other in her living room to eat. On the floor with a coffee table between us, aluminum tree there beside us, gifts underneath. I had gotten her skis. Not much of a mystery even all wrapped up. . . . We'd been thinking about a trip to Colorado."

I had a couple of Christmases like that, too. In my mid-twenties. But with guys. In retrospect, I didn't appreciate those holidays enough. I didn't realize then that there'd be decades—all of my thirties and forties—without celebrations like that. When I'd be a guest at other people's holidays, if I celebrated at all. Even two people can be family enough to give holidays a charge, a kind of specialness. Maybe if I'd had a different relationship with my father growing up, he and I could create that sense of family between us—though as it is, the idea strikes me as a joke.

"At least yours were with guys," Dave says. "After Lauren went to bed, I snuck out to go cruising. No Scruff back then, but there were places you could go. A ton of guys looking to get off after spending the night with their families. Maybe after pushing down that side of themselves all day, it came busting out. Now it seems like a shit thing to do, ducking out on her like that."

"You were young and horny," I say, dismissing it. But I don't dismiss it, not really. For a moment, I sit with it, the toll that must take on both parties—the one who goes cruising and the one alone at home who would probably feel it, some kind of loss, even if she couldn't point to exactly what was going on. "You ever think about contacting her?"

"Lauren?"

"Yeah, Lauren. Just to talk, explain some stuff, hear some stuff. An after-action report. She's probably on Facebook."

"No. I don't know. . . . What would I say to her?"

"You don't need a map of how the conversation would go. You say hello, ask what her life is like. Listen to what she says. She might have questions for you, too."

Dave is silent, picking up his beer and taking a deep pull from it. I lean back, watching him. I can see it in his face now, and—though he laughed when he said it—from his obvious embarrassment about having ducked out on her at Christmas. That time still churning in him.

"Shit, no. Facebook? I'm not on that. I don't need to be part of Mark Zuckerberg's algorithms." He pauses. "I guess there'd be pictures of her on there."

"Yeah. Probably pictures. Pictures of her with her husband, her kids if she's got any." I wince after saying that, unsure if I've poked a sensitive spot. Maybe it's the beer talking; I might be overstepping.

Dave drains his glass and claps it down on the table. "The trick is to have a nice family Christmas and want nasty pig sex with the person you're celebrating with," he says. "Not go find some guy at a rest stop."

I nod. "That is the trick."

THE OREGON DISTRICT is hopping. The fun part of it is just a few blocks along Fifth Avenue, but it's the only place in Dayton where there's any street life. There are a dozen bars, a few non-chain restaurants, and the coffee shop-*cum*-bar on the corner, where Dave and I met up. Also a handful of quirky shops. One specializing in fair-trade bric-a-brac, another for handmade jewelry, a third dedicated to music on vinyl. The buildings in which the businesses are housed are old for this part of the country, so there's atmosphere, a funkiness. Plus on weekends there are wooden barriers closing off this section of Fifth to traffic. It's like someone took a length of the French Quarter, soaked it overnight in Midwest bleach, and plunked it down in the middle of Ohio.

A few minutes later, Dave and I are walking the length of it. It's a nice night, warmish, and we're walking close, our shoulders knocking against each other. It feels good being out here with him, like a real date. Someone looking at us would assume we're together, would see it in our body language and the way we're dressed—duded up to the same level. I feel proud to be out here with him.

It occurs to me that I don't know what I'm waiting for.

"Hey." I stop and put my hand on the side of his arm, stopping him. When he turns, I lean in and press my mouth against his. But it all happens too quickly and too forcefully. The kiss is clumsy enough to knock us both off balance.

He steps back, rights himself, and then looks around. "Shit," he says. After a moment, we start walking again.

"That a problem?" I ask, willing the nerves out of my voice.

"No, it's good. Real good. Just a surprise."

We walk another minute before he stops. "There." He points across the street to the front of a candy shop with an old-fashioned recessed entrance—two large glass display areas jutting forward on either side of the door, making a kind of alcove. The store is closed; there's only a dim yellow light on in front, illuminating the displays. As we walk over, I see that one of the display areas is filled with an underwater scene. All candy. An orca is suspended in the middle of it, carved from what looks like white chocolate with dark chocolate coloring its back. The ocean floor below it is crushed nut brittle. Colorful boiled sweets in the shape of shells are half-embedded there. It's magical. We step between the cases and examine the scene. I put a palm on the glass.

"Thar she blows," Dave says.

Graceful curves along its body: the orca is mid-dive, its tale raised above it. Dave puts a hand on my shoulder, squeezes, then cuffs the back of my neck.

"How would you even begin making something like that?" I ask. "Molds, yeah, but you'd have to make those, too."

"I don't know," he says. "You'd need a lot of patience." The orca's mouth is open. Stepping in close, his body right behind me, Dave points out the row of triangular teeth. They could be made of crystallized fruit. Or maybe ginger.

I turn to face him, and he brings his face forward. A tentative kiss, much softer than before, much gentler than I was expecting, his mustache up against my lips and beard. We hold it for a few seconds before he brings his face back and exhales.

"Woof," I say.

He brings his face forward again. I come forward, too, pressing my chest against his. After a moment, I bring my hands up to his shoulders, and he puts a hand against my back, pulling me in, pressing his crotch on mine. We kiss like that for what feels like a long time, though it's probably only four or five minutes. When I step back, Dave brings a hand down and cups the front of my jeans, my hard dick, squeezing down near the head of it. "Nice, buddy," he says.

I do the same to him, put my hand on the front of his jeans and feel the hardness there.

"Hey," I say. "You just want to get takeout and head back to your place?" Earlier we'd talked about going to the Brazilian steakhouse right next to the coffee shop.

"Your place," he says, correcting me. "My roommate's a dick, and he's got work in the morning. Plus my place is a shithole."

I remind him about my father, that we'd have to keep it down. He nods.

Before we leave the alcove, I turn for a last look at the underwater scene. There are a couple of starfish, too, which might be covered in toasted coconut, and off to the left—I'm not sure how I missed this before—a sunken freighter on its side, mostly milk chocolate but decorated with mint-green moss. A cannon ball has punctured the hull. Shards of chocolate are broken off around the hit, with gummy worms pouring out. It's incredibly cool, but also a little eerie. Maybe the people making the display figured something that magical needed a little darkness, like how they put salt in caramel to make it sweeter. If the ship were real, it would be filled with bodies.

IT'S NEARLY ELEVEN by the time Dave and I get back to my place with cartons of Chinese food. When I put the bags on the counter, I feel him come up behind me. I turn, and we begin making out. The house is dark, only the light over the stove on, and absolutely quiet except for the ticking of the kitchen clock. I kiss along his neck, down to the hair curling up from his shirt, smelling it. He puts his hand down the back of my jeans and underwear, palming me there, pulling me close.

After a few minutes, I point down the hall and we head to my bedroom. There's a light in the closet that's gentler than the overhead, so I open the closet door and turn it on. It's just enough to see by. Dave unbuttons his shirt. His chest is covered in curly brown hair, but his stomach is smooth, protruding a bit. I lean in and kiss him, my palms on his chest. Then he reaches up, brushing my hands apart and away from him, and unbuttons my shirt. I'm much hairier than he is, dark brown hair covering my chest and stomach. "Oh, that's nice," he says, running a hand across my pecs.

He leans down and kisses my chest, quickly dropping to his knees to kiss my stomach, then down under my belly button, and lowering to kiss the front of my jeans. He presses his face against my crotch, making the front of my jeans hot. Then he unbuttons my jeans and yanks them down, along with my underwear, and takes my dick in his mouth, his face up right against my crotch, and draws back with a long slow suck. For a moment, I think I might come right then, feeling him draw up the length of my dick, holding the head in his mouth, so I step back. He looks up. "I've wanted to do that for a month," he says.

I sit back against the edge of my bed so I can pull my jeans the rest of the way off, and Dave finishes taking off his shirt and lays it gently across my dresser. Then he pulls off his own jeans and underwear. His socks, too. I'm only half undressed—my shirt is still on—but I stop to look at him. Dave must be in his late forties or early fifties; he's not young. But his body is beautiful. Not the chiseled look of a bodybuilder. He has a gut, not a ton of definition in his shoulders. But there's a solidity to him. He's broad with a nice chest and muscular forearms covered with curly hair. His legs are thick, substantial. His dick sticks straight out, also thick, maybe five or six inches with a big head. The whole package is pretty damn stunning. I tell him that it is—that's the word I use—as I finish taking off my shirt.

"Take your socks off," he says. But he doesn't wait for me to do it; he gets down on his knees and slides my socks off, one at a time. Then he brings his face up to kiss my balls, his mouth warm there.

I run my hand over his head and then across his shoulders. Soon he is sucking on my dick again, and he reaches up and puts a hand on my chest and pushes me back so I fall on the bed. He sucks on me for a while before pushing my knees up, so he can lick underneath my balls and tongue my ass. I close my eyes and let him. It's not something I usually let guys do; it's almost too intimate. But this feels different. Not safe, exactly, but like the vulnerability is, has got to be part of the act. Like that's the point of it.

"You like that?" he says.

I do like it. Because it's him doing it. But I don't answer. I don't want to risk saying anything that might break the moment.

When I open my eyes, Dave is coming up on the bed, above me, and I can feel his chest, his dick, and the heft of him settling on top of me. It's intoxicating. I reach up, my arms on his back, and press him onto me hard, bear-hug style. He presses his mouth on mine and rocks back and forth, his dick rubbing against my stomach.

I let myself have a few minutes of this, but then I get a little uncomfortable with him holding me down, being fully in control like that. And maybe I just want to let him know at the outset the full range of what's possible here. I push my body up, hoisting Dave's weight, using the bed for leverage. He quickly realizes what I'm doing and lets me roll us over so that I'm on top of him. I do the same thing he was doing, kissing him, rocking myself on him. Then I raise myself up, sit between his legs, and begin sucking his dick. While I'm doing it, I take my left hand and reach under him, rubbing my pointer finger against his ass, feeling his sphincter, then working my finger in a little bit. I can hear he likes it; can feel in my mouth that he's making more precum.

"You got any lube?" he asks.

I stretch out on top of him so I can reach the nightstand and fumble around until I find the small bottle.

Dave gets up and sits on the bed, near the edge, on the back of his heels. At first the position seems strange. He's got his back to me, legs folded under him. But it allows a lot of access to his body. I stand up and get behind him, then reach under, between his feet, and feel his dick, his balls, and press the pool of lube in my palm against his hole. I massage him there, working a finger fully into him. Then get more lube and run my palm up and down on my own dick, making it slick.

"Go slow," he says, turning his head toward his shoulder to glance back at me. He sounds a little nervous. Then laughs. "It's been a while since I've done this."

I ease my dick into him, just the head, which I gently move in and out until Dave says, "Just give me it all," breathing heavily. Then I do. I'm standing against the edge of the bed, and I let my torso fall forward until my chest is against his back and my hands can reach around and under him. He has his head down, eyes closed. I hold his dick in my right hand and move my hips back and forth against him. In a minute, Dave reaches under to pull my hand away from his dick. "Not yet," he says. I continue to fuck him slowly.

After a few minutes, he pulls away, turns, and exhales. "I need a break." We kiss for a while, me still standing, him sitting on the bed, until he pulls me down onto the bed on my back and moves my legs apart. "Where's the lube?" he says. He feels around on the bed until he finds it and then begins massaging my asshole, finally working one of his thick fingers inside me.

This feels great, and it's a little uncomfortable. Both things. He must see that on my face because he pauses to ask if I'm good. I can see concern on his face, and it reminds me of a moment in Hansen's barn. I'd stumbled getting off the ATV, and he came over to steady me. The same look—a widening of the eyes, a tenderness. "Hell yeah," I say, but my voice is almost a whisper. I bring my hand up and touch his face. He smiles.

Then he brings his crotch against me and tries to put his dick in me. I feel the pressure of it against my body, and I want it, but I'm tight. Dave spends a few minutes doing this, pressing himself there, easing off and trying again, and it becomes pretty clear that it isn't happening. Not this way.

"You want to try sitting on me?"

I get up, and Dave lies down on his back. He jerks himself off as I straddle him, then I work a finger into myself a few times before lowering onto him.

It takes a while to get his dick inside me, just the head. It feels immense back there, and I'm grimacing.

"We don't have to do this," he says.

"Maybe if we could just take that telephone pole out of my ass and put your dick in there, instead."

He laughs, and then I do, and that helps. Slowly over the next few minutes, I lower myself fully onto him, feeling his hairy legs against my ass, my weight against him. We're silent, moving together, and I jerk myself off for a minute or two before stopping. It's all I can take; I don't want to come yet. Dave raises and lowers his hips, drawing himself in and out of me. I lean forward, putting my palms on his chest.

"You doing okay, buddy?" he says. He puts his hands on my shoulders and lifts his head toward me. I lean down so we can kiss. Our mouths just barely reach.

"God you're tight."

Dave starts pumping his hips faster, and it feels like he's bucking underneath me. It's not entirely comfortable—it's almost uncomfortable—but it feels good. Part of me wants to tell him to slow down, but he's fucking pretty hard, and getting harder, and I think it's too late to slow him down.

"Oh shit," he says. And then I feel it inside me, the cum shooting out of him. I feel how much wetter it is back there, how much hotter. The discomfort is completely gone now; he's bucking in and out of me, and I don't want it to stop. I reach for my dick as he lowers and relaxes, catching his breath. But he puts his hand over mine, stopping me from moving it. Then he lifts his head a little toward mine, so I bend forward to kiss him. Again I try moving my hand on my dick. I'm ready to shoot.

He restrains my hand. "No. You want to come in me?"

"Didn't you already come?" I know he did. I felt it, still feel it.

"I want your jizz in me," he says.

He gently pulls out of me, and I get up. He rolls onto his stomach. I run a hand down his back, along the wings of curly brown hair on his lats, then over his backside to his asshole. I slide a finger partway inside him. "You're gonna need more lube," he says.

It doesn't take me long. I can feel Dave's cum in the back of me, the heat there, can feel my chest against his back, my face against the side of his. Can smell his mustache, feel his breath. While I'm fucking him, he grabs my right hand down near his waist and squeezes. I come almost immediately.

I tend to stay hard a while after, so I don't rush to pull out of him. I want to stay inside him for as long as he'll let me.

"I like that," he says. He says it quietly. Our faces are very close, his against the pillow, mine against the back of his neck.

"You like me fucking you?"

"I like all of it." His eyes are closed.

For a few moments, I think about how I like it, too. Just like Dave said, how I like all of it. With him. How it feels like we've exposed ourselves to each other, have somehow transgressed with each other, a private thing we've exchanged—a vulnerability, even a shame. We have made a mess of each other. I mean that physically. We're covered in each other's cum and saliva. And probably some of each other's shit, too, to be completely honest about it. Not that the sex was especially dirty. But there's also an undeniable psychological messiness. I am lying here on my bed with him, but it feels like we're somewhere else, a half-interior space, an intimacy that's all unshaped and animal, one which required a very complicated un-peeling of the human to get to.

"You're looking for a boyfriend, aren't you?" Dave says, still speaking very quietly.

The question startles me.

"I don't know." That may be a lie. Then it occurs to me that I've got Dave's cum inside me, that our bodies are pressed against each other, that my dick is still hard inside him. Why lie? Why lie *now*? Doesn't this much closeness call for the truth?

"I don't know," I say again. "I've lived my entire life alone. I'm not sure what I'm capable of."

Dave doesn't say anything.

I continue talking; I want to lay it out for him.

"Even as a kid," I say. "Mostly what I remember was waiting around for people to come home. Waiting in front of the house until my mother would get home to let me in, watching cars go by, checking each to see if it was hers. Or walking through the woods behind the house alone, pretending I was a ranger on some Dungeons and Dragons quest. Being alone is what I know how to do. It's not so different from what you said about your own life. It's been twenty years since I've been in a relationship, and I sucked at it then. Just antsy all the time, you know; waiting to be by myself again. Like I needed to get out. But I think it could be different now. Maybe just because I'm getting older. I feel it now; being alone feels like isolation. I was content back then just to be in my head all the time, but now it feels like it would be nice to have someone regular around, just some company. When I was asking before about the holidays, I think that's what I was asking you, Dave. If you feel any of that."

I stop, sure I've said too much. Normally that would really worry me, but I remind myself that he is here, underneath me, listening. I am soft now, barely inside him. But we are close. Very close. I move my head over and kiss him—a half kiss on the side of his mouth since his face is against the bed.

"It's tough," I say. "It's partially a numbers game out here. You know. There just aren't a lot of guys around. Of those that are, a lot are in relationships—with men or women, doesn't matter. A lot of the others are too young or too old. And of the remaining guys—we couldn't be talking more than a hundred men, right?—how many would you actually want to talk to, much less fuck?"

It feels like I can't stop talking.

"I don't think it's just sex, either. I think that kind of sexual attraction is psychological. That if you want someone like that, there are reasons beyond the animal. Some kind of fit, something in you that answers to something in the other guy. It's rare for that to be mutual. When I was in my twenties and thirties, I shrugged it off. I fucked guys I had that connection with, and I fucked a lot more guys that I didn't, and the only difference in my head was that some lays felt better than others. But now I realize how rare that connection is. I think it's the body's way of nudging you along: *here*, you know, saying, *here is a thing you need. Stop here. Come back here. Return to this.*

"So maybe I am looking for a boyfriend," I say. "Someone to do holidays with. Or maybe I am not looking for someone like that, so much as I think you could be that guy. That you could be that guy for me." I pause. "And it seems like it's possible you're feeling that, too."

Now I do stop talking. My heart is pounding. I fear Dave must be able to feel it against his back, so I shift my weight off him, to the side of his body, though I am still resting against him. All he asked is if I'm looking for a boyfriend. I should have just said, "I'm open to it. Why do you ask?" Nothing more than that and clammed up. Why should I be the one with his ass hanging out in the wind? Dave remains quiet. I go quiet, too.

After a moment, he says, "Okay."

That's all, just "okay."

I wait. I think about saying something else, reminding him what he told me about his history, about how many years it's been since he was with a guy—with anyone—as if to argue the point, or to insist, *look, it's the same with you.*

I feel a rising panic in my chest and shift my body completely off his.

Dave turns onto his side toward me, so we are facing each other. "It's cool, man," he says. "I just need to think about it." Then he presses himself against me, and we kiss. Not a quick kiss, but a real kiss, a deep making-out kiss with his tongue in my mouth. And he keeps it there. We kiss long enough for him to get hard again. At some point, he rolls over so his back is toward me, and soon I can tell—because of the way his breathing changes, because occasionally his arms jerk out a bit—that he's asleep. I know I won't sleep. I don't even try. I try also not to think too much. I lie up against him, my chest half-resting on his back, listening to him snore all night, and enjoy the feel of his body as much as I can.

DAVE GETS UP not long after sunrise. I might have slept a few minutes here and there. It's hard to tell. At the moment, though, I feel clear-headed, at least partially because my stomach is empty. I'm going to be a wreck this afternoon.

My father is awake, so I get out of bed when Dave does. We both pull on our underwear and jeans. No shirts though it's cool in the house. I leave the bedroom first. My father is at the sink, washing dishes. I point Dave down the hall to the bathroom, then go in to let my father know I've got a guest.

"Hey Dad," I say, walking into the kitchen. "I've got a friend here." I sit down at the table. My father continues washing up.

He turns from the sink. "I put your Chinese in the fridge," he says. "Do you want me to put on some coffee?"

I tell him that would be great. I'm going to need it. I sit for a few moments and think through what happened last night. I had mostly avoided this train of thought lying in bed, but now that I'm up, I don't seem to be able to. Dave is here, still here, and there might be something else I should say to him. Like I'm a damn lawyer. Like this might be the last chance I have to make my case.

The toilet flushes and a few moments later, Dave comes in. He's got his blue shirt back on, untucked, partially buttoned. I introduce him to my father, who can be gregarious with new people. This jarred me when I was a kid. I'd always thought of my father as sullen, quiet, quick-tempered—then I came to work with him one day, and on site he was a different person, smiling, asking people how they were, slapping them on the back. Some of that comes out now. He goes over to shake Dave's hand, says he's glad to meet him, offers him a cup of coffee. Then he says he's going to make oatmeal and Dave is welcome to have some.

Dave calls my father by his first name, Peter, which is also jarring to me. "Thanks, Peter," he says. "I'm going to head out in a minute. Though I could use the coffee if you've got it made."

My father begins talking about the weather, getting past the worst of winter, spring being just a couple of weeks away. He asks Dave how he feels about winter and says that he can't stand the cold and darkness anymore. Dave says that my father should move to the Sunbelt, and my father runs with that, talking about the desert Southwest. While he's talking, my father brings over a mug of coffee and sets it in front of me, then hands a mug to Dave, who remains standing. My father sits across from me with his own mug. He gestures to Dave to sit.

What would I say to Dave? Maybe I've already made my case. But I want him to know that I wasn't talking about instant marriage last night, that I'm not "clingy." I'm the furthest thing from it. Not even much of a romantic, I don't think. Just that after decades of seeing the world from the other side, seeing couples and not being one of them, I'm wondering what, if anything, is so different about me. I was trying to tell him that I would be willing to try. With him, I would be willing.

Dave is describing the weather out in LA. My father says he doesn't think much of that city, but he agrees it's perfect weather. I sip coffee, watching Dave talk. He is leaning against the kitchen wall closest to the table, smiling, listening to my father, speaking easily. He looks comfortable standing there, and warm, open.

Then Dave puts his half-finished mug on the kitchen table and announces he had better get moving. My father asks if he's sure he won't have a bite before he goes. I stand up to walk Dave to the door for a chance to talk to him in private. My father stands to shake his hand again, so I say that I'm going to see Dave out. He and I walk to the foyer.

Dave sits down on one of the chairs in there to put on his shoes. I come over and kneel next to him, so we're about eye level.

"Your father's a nice guy," he says, not looking up.

"Hey, I had a good time with you last night," I say, looking at his face. I run my palm up his arm to his shoulder.

"Shit," he says. He pauses, finally looks at me. "I had a good time, too. A really good time." He pauses again. "I don't think I can do it, Mike. What you talked about last night." He stands. I can see it in his body language, can feel it like electricity crackling off him, that he wants to get out of here as quickly as possible. I know this because, over the years, I've put out enough of that same energy.

I stand, too. "You don't think you can do it? Is that all you're going to say to me?" My voice is louder than it should be. I feel myself tensing. Decades of experience have taught me that it means nothing—that we fucked, that I admitted something to him, that I saw a possibility in us and said that I saw it. But in that moment, it feels like he owes me more.

"What else should I say?"

"You could tell me why you can't," I say, quieting my voice. I can't make it calmer, only quieter. "If you're just not into it, not into me, that's one thing. Lay it out. You seemed into it when I fucked you last night, but if you're not, you're not. But if it's something else, you need to let me know. I wasn't talking marriage, Dave. Just dating and seeing where it goes. Getting to know each other. I said too much last night.

Partially it was the beer, partially the sex. But whatever I said, I'm not talking about a marriage proposal."

"This shit ends badly," Dave says. "It always ends badly. I like you, Mike. I like you a lot. There's something real and honest about you. I can feel how much you take in, how much you're present for. And you're sexy. I did like it, you fucking me. If I was going to do this, if I was—but once guys start expecting things of each other, and start demanding things, it becomes a mess. I just don't think I can do it."

"You're like fifty, right?" I ask, stepping back, my voice colder.

"Fifty-three," Dave says.

"Yeah, it usually happens by that age. Fear. Cynicism. Some bullshit like that, and guys shut it all down, all their capacity for a certain kind of connection. Just take a wrench and tighten that shit off."

Dave mutters, "I'm sorry, Mike."

I want to throw that "sorry" back in his face. Instead I say, "You're not even going to try. There aren't all that many opportunities, Dave. Not that many left for either of us. You think it's gonna get easier when you're sixty?"

He says it again, "I'm sorry," and pauses, looking at me for a long time, as if he's about to say something else. Then he pulls open the front door and lets himself out.

WHEN I TURN from the door, my father is there, right in the doorway behind me, blocking my way out of the foyer. It startles me seeing him there.

"Did you hear all that?" I say, my voice sharp.

"Did you guys have a fight?" my father asks.

"No, Dad, he just had to head out."

"Did you tell him to leave?"

"I didn't tell him to leave. Actually, just the opposite, Dad. I wanted him to stay; I asked him to stay." I feel trapped in the foyer, waiting for my father to step away from the doorframe so I can go back to my room.

"Maybe you should have offered him some breakfast," my father says. "We have oatmeal and eggs. You could have made him something to eat."

Of course his assumption is that Dave left because I was somehow unwelcoming.

"He wanted to go, Dad, there was no way to keep him here. If there was, I would have done it."

"You might have tried, Mike," my father says, finally turning away, out of the doorframe. "If you're nice to people, they stick around."

Maybe it's because I didn't sleep or because this is typical of my father—this starting assumption that I did something wrong—or because Dave left, because Dave just goddamn left, but, for whatever reason, I feel instantly furious. "Did it even occur to you that I might not have done anything wrong here?" I say. "The guy left, okay? He didn't want to spend any more time with me; he was done; we had sex and he was done, so he just left. There was nothing I could do about it."

I can tell the word sex has made my father uncomfortable. Good. He shrugs and walks into the kitchen. I follow him in there.

"What's the shrug supposed to mean?"

He sits down at the table, in front of his mug and laptop. "It seems like a lot of guys don't stick around. It seems like you have sex with a lot of guys, and none of them stick around. There's got to be a reason for that."

"Maybe you're the reason," I say.

"Am I cramping your style, Mike? I don't have to stay here. If you need me to leave, you let me know. I don't need to stay here." My father looks angry now, suddenly in full fight mode. He's old, but he's not so old that his anger has lost its bite. His face is screwed up into a sneer that still feels threatening. This is how it's been all my life. He is a man who can be made furious with a single word. Again: good. Let him be furious.

"Not you in my house," I say. "You in my head. If I drive people away, I guess I had a good role model for how to do it."

My father stands again.

"'*Who the fuck needs you?*' Remember that? That's what you said whenever anyone pissed you off: me, Sarah, any of our relatives. I'm pretty sure you even said it to Mom a few times. You were always ready to walk out. You think she would have stayed around for that if there were no kids, and she was like Dave and had some experience living alone? Shit, Dad, it's a hell of a lot harder keeping someone around when they actually have the ability to leave."

Now my father should start raging, shouting in my face—calling me some pretty awful names. Saying fuck every other word. He's never gotten angry enough to call me a cocksucker, not yet, but I'm sure he's thought it often enough. Even now, I suspect my father is capable of shouting me down. I hear that edge, that fury in his voice when he gets started on Obama. It's been years since he and I mixed it up—since before my mother died. And that's what I'm expecting now. I'm braced for it. I want it. To hell with him if he can't even pretend to be on my side here.

But he doesn't do any of those things. He just takes a minute, looking at me, and sits back down. "I'm sorry the guy left," he says. "I guess you liked him. I'm sorry he left."

"Oh fuck you, Dad," I say. I spit the words out, gritting my teeth. I can suddenly feel tears behind my eyes, the pressure of them against my face. I don't know if it's frustration at my father or because of Dave, but I can feel them coming, and "fuck you" seems to hold them off for a second. But only for a second. I say it again, barely getting the words out, and turn so my father won't see my face. I go to my bedroom, lock the door behind me, get into bed, and lie there seething—my head running down all the times in my life my father didn't, wouldn't, couldn't say one gentle word to me.

Soon, I'm not sure exactly when, I fall asleep.

13

WHEN I WAKE UP, it feels very late in the day—some combination of my mood and the quality of light in the house, the result of an overcast sky. Everything is still. My first thought is to text Dave. I don't think it will do any good, but I decide to do it. I have to.

I find my phone on the kitchen table. My father has left a Post-it on the screen, which is unusual. We're not in the habit of leaving each other notes. It says that he's having lunch with Beth at Bob Evans. And "Sorry we fought." He signed it "Dad." For my father, this is a significant concession. I still don't feel very warmly toward him.

I remember the Chinese food, and I wonder if being out all night has made it dangerous. Pork? Maybe trichinosis, whatever that is. I get it out of the fridge, grab a fork from the sink and run it under the tap for a few seconds, and eat from the cartons, standing up. I eat fast, a lot of it, and fill a glass with tap water to wash it down when it starts to feel clumped in my throat. Pretty quickly I become nauseated and stuff the cartons back into the brown bag. I finish the water, look around the kitchen, and see my phone.

What can I say to Dave that won't make things worse? Be more direct about liking him? Could I be *more* direct? I was already perfectly clear. Too clear. More would only push him further off. Insist on how uncommon a chance this could be? As if the heart worked like that, calculating odds, making strategic assessments. Maybe I could just tell him that he can contact me whenever he wants to. Like I'm a fucking doormat.

I walk over to the table and check my phone. Matt texted. Actually, he texted twice since last night. That makes me feel worse.

I walk back to the sink, take another swig of water—right from the faucet this time—and swish it around my mouth like it's mouthwash. Then I spit it into the sink, run the tap for a minute, and go back to my room. Back to bed. I stay there the rest of the day.

I DON'T SEE my father again until the following evening. I wake up at midnight, shower, clean my teeth properly, and start a novel called *Mrs. Kimble* that one of my students recommended, handing me her paperback copy. The novel keeps my interest, bringing me into the world of three women semi-abandoned by their husbands, or husband—it's the same guy—and I read until sunrise. Then I throw things in my bag and head off to school, figuring that if I get there early, I can prepare for class.

I do get there early, and I don't prepare. Don't do much of anything. I sit at my desk in the adjunct office and finish the third section of *Mrs. Kimble*. I head to the Keurig in the copy room three times to make a new coffee once each previous cup gets cold. At around 8:00, one of the secretaries peeks in to see if anyone is in there since the door is open. I lift a hand to say hello, and she asks if I was "burning the midnight oil." I smile and nod, and she leaves. Fifteen minutes before class, I'm on the edge of saying fuck it and canceling, but then I figure I can just give them some group work and hastily invent something lame. I don't feel like I can look at them, my students. Don't feel like I can look at anyone.

But class goes fine. Or badly. I'm not sure which. Probably the students don't notice any difference. Afterwards, I don't go home. I don't want to face my father. Instead, I drive out to the reservoir, which has a paved path, a loop about three miles. I walk it. Then I walk it again.

The first time I was with a guy, I was thirteen. I didn't know I was gay. I had thoughts or feelings, but no word to organize them into an identity. I guess I felt my impulses were shameful, but I didn't know what they were exactly. That first time happened on a snow day. After I got the call that school was closed, I walked down the street to the house of a friend, a kid named Marc, who was taller and darker skinned than I was. He'd moved to town the previous summer. We became friends pretty quick.

Marc had the idea that we could make money shoveling driveways that day, just going around knocking on folks' doors and asking. I was a shy kid, but I went along with it, and it got easier and easier all day. I don't mean the shoveling; that stayed tough. But knocking on doors, saying "Shovel your walk?" to whomever answered. We were out there for hours, and we got jobs. Way more than I was expecting. It was sundown by the time we got back to his place. We were tired but victorious, counting out our money on the living room couch as his mother fixed dinner. Maybe we had sixty bucks between us, but it seemed like an enormous sum, like it had been a miraculous day, making money materialize out of the weather. After we ate, he asked his mom if I could spend the night.

I don't know how we got onto it. I guess we had money, so we decided to play poker. We played for hours, and it didn't go well for me. But Marc gave me my money back. That seemed a little miraculous, too. He just gave me back my half and said we should change the stakes. We started playing for back massages, which we counted out in seconds. You could bet thirty or sixty seconds, the guy doing the massaging counting down the time in his head. Things escalated from there.

We must have passed the whole night doing that because what I remember most clearly is the silhouette of Marc against a lightening sky. We turned off his desk lamp after each poker hand for the touching part. Touching each other, soon rubbing each other. I remember the sky through the windows brightening to purple behind him, and him pulling my underwear down and then leaning there, between my legs, just touching me. Not jerking me off like a guy would do now, just feeling me, patting the area, putting his palm against my dick, my balls, holding his palm there. At some point, I came.

I immediately felt deeply ashamed. I think I went to bed right away, without much of an explanation or excuse, just turned my body away from him. The next morning, I was hellbent on getting out of there. I didn't even stay for breakfast. I left right after we got up. Marc and I stopped being friends after that. I say that as if it was a spontaneous natural occurrence, that our friendship just happened to stop. The truth must be that I stopped it. I must have stopped calling and returning his calls, stopped talking to him at school, stopped sitting next to him on the bus, stopped responding to him at all.

All this was more than thirty-five years ago, and I still feel bad about it. The late 1970s, homophobia everywhere, a staple of television situation comedy. AIDS about to happen. It was a fucked-up moment that was quickly followed by a more fucked-up moment. I wonder what I must have felt or understood to cut Marc off like that, the disgust and shame I must have carried. How much the disgust of that cultural moment was inside me. And how he had taken the brunt of it.

Walking around the reservoir, thinking about Dave, how Dave ditched me, about how many guys I've ditched, I can't help but feel that the sickness of that era continues in my body. I know things are different now. People talking about a gay-marriage decision by the Supreme Court this summer, kids coming out to supportive peers in high school or even earlier. But this, right now, isn't my era. It's like I've been misshapen by a disease that people get vaccinated for nowadays, like my body has been twisted by Polio, but now Polio has disappeared, exists only as a hard-to-believe story. As in, "Can you imagine people once had to live with that?" But it's not my body that's twisted. It's my head, my heart.

Dave was there, too, I know. Formed by the same era. Maybe that's part of what made the connection I feel possible. He had seemed like a chance at some kind of redemption, like a last chance.

I DON'T GET home until after six, and by then I'm dead tired. My father comes out of his room as I'm walking in the door, setting down my school bag and taking off my coat.

"Where were you?" he says. "I called."

I nod. "I'm sorry. I turned my phone off during class."

"I made dinner."

My father starts walking into the kitchen, and I follow to see a couple of pots on the stove and a dish of something covered by tinfoil. I walk over and peek under it. Meatloaf. I haven't eaten since yesterday, the rot-gut Chinese. I become aware of my stomach.

Maybe I should apologize to my father, but I can't bring myself to do it. He reaches into the cupboard for a plate and hands it over to me. I'd prefer to take the plate of food into my bedroom, just eat and pass out. But I load up and sit at the kitchen table, hoping he doesn't say anything about yesterday. Or that he doesn't say anything at all. That's my concession, sitting at the table. My father immediately starts talking about my mother's car, and something about Beth's car, and about new cars in general, and driving stick. I nod every once in a while and try to ask a few questions.

THE REST OF the week feels hard. Even moving my body feels hard. There's a heaviness to my limbs and in my head. On Tuesday I oversleep and get to Lowe's twenty minutes late. Rob calls me out as soon as he sees me, but his voice barely registers. "This isn't a cocktail party, Breck," he says, walking up as I'm hustling to help another guy bring a palette down from the top of a shelf. I'm gating the end of the aisle when Rob comes over. I apologize and mutter "car problem" without looking up. He stands there a long time staring at me, waiting. I don't meet his eyes. "Be on time," he says, "or don't come." Then he stalks off.

On Wednesday, I do cancel class. The students won't care anyway.

At least on Thursday I get to Lowe's on time.

I try not to check my phone. All week, I try. There's no text from Dave, and I feel it—the absence of a message, the not-vibrating—every time I bring the phone out or pat my pocket. On Thursday morning, I decide to text him. Just a hello. Something casual. Or maybe an apology: *Hey, I'm sorry I was a dick this weekend.* But I don't want to apologize. Was I a dick? I don't think I have anything to apologize for. I don't know. I just want to hear from him.

Finally, I decide not to text. He knows what there is to know.

MATT REACHES OUT again on Wednesday, asking if I'm all right. *I haven't heard from you. . . .* I know I need to respond to him, but it takes me until Thursday morning to think of what to say. I eventually just thank him for checking in, and, by way of an apology, say I had a rough weekend. He texts back *Gotcha*. Just one word: *Gotcha*.

I spend most of Friday on the couch, surfing the internet and chatting with guys on Scruff, grateful for every new woof or unlocked album, the penny-ante rush of it. Whole blocks of hours get leveled this way. By 3:00 p.m. I feel disgusted with myself for doing nothing all day. Then I agree to drive out to some guy's house in Middletown. "MedinaStud." He's got a scenario in mind. It involves the back of his couch. Maybe I agree to it just to get out of the house. Factoring in the drive, it should take two hours.

When I get there, the guy unlocks his door and immediately starts taking off his clothes. He's a big guy, muscular, early thirties, brown skin, wearing tight gold bikini briefs. When I move to kiss him, he steps back and puts his hands on my chest, holding me off. I just can't get hard after that. He bends over his couch, and I try rubbing myself against the back of him. Nothing happens, and I start to feel ridiculous—small, puny, and old next to this gorilla of a guy. After a few minutes, I tell him this was a mistake and that I have to go. He looks relieved. When I'm back on my own couch again, it's a little hard to believe that the previous couple of hours actually happened.

More or less, that's how the weekend goes, too. I read. I eat some. I try unsuccessfully to stay off the app. I spend a lot of time in my room. My father knocks a couple of times to tell me he's going out or to ask if I want anything from the store. I remind myself that he's trying and force myself to thank him, but I do it without opening the door.

THE NEXT FEW weeks pass uneventfully, too. Daffodils come and go, and the giant forsythia by the side of the house starts to bloom. I expect there will still be a last-minute snowstorm. There's always one of those around here.

Matt doesn't text again. I don't cancel any more classes. I consistently make it to Lowe's on time and try to be friendly to customers. My life returns to what it was before I met Dave, though it feels flatter, somehow bleached out. I do spend a lot of time mulling my errors. That's how I think of them, "unforced errors," as if this were a football game. I decide I should have been more careful about Matt, or at least more straightforward with him. I wonder if the only thing wrong with him is that he liked me too much or was too eager to hang out. Maybe in my head that's sufficiently disqualifying.

And I think a lot about the unforced errors I made with Dave.

How it would have been safer to drift into a relationship, to spend time with him and just see what developed. I remind myself that he asked me, directly, if I was thinking about a relationship. In a way, the same question that gets asked on the apps: "What are you looking for on here?" It's a useful question—and a safe one. The answer can be anything from a specific sexual act to an invitation for coffee. To a boyfriend. It's like asking someone to open his hand, to show what kind of weapon he's carrying, or to show that he's carrying none at all—but without showing what's in your own hand, without betraying any assumptions or making any concessions. Is that what Dave was trying to do? In any case, I've seen enough of how men react to know that my answer, however *true* it might have been, was piss-poor strategy. Honesty may be good policy, but as a strategy, it sucks.

One afternoon at Lowe's, I even think I see Dave coming out of the plumbing aisle, rounding the corner toward me. Plumbing is far down the store, and the guy turns away pretty quickly. But it looks like him, buzzed head, the mustache, a black T-shirt, jeans. A little gut, wide shoulders. I stop what I'm doing—walking a customer toward the rolls of vinyl flooring in order to help her measure it out—and head after him as fast as I can without drawing attention to myself. I dart away from the customer without explanation, my heart racing. When I get to Plumbing, I look up and down the aisle. Dave's not there. Then I glance down the aisles to either side, and head back to Flooring via the front of the store, by the registers, just to make sure. When I get back to the customer, she looks mighty put out. I don't want her to talk to Rob, so I apologize three or four times, making up a story about seeing my ex-wife down there. She finally laughs, and I relax. Then we get down to measuring her vinyl. For weeks after that, I can't help myself. Every time I'm at the store, I glance around for Dave.

FOR EASTER, my father asks me to drive him out to Uniontown, where my parents lived for most of their fifty-plus years together, to the small graveyard out there. He could drive himself just fine, but it's over four hours, and I feel better ferrying him over. He wants to leave flowers. He goes out and buys them the day before, not cut flowers but potted bulbs: two containers of daffodils and one of orange tulips. I see them on the kitchen table that afternoon. He got a foil balloon, too, on a plastic stick. It reads, "Happy Easter!"

We head out just after 7:00. If I was by myself, I'd do the drive straight through, but I figure my father needs breaks, so we stop every hour or so. I encourage him to stretch his legs, use the bathroom, get something from the quick mart if we're at a gas station.

The last place we pull into is a rest stop set back from the interstate. No gas station, just a small building—really a shed with a corrugated roof—and a couple of wooden picnic tables. We both get out. I head over to use the bathroom in the shed. When I get back, my father is seated at one of the tables, gazing into the parking lot, watching families pull in.

"You good to go?" I ask.

"I need a root canal," he says. "I went to the dentist on Friday, and she said I have pus under my tooth. There's an infection."

"Ouch. Sorry to hear that, Dad. Will insurance cover it?"

He waves off my question—literally—with his hand. "She's about thirty-five. She's got her own practice, a husband, two kids. She didn't tell me that, mind you, but she's got a picture of the four of them up in the waiting area, on the same wall with her diplomas."

"It sounds like she's got a good life."

I'm antsy to get back on the road. We've got at least another hour of driving ahead of us.

"But does she know how good?" my father says. "I guess nobody ever really appreciates how good they have it. We walk around muttering about work or things that piss us off and don't stop to realize how lucky we are."

"Not everyone has it that good. It sounds like your dentist has a good life. You and Mom had a good life, too. You had decades of good health and peace. A nice house. You had work. No one really got sick. Those were good years. Good decades." I say all this because I think my father is feeling sorry for himself. I want him to balance his grief with a sense of gratitude for what he had. It's been more than four years since my mother died. Isn't that enough time to get beyond pure grief? But my motivation is partly selfish, too. After a while it gets hard to hear someone grieving for the loss of more than most people ever have, more than you will ever have. "A lot of people lose their husbands or wives at fifty," I say. "Or forty. A lot of people lose kids."

My father nods. He's still looking off, toward the parking area.

I sit across from him. "You know, Dad, when I lived in Jersey in the early '90s, guys were dying everywhere. Those guys were in their twenties and thirties, just starting their lives. Think of everything they didn't have—a lot of those guys had no partner and no family, no time to do or make anything in the world. Life can go that way, too." I pause, waiting for my father to respond.

"I like spending time with Beth," he says.

I inhale, filling my chest with air, and hold it for a minute. Maybe he hasn't heard me. Maybe he simply doesn't want to engage with the topic of AIDS.

"You *should* spend time with her," I say. "There's nothing wrong with spending time with Beth. Mom would have wanted you to spend time with her. She worried more about you than about herself, and she was a practical woman."

"You think your mother would have wanted that?" He finally looks over.

"I'm sure of it, Dad," I say, fully shaking off what I'd been trying to say before.

Then I stand, and he takes the cue and stands, too.

Back in the car, we are quiet, my father sitting with the flowers on his lap, his arms around the pots. He didn't want to put them on the back seat, afraid they'd spill.

I think about our conversation, about what constitutes "good years." By my own logic, these must be good years for me now. I've got a house, steady work. I'm healthy. A lot of people never have those things, either. But though I can wrap my mind around the idea, in my chest, in my heart, it falls flat.

When we get to the graveyard, my father places the flowers in front of my mother's headstone and kneels to talk to her. I sit on a stone bench a few lanes over, in front of another grave, to give him some privacy. She put up with a lot, my mother. She had a job as a receptionist in a veterinarian's office for most of my childhood, up until she was almost sixty. That whole time, she also had the job of keeping my father happy, which involved the usual stuff—child rearing, making dinner, cleaning—but also tolerating his sudden rages. She was always fiercely protective of him if my sister or I criticized his behavior, even his shouting at her, saying that everything he'd ever done, he did for us. I wonder now if she enjoyed it, if she experienced her fifty-eight years with him as good years.

Then I decide to text Matt. Maybe it's seeing my father kneeling there, wrestling with unresolved things. It's been almost a month since Matt and I have had any contact, and I know it's my fault. So it suddenly seems urgent. I take my phone out. I type *Hey, this is Mike*—and begin to think about how to explain my absence. Maybe I've been in mourning; maybe that's the word to use. But how to help Matt understand what I've been in mourning for? I finally decide to keep it short. I apologize to him for flaking out. That's really what I need to do—a simple, straightforward apology.

He doesn't text back.

14

BUT A WEEK LATER, I run into Matt at Walmart. I'm still feeling somber, but at least I'm up, getting things done. I'm in the garden center. I've got a bag of crabgrass preventer in my cart—it's a hair late for it, but close enough—and I'm pausing before a table of annuals, thinking I might put a few by the front door in the ceramic planter where the mailman usually leaves my letters. Maybe if there were flowers there, he'd stick the letters in the door slot like he's supposed to.

I hear a voice, loud, coming from behind me. "It isn't Halloween, but there, I think, is your ghost!" I turn, holding a six-pack of begonias, to see Maria pushing a full cart, a garden hose coiled on top. Matt is walking beside her. Both wear sour faces.

"We're going to need to call the Holy Father to come perform an exorcism," Matt says.

"Yes," says Maria, holding up a pointer finger. "I will call the Holy Father. Father, Father, there is an asshole ghost in the garden center, and you must banish him!" Then Maria marches toward me, leaving her cart with Matt, who slowly pushes it forward. "Why did you disappear on my brother," she says. She comes close enough so she can smack me on the shoulder with the back of her hand. "What, you are not one of these guys that does this, that simply stops responding to somebody, like to hell with you . . . like you never existed . . . I don't know you . . . I got all I want from you and now you can drop dead. Mike, tell me you are not one of these guys. But maybe I see in the event that you are one of these guys and I just didn't know, eh?"

Maria is standing right in front of me, maybe a foot away, so there's no avoiding her glaring face. Matt pulls the cart up alongside, and then they're both right there, glaring.

I swallow a burst of nervous laughter and decide I just need to own this.

"I was having a tough time—"

Maria smacks my shoulder again. "You're having a tough time, you text your friend that you are having a tough time and your friend comes and you have a tough time together. Or a good friend comes, and the time gets a little less tough, eh? I will tell you why you did this. You did this because you are one of these guys that does this! Now we know you are one of these guys."

Matt puts his hand on Maria's shoulder to get her attention and gently guides her back away from me. "Let me talk to him," he says.

"Okay." Maria steps back a few feet. "But I am going to stay right here."

Matt turns and gives her a look.

"Okay, fine," she says. "I will be in the linens area." She wheels the cart away from us.

I start apologizing as soon as Maria is out of ear shot.

"Groveling in a Walmart," Matt says. "Not very dignified. Actually, just being in a Walmart is not very dignified. We're supporting starvation wages and the production of crap."

"If it would be better," I say, "I can grovel somewhere else."

"No," Matt says. "No groveling, no bullshit. But if you want to tell me the truth, I'll listen."

I think about how to say the truth. Is there any way to do it which isn't awful? *I liked some guy more than you.* But there's no quantitative comparison to be made. I liked—and like—Matt a lot. But Dave was a different feeling, just a different thing. A rare one. I think about how I might say that.

"I'm not going to leave Maria alone in linens all day," Matt says. "If there's something you want to say, now is your chance."

"Okay, okay. I like you a lot, Matt—"

Matt turns and starts walking toward linens.

I immediately start walking, too, and fall in beside him. "Hey, you didn't let me finish."

"Do you need to? Any explanation that begins 'I like you a lot' isn't going to be the truth—or at least not much of it. You had a chance to tell me the truth, and you took a pass. You know the expression, 'man up'?"

"Okay," I say. "I was sort of dating this other guy named Dave, and he ditched me, and I—Matt, I think I could have loved him. Or maybe I did, if you can after three dates. Love him." As I say that, it feels like a wave of grief is swelling up inside me, about to crash out.

Matt turns. He studies my face. "Why didn't you just tell me that? You weren't violating any agreement we had. You were into another guy. It didn't work out. Fine. I don't see what that has to do with you ghosting me. If we had an agreement and you were breaking the rules, that's one thing—not that it would justify ghosting, but you would simply be an asshole and I'd need to know. But I wouldn't have been angry if you were dating someone else. What assumptions were you making about us, Mike?"

I have no idea what assumptions I was making. That's the truth.

I suddenly feel confused. "I don't know. I was just really crushed when the guy ditched me."

"Yes. It hurts being ditched. And being ghosted is the worst form of it."

"Yeah, I know, Matt."

"Maybe you do," he says, looking me up and down. "Okay, look. I've got to get back to Maria before she chooses gold lamé sheets or something equally awful. But you may buy me dinner. Thursday. Somewhere decent. You can explain yourself more fully and apologize again, and I'll get a free meal out of it."

The thought of dropping fifty bucks on dinner right now makes me hesitate, but only for a second. I want to tell Matt the truth. I need to—as a kind of atonement and because I need to talk about Dave, about what happened, and there's really no one in my life I can do that with. Matt names a Thai restaurant in town, a moderately priced one, and says he'll text me. Then he heads off.

That afternoon, I put down the crabgrass preventer and plant the flowers—marigolds, it turns out. The pot gets too much sun for begonias. It feels good, kneeling there on the stoop, digging out fistfuls of dirt. (There's a hand trowel somewhere in the garage, but I don't go look for it.) I'm glad I'll have a chance to talk with Matt. To make things right. I haven't done enough of that in my life. Maybe I haven't always had the chance to.

When I look up from the planter, my father's there in the doorway, watching me work. He gives me a thumbs up.

I GET BACK from class Monday in a better mood. It's an easy day. The students are giving presentations on their research papers. I sit in the back of the room and raise my hand to ask a question every now and then when the class's questions peter out. We applaud at the end of each presentation, and I think everyone goes home feeling all right. It's starting to get warm out; only a couple of weeks remain in the term. It seems like gentler days are ahead.

My father isn't in a great mood, though. He and Beth went to a deli after the gym. He ordered a cheeseburger, so he doesn't want dinner. I find him sitting on the couch, the remote in his hand. He's not so much watching anything as flipping channels. He seems distracted, like something is nagging at him. I've just changed out of my work clothes into a T-shirt and jeans. I'm thinking I'll dig out a small mugho pine in front of the house, one of a line of three. It died over winter.

I ask him what's up.

He doesn't look at me. CNN is on, a panel of talking heads discussing Obama's meeting with Raul Castro, the implications of opening an embassy. "Your president is sitting down with murderers," my father barks.

I take this as a sign that he's all right and head outside to dig up the pine, which I do in short order. It's only been in the ground a couple of years. I'll be at Lowe's tomorrow; I'll pick up another. Usually there's something a little banged up that the Lawn & Garden manager will let me have for five or ten bucks. Maybe I'll be able to find a small Japanese maple that some kid has snapped a few limbs off of.

When I come back in, my father's still in front of the television, now watching *Wheel of Fortune*. I rinse off and then return to the living room to find that he's fallen asleep with the television on—a documentary about some very small cat species, the rusty-spotted. He wakes when I sit down in the lounge chair and ask if he's ready to turn in.

He seems startled and sits up. "The cheeseburger didn't sit so well," he says. "I had a cheeseburger and a Diet Coke. I wonder if the food was stale or something."

"Are you feeling nauseous?"

He nods and slowly picks himself up, rubbing his chest as he does.

"You need anything? We have some Pepto Bismol."

"No, no, I'm just going to go lie down." He walks off to his bedroom.

I stay up for another couple of hours, watching a few episodes of *Law & Order* and chatting a little on Scruff, though my heart isn't in it. It seems clear that what I'm looking for—who I'm looking for—isn't on there. Though I imagine that he is, and imagine chatting with him, maybe him pretending to be someone else. Because he wants to talk to me and that would be a safe way to do it. But if he's on, he's lingering behind one of the faceless profiles. Maybe sitting on his couch eating a bowl of cereal, exchanging compliments with some guy in Australia or Montreal. Someone not close enough to be real, though the guy responds in real time. A voice that will never say it wants to be your boyfriend—or will never do more than say it. I feel a burst of futility in my chest.

Before heading off to bed, I stop to listen at my father's door. I hear snoring.

MY FATHER TEXTS me at work the next day a few hours before quitting time. It's been a decent shift. I've got a new shrub—another mugho pine—set aside for me. It looks like some kid took it for a bench, cracking off a good third of it, but I figure it will recover pretty quickly. And Rob has kept off my case. In fact, for most of the afternoon he lent me out to Lumber. We unload, move palettes, stack wood, and make jokes about everything from politics to the glory that is working for Lowe's. I've got my phone on vibrate, and I don't check it right away, not until I get a break. I've already been called out for that too many times. I keep thinking that it could be Dave, and it's like carrying a scratch off ticket, knowing I've got a text waiting. Small chance of a big payoff, but still a chance.

So I'm a little disappointed when I see it's my father. A little surprised, too. He rarely uses his cell. In fact, he asked me to install a landline when he moved in, which I didn't do.

His message is brief: *I am at Miami Valley. I am OK. I am going to stay for tests.*

I text back: *What's going on?*

Then five minutes later, I text: *I'm still at work. Should I come by?*

I wait another minute, looking at my phone. Then I start to type a third message, telling my father I'll head right over. Then I'm not sure if I should head over. I slide the phone into my back pocket. I've got another hour here. It seems likely that my father will still be there at 4:00 when I get off. But it's a good half-hour drive there, and at rush hour, it will take longer. The idea of telling Rob I need to leave early makes my stomach knot. But I do need to leave early. It's only an hour, and Rob can't need me that badly if he lent me out to Lumber.

Rob isn't pleased. He shakes his head side to side as if I were a delinquent, but I hold up my phone showing him my father's text and he says, "clock out." I decide to wait until Thursday to load up the pine.

My father texts en route. Again he says he's okay and that I should come by later. I text back—the magic of voice dictation—and say I'll be there around 4:00.

He texts again as I'm parking the Celica. He's in Emergency, he says. Waiting for an ambulance. So I start the car again, drive around to the Emergency entrance, and park there. I see my father as soon as I enter. He's in a gown, sitting in a wheelchair in the waiting area. An older woman sits beside him, talking. She's turned toward him, but I can see she's got gray hair pulled into a ponytail and she's wearing a baggy blue sweater that falls below her waist, almost becoming a dress. Both of them look up when I walk over.

"Hey Dad, are you all right?"

My father nods. "Yeah, kid, I'm fine."

The woman—speaking loudly—says, "You're not fine, you're having a heart attack."

"I'm having a heart attack, but I'm fine." My father shrugs.

"Right now?" I ask. "You're having one right now?"

"My EKG was normal," my father says. "But my enzymes indicated there was something going on."

The woman turns to me. "The enzymes indicated a heart attack," she says. Then she holds out her hand. "I'm Beth. I told your father to get to the hospital. It *sounded* like a heart attack."

Beth is an assertive woman. I see it in her face. The set of her jaw, how she leans forward to talk. She's also put together. She's wearing blue eye shadow, and her glasses are covered with rhinestones. I think she's wearing lipstick, too—a pale shade.

"I'm Mike," I say, shaking her hand. "Thank you. It sounds like I owe you some thanks."

"I've seen heart attacks before. Not like in the movies where someone clutches a hand to the chest and cries out and collapses. Maybe they can be like that sometimes, but not always." Beth jabs a finger in the air to make this point. "Sometimes they are slow, creeping affairs. You're walking around, getting your hair done, frying up dinner, and you're having a heart attack the whole time! Your father has been having a heart attack since we went to that deli last night."

"A minor heart attack," my father says.

"No such thing," says Beth.

"Can you go home?" I ask.

It turns out my father can't go home. In fact, he has to go to another facility, a heart center north of Dayton. The three of us wait for another twenty-five minutes until a nurse with a clipboard comes over and announces that it's time for him to go. While we're waiting, I learn a few more details. My father had a dull ache in his shoulder and thought it was from the gym. He told Beth about it when she called this morning to see if he was feeling better. She notes that he didn't look great last night. On the phone, she'd told him she was either going to call an ambulance or come over there to pick him up. He refused both options, and she employed both—arriving at my place about ten minutes before the ambulance did. The EMTs convinced him that he should at least come get checked out. Beth's manner is triumphant, but not grating. She's funny, too. She does an impression of my father's face when the ambulance pulled into the driveway. She says that if he wasn't already having a heart attack, he would have had one right then.

My father shakes his head a little bit. I stifle a laugh.

Beth and I see my father into the ambulance, but neither of us is allowed to ride with him. So I offer to drive her to the heart center. We walk out to my car, and then Beth waits patiently, watching as I clean out the passenger seat, throwing things in the back: assorted papers, a couple of books from school, my Lowe's vest. She sees the latter and notes that it's impossible to get anyone to help in those places. I agree, but the comment feels a little accusatory.

As soon as we're on the interstate, I thank her again for helping my father and tell her that I'm glad they have become friends.

"Oh yes," she says, leaning back with her purse on her lap. "I'm glad, too. It's nice to have someone to do things with at my age. When Phillip died—that was 2007 . . . he had a heart attack, too, a much more serious one than your father's seems to be—I spent a number of years not doing much of anything. But that's not good; a body needs to do things to live. A mind without stimulation collapses inward. So I started doing things alone. Going to the movies alone, going to coffee shops alone. Oh, I had girlfriends and I met them for lunch here and there. But I had decided I wasn't going to spend all my weekends in the house, you see, and I didn't."

What Beth did do was a lot of "table for one" dining and walking around malls by herself, but eventually she started taking classes and traveling. She even took a solo trip to New York City when none of her girlfriends would accompany her. She saw *A Tale of Two Cities* on Broadway, ate good Italian, and walked up Fifth Avenue to Tiffany and Versace.

Beth talks a lot, which makes the conversation easy. She tells me about her son in Tucson, Henry, who she adopted when he was just a baby. Henry's biological mother was Beth's best friend; the woman was unmarried and died of breast cancer soon after Henry was born. Together they had decided that Beth would raise Henry.

Even when his biological mother was alive, she says, she felt like Henry was half her baby.

"I went out there a few times, too, after Phillip died," Beth says. "To see Henry and Adara. They have the space now; their twins are long gone—I mean grown up, making their own lives—they're not *gone* gone! All this talk of people going, I need to be more careful how I speak. The twins are very much here. I'm going to ask your father to come out to Tucson with me next time I go."

I raise an eyebrow. This seems like an unlikely proposition. "Are you and my father dating?" I ask. It's patently none of my business.

"No, no, no, we're not dating. Or, if we are, it's three of us: your father, your mother, and I. Or maybe four of us, maybe Phillip is in there, too. A little. Or maybe your father and I *are* dating. What does dating mean when you're in your seventies? Well, I suppose it means whatever you want it to." She puts her hand on my arm. "Does it make you uncomfortable to think of your father and I dating?" she says. She leans in.

The question startles me. "No," I say. "Not at all. By all means, whisk my dad off to Tucson. I'm just glad he's getting out. He doesn't get out enough. I mean, socially."

"I get that sense. He's easily made sad. But you can't rush grieving. When he's ready to be done with it, he will be done with it." Beth pauses. "Though there's not always enough runway. It does seem possible to acquire more grief than you have days left to grieve it in."

I ask Beth what a person does then, and she doesn't answer right away, so I turn to look at her. Her brow is wrinkled, and she's looking forward, into the road ahead. Another moment passes, so I turn my gaze back to the road, thinking she has let the subject drop. But then she speaks up. "You can be miserable. You can be miserable, or you can find a way both to grieve and enjoy your life."

Then she tells me more about Henry. An engineer. Served in the army, in Iraq. He was stationed in Germany for a while, too, and married a woman when he was out there, Adara, who was in the country as a guest worker. Beth and Phillip flew over for the wedding, which was just the four of them in a clerk's office. She eventually asks if I would like to get married someday. Apparently, my father has told her that I'm single. I am about to say that gay marriage isn't legal in Ohio when I realize that Beth must not know I'm gay. She means married to a woman. This doesn't surprise me; it wouldn't be an easy thing for my father to bring up. But it doesn't much please me, either. Beth is probably in her early seventies. I don't know her religious affiliation, and we've got to be in the car together for the remaining ten minutes of the ride out and the whole ride back. And of course, if my father and Beth have any kind of friendship, I don't want to say anything to jeopardize it.

"I would," I say tentatively. "I don't know if I've got it in me, but if the right person came along . . . or maybe if the right person had a change of heart, if circumstances aligned just right, I'd be willing to give it a try. As an experiment, just to see how it would go, to see what I might be capable of."

"That's a pretty cavalier attitude toward marriage," Beth says. I didn't at all mean it as cavalier. Just the opposite. But I wonder if I should have been more careful about saying even that much. "An experiment! If you tell a woman that, she's going to run gangbusters in the other direction."

I feel like a fraud not correcting Beth, but I laugh and nod. "Maybe that's the plan."

"You didn't learn that attitude from your father," she says. "He took his marriage to your mother very seriously."

How well could Beth possibly know my father? Clearly, there's a lot of stuff she hasn't seen. Not that my father played around on my mother, or that he ever thought about leaving her. Just that there might be a difference between taking something "very seriously" and never really considering that there might be other options. But the truth is that I have no idea what was going on in my father's head when my mother was alive—especially in their thirties, forties, and fifties, before the gravity of old age and illness pulled them into a close orbit.

"I guess he took his vows seriously," I say. "I don't think he ever really considered leaving her."

"I'm not religious," Beth says. "I do not believe. I have wanted to believe. I think life is easier, often better, for those who do. But you can't reason yourself into believing. I do put stock in vows, though. Your father kept his, and that's something to admire."

I push back a little. I can't help myself. I just met her, and she's telling me about my own father. "I'm not sure," I say. "A person can keep a vow out of love and dedication, or just mechanically, because he doesn't know what else to do."

"No. There are always other options, other choices. People drink, they get fired, they are physically abusive, they walk away. A lot of people walk away. Your father did none of those things. All of that is keeping your vow. And almost sixty years of keeping your vow is not a coincidence; it is something to admire."

At first it strikes me as a low bar to clear for admiration—simply staying put—but maybe Beth is right. I haven't been with anyone for as long as three years, much less sixty. Doesn't it ever become mechanical? Do you have to keep deciding to stay, moment by moment? The mindset escapes me utterly.

"You don't know what you don't know," says Beth. "Henry doesn't either. It's part of the experience of being someone's kid."

I look over again and see that she has turned toward me, smiling with full teeth. I laugh.

IT TURNS OUT that The Center for Cardiovascular Medicine is not an independent building, but just the wing of an old hospital with a new entrance opening onto a large rotunda with a terrazzo tile floor. There's mica or some other reflective material mixed into the polished cement, so the rotunda glitters. As we walk in, Beth grabs my arm and says she feels like we're entering a ballroom.

A receptionist at the front desk directs us toward a hallway to the left, and we quickly move out of ballroom territory. The corridor is drab gray with framed nature prints every few yards—a lot of meadow scenes. At the end of it we find another waiting room, and it's there my father sits, again in a wheelchair, leafing through *USA Today*.

Beth and I settle in beside him, and we wait for more than an hour. My father starts talking about Obamacare, and since he and I have been through that a hundred times, I find a recent *New Yorker* on the table next to me and read through an article about Xi Jinping, the president of China. I glance over to see that Beth seems to be listening to my father go on about socialism. When she responds, I don't think she quite agrees with him, but I do my best to tune it out. Eventually a nurse comes over to announce that they have a room ready, and at that point my father tells Beth and me to go home. He makes us go over the details of the trip back a couple of times—that Beth's car is at the other hospital, that I'm going to drive her there, that we know what room he's going to be in at this facility—and then he assures us he'll be fine. I speak to the nurse before heading out, and she confirms that he's in no danger and that a specialist will be around to see him early tomorrow afternoon. So Beth and I go. I lean over and give him a hug before we do, which is awkward and brief, and not just because he's only half-risen from his chair.

15

THE NEXT MORNING, my father rushes me off the phone because his breakfast has arrived. He says I should come by after my classes. "No, no, after. Come by after." It's very important to him that I don't cancel class. So I don't. I'm not sure how worried I ought to be about him. He doesn't sound especially sick, but my father may well be like a cat in that respect—by the time he starts acting sick, he's *very* sick.

I teach—the second day of presentations, so it involves a lot of sitting in the back and applauding—and then head up to see him. It's after three by the time I get to the heart center, which is much busier now, with groups of people scattered around the rotunda, and the tables in back, near the snack kiosk, largely filled. I head right up to see my father and find him sitting up in bed, watching Neil Cavuto interview some Republican congressman about "the recklessness of this current president." That's the phrase I hear when I walk in. The bed on the far side of the room looks recently vacated, with a paperback open face down on the nightstand. My father has a roommate.

"Hey, kid, there you are," my father says, jabbing the remote control at the television to shut it off. I pull a chair up to the side of his bed, and he asks about my day but cuts me off before I say half a dozen words.

"I had a heart attack," he says, his face suddenly heavy.

Did the specialist give him some bad news?

"Yeah, it seems you did, Dad. Are you feeling all right?"

He nods.

"What did the specialist say?"

"I've got blockages in both arteries, but they don't seem very concerned. I'm going to get a couple of stents. They've got me scheduled for Friday."

"Friday? And it's all right to wait till then?"

"I guess it is," he says. He puts his hand on his chest, feeling around. "It's a strange sensation, my heart is in there beating, but not all that well, apparently."

"The stents will fix you up."

"I'm getting old, kid. Do you know who was president the year I was born?"

"Roosevelt." He's asked me this before.

"Roosevelt." He nods. "I don't remember that, of course. It was during the Second World War, ancient history now. We had an icebox. I remember the icebox. When I was a kid, they'd deliver blocks of ice to your house."

"It doesn't seem like a very efficient way to keep things cool."

"It worked! Surprisingly it worked. But it was a different world. We didn't have a television until I was sixteen. Black-and-white, the screen maybe twelve inches across." My father glances over his shoulder at the cluster of machines he's hooked up to, rendering his vital signs in brightly colored waveforms and numbers. "It's almost too much change for one person's lifetime. My brother Frank said that before he died—that it was like he wandered into a different world, and he missed the first one."

I agree that the world is different.

"Frank's world was my world, too," he says. "I'm not sure what I'm doing in this one. Your mother was my connection to that past world, but now I'm shipwrecked in this one with a bad heart."

I have no idea how to honor what my father is saying. My impulse is to tell him it's not so bad—neither his heart nor his sense of being shipwrecked. And that's what I eventually do say, but I kick myself for the words even as they're coming out. They sound dismissive, even invalidating. I'm also not all that sure they're true.

My father shrugs. "I've got to change a few things."

"It can't hurt to change a few things," I say.

"You, too. You've got to change a few things, too."

I assume my father is talking about diet, so I ask if the nutritionist has come to see him yet, but he starts going on about his own father, who was in a wheelchair for the last decade of his life. My grandfather fell down the stairs in his apartment complex when he was in his mid-sixties. That one misstep put him in a chair until he died. My father says that his life ended ten years before it actually ended. Then he asks what I thought of Beth.

"She's got some fight in her," I say.

"She was here this morning. She brought muffins. Honey bran, try one." He points across the room at the built-in shelving and dresser, and I see a Tupperware box on top of it. "She's trying to sell me on coming down to Tucson for a week with her. She says she'll teach me how to cook heart-healthy meals."

I pass on the muffins. I can tell by my father's face he didn't think much of them.

"I just had a heart attack," he says, waving his hand forward in a gesture of dismissal. "I'm not going on any trips." Then after a beat he adds, "Maybe I'll go."

"She asked if I wanted to get married someday."

My father snaps his head toward me, concern in his voice. "What did you tell her?"

"I didn't tell her I'm gay. I wanted to."

He's silent a moment. "That guy who was at the house a while ago," he says. "Dave. You liked him, didn't you?"

Hearing Dave's name—especially from my father more than a month on—makes me flinch. How is it possible he even remembers him? My father never paid much attention to my life, much less my emotional landscape. For a moment, I'm thrown back to that morning in my kitchen: the small talk, my father at the table, Dave leaning against the wall. Blue shirt untucked, holding up a mug. Just standing there in my house like he belonged there.

My father says my name, and I look up.

Then someone comes in, a loud, peppy guy in his mid-thirties who introduces himself as "Joey the Dietitian!" and for the next twenty minutes I sit and listen as Joey tells my father about healthier choices. He's got pamphlets, which he opens one by one on my father's lap, revealing glossy pictures of food. My father's roommate is wheeled back into the room a few minutes later, too—an overweight guy at least twenty years younger than my dad. They're on a first name basis. He gives my father a big "Hi, Peter!" My father goes into full gregarious mode, almost struggling to get out of bed, to introduce me. The hospital room suddenly seems like a party.

My father isn't scheduled to get his stent for another few days yet, so I decide it's time to head out. But before I leave—right before—I get up and go closer to his bedside to speak more privately.

"Hey Dad," I say. "Remember the fight we had, you know, after that guy you mentioned had left? I just—I'm sorry about that. I shouldn't have said that stuff to you."

"I wanted to tell my old man to fuck off lots of times," he says. "I don't think I deserved it as much as he did."

"No," I say. I think about putting my hand on my father's shoulder, even leaning in to kiss his cheek. It seems like the right thing to do, like what would happen on a television show. "I don't think you deserved it, either." I'm not sure that those words are true, but for now they're close enough.

LATER THAT NIGHT, I text Matt to see if we're still on for dinner the next day. The house feels quiet without my father in it. He usually stays in his room with the door closed, but there's the sound of his television through the wall and him peeking in when he goes to the bathroom or kitchen. And just the fact of him being there.

I lived in apartments until eleven years ago when I bought this house. Being alone is different in an apartment. There are people around you, to the side, above, below. Even if they are in different units, you always know they're there, buzzing in the hive. But in a house, you're alone inside the structure. It feels different; the silence feels different. It took me a while to get used to it when I first bought this place, and I find I'm startled by it again.

So I spend the night on Scruff.

One of the guys I chat with lives in central PA, about four hundred miles away. Richie. Mid-forties. He's got a long, blonde beard, an arborist. We talk about driving out toward each other, that it would be only three or four hours for each of us. A ridiculous notion. Impractical, at least. But we discuss in detail how we might do it. Find a campground somewhere, hike until it gets dark, what we'd bring to grill, then how we'd spend the night in his two-man tent. And what kind of sex we'd have in there. Exactly what kind. What we'd do in what order. Talking about it as a way to experience it. In a novel I read last year, something set in feudal nineteenth-century Japan, one of the characters is an addict. He's got a private room in his house, and he stays in there all day, smoking opium as his family goes to ruin. I don't pretend to understand the human brain—either its chemistry or psychology—but I think the apps must be similar to opium: whatever happens chemically, serotonin or endorphins or something else releasing in the brain when you first meet someone, that rush of fantasy and possibility and desire. And how the world outside fades, at least for that interval, for however long you can draw it out. Sitting there on the couch, curled over my phone, I picture myself like the character in that novel, hunched in his dark office with that sickly sweet smoke, his family growing desperate. When I finally pull myself off the app, it's almost midnight. I got to bed thinking that I ought to have washed the dishes or even done my father's laundry, so he could come home to an orderly house. The old man is right. I do need to change a few things.

MATT TEXTS THE next day to confirm dinner. I was beginning to wonder if he'd changed his mind or if he just wanted me to sweat it a bit. It's 3:00 p.m., and I'm out in the yard up to my forearms in mud when my phone buzzes. I quickly finish up, then head around to the back of the house, to the spigot, to rinse. His text reads, *What are you up to?* I text back, *Just finished planting a mugho pine*, and he responds by asking me if that's some sort of euphemism. I send him a picture of the pine, which is roughly the size of a beach ball with a bare patch on one side. I text him about my father, too, that I've got to go see him for a couple of hours, but that I'm looking forward to dinner. We agree to meet at 7:30.

Matt is already seated and drinking a glass of red wine by the time I get to the Green Elephant Trail. He asks how my father is as I'm sitting down.

"I think he's okay," I say, unfolding my napkin. "His friend Beth was still there when I left, so he's got company. Beth and the guy in the next bed, Jack. All three of them were watching *Jeopardy*, pointing at the TV, calling out answers. It seemed like a good time to duck out."

The waiter comes over and asks what I want to drink.

"But he's more subdued than yesterday," I say. "He must be afraid. He's getting a stent put in tomorrow. A couple of stents."

Matt sips his wine. "It's an easy procedure," he says. "You're awake the whole time. They even set up a monitor so you can watch it go in." He tells me his mother had a stent put in back in Italy, and she recovered just fine.

After we order, he gets down to business. "So what about this Dave guy?" he says.

"What should I tell you?"

"Let's start with the time frame. How long have you known him? Is this an ongoing thing?"

"I met him right after I met you. Maybe the following week. We only went on a few dates. Well, three." I tell Matt about the water heater, the cornfield, and making out in a candy-store entryway.

Matt rubs his chin. "And I assume you're leaving out the sex for my benefit?"

I nod.

"But you guys fucked?"

I shrug and half-smile, unsure how to answer. Maybe Matt wants the salacious details, but I'm not going there, not about my night with Dave.

Matt waits a moment, then starts up again. "So you fell for this guy hard and quick?"

"Yeah, I guess I did."

"That's a crush, Mike. You understand that, right? I'm not knocking it. Great things can happen with crushes. The uprush of all that tingly energy. It makes people crazy. They write hundreds of sonnets and marshal conquering armies."

"You're not really a romantic, are you?"

"I am," Matt says. "If you take out the bullshit parts. I'm all about flights of passion; I just don't lose sight of what they are. What does this guy look like?"

I describe Dave. Beefy, furry, square jaw, big nose. Kind of a pornstache. Matt listens closely.

"Flight of passion. I hear it in your voice. You wanted to fuck him," he says.

That seems harsh, but I try not to react. Maybe Matt's jealous. "I guess love at first sight is off the table?"

"That's a story written backwards. If something works out, you look back after thirty years and say it was love at first sight. For all the times it doesn't work out, you look back and call it hormone-stupid."

"Then it could be love at first sight," I say. "We've got to wait a couple of decades to know for certain."

Matt takes a sip of wine. "I thought this guy ditched you. We already know the outcome."

Our food arrives at just that moment, which is fortuitous. The word "ditched" stings. Now I do want to push back. Hard. Jealous or no. *Fuck you, we don't know the outcome. Not for sure, not yet.* But then I remember that I'm here to be honest with Matt, that I was a dick to him. And besides, "ditched" is the right word. Or something worse than ditched. I take a breath.

"He more than ditched me," I say. "I laid it on the line for him. In bed. Post-coitally. I don't know what got into me. I told him I liked him. And how much."

"Cum drunk," Matt says, nodding. Then he sets down his fork and looks up at me. "Did you tell him you loved him?" He seems really horrified.

Maybe this dinner is a mistake. If Matt's here to punish me, to rub my nose in how badly things turned out, it's definitely a mistake.

"Look, I told him I could see myself in a relationship with him. That's all. That it had been a very long time since it happened, since I'd been with anyone, and I could see myself with him." As soon as I say this, I flush deeply with shame. For having been rejected, maybe. For having exposed myself and been rejected. My impulse is to get up from the table, go to the bathroom and breathe. But

I don't. What I said is what happened, and I just try to accept it. I stay seated.

"I'm not surprised that sent him running," Matt says. He picks up his fork and continues eating. "It would have sent you running, too. Basic dog instinct. When something runs towards you, you run away. When something runs away from you, you chase it. Has nothing to do with whether or not this guy likes you. Just dog instinct. You ran at him too fast."

"Yeah, I get that. But how the hell are you supposed to get close to a guy if you can't move toward him?" My voice comes out louder than I mean it to. I'm upset now, and maybe that's what Matt wanted because he eases up.

"Calm down," he says, reaching across the table to put a hand on my wrist. "Think dog. You approach slowly and talk in a soothing voice. Anyway, it doesn't mean this guy doesn't like you. Not necessarily. He *may* not like you. But sometimes dogs circle back to smell the area where you've been because they're still curious." It feels like a concession, Matt saying that—albeit a small one. It gives me a little hope.

He puts another forkful of Pad Thai in his mouth, chews, and swallows. "Now on to us. What about your predilection for ghosting?"

"Who said anything about a predilection?"

"Isn't this something you do a lot?" Again, a hardness in his voice.

I exhale. Right. I want to answer honestly. What does "a lot" mean, anyway? Ghosting is something people do. Guys have ghosted me dozens of times. Hundreds, I bet. Do I do it more than other people?

Matt reaches over with his fork, nabs a shrimp off my plate, and eats it. "That's good," he says. "I think I like yours better than mine."

"We can order another one for you."

He jabs his fork forward. "You need to learn how to share your food. Speaking of dogs: you are not one. Now about the ghosting."

"Okay. Yes. It's something I do a lot."

"Well, walk me through it, what's the thinking there?"

"Do you want another shrimp?" I ask, pushing my plate toward him. He makes a sweeping gesture with his hand, indicating that I should keep going. "It's easier. Easier on all parties concerned, isn't it? No one likes to hear that you don't want to hang out with them."

"It's easier on you," Matt says. Then he spears another shrimp off my plate, gesturing with it as he talks. "For the ghostee, it's always better to hear directly that a person is no longer interested, so he can close that door and move on. And hate you, if necessary. You and I had talked about getting together, so there was an asterisk in my weekend, an instability." He pops the pilfered shrimp in his mouth. I start to respond, but he puts up a finger to stop me while he finishes chewing. "That's not a big deal," he says, swallowing. "An instability in a weekend. But when you ghost someone, you put an asterisk in their emotional life, an instability *there*. And the more interested the person is in you, the bigger the asterisk. That is a big deal. Don't do it anymore—"

"Besides, I didn't text because—"

"Ahh. Say you won't do it anymore, then you can continue with what you're going to say."

"Matt—"

He puts up a hand. "Just say it."

"I won't do it!" I say. "Won't do it anymore." I'm still not sure I ghost more than other guys, but I take Matt's point; it can hurt. He nods, authorizing me to continue. "But what I was going to say is that I was down that week; I was just feeling really down. I didn't feel up to contacting anyone."

"You couldn't send a short text? No excuses. You couldn't take five minutes to text me?"

Matt looks at me, holding my gaze. He's right. I know he's right. I shrug and let my hands fall into my lap. I say I'm sorry, and Matt nods and says, "very good." After a moment, we go back to eating.

When Matt speaks again, his voice is markedly more gentle. "Are you still down?"

"Yes," I say. "Maybe not. Yeah, yeah, I am. The possibilities feel diminished."

He asks what possibilities, and I say, "All of them." Then we start talking about falling in love, and Matt tells me a little more about Javier, who he says could be quite romantic: good chocolate, candle-lit dinners, champagne. Early on, he surprised Matt with a weekend trip for his birthday. Matt thought they were going to eat at a new Spanish place east of the city, but Javier kept driving out on I-10 until they reached New Orleans, where a bed-and-breakfast reservation awaited them. Javier had arranged everything: cat sitter, weekend bags, spa passes. He'd even packed strawberries for the five-hour drive. It all sounds pretty spectacular.

"So what went wrong?" I say. "Didn't you tell me the last year was bad?"

"Abysmal," Matt says. "That was my word. But nothing went wrong, we just stopped taking walks, stopped fucking. Javier decided to stay out in LA an additional month and that turned into three. The energy was spent. Whatever energy he and I had, it took four years to burn through it. The abysmal part was due to not acknowledging what was obviously true: that we were done."

The waiter comes over to collect our plates and ask if we want dessert. Matt tells him no, glancing over at me mid-sentence and saying, *sotto voce*, that we'll be going for gelato.

When the waiter leaves, Matt continues. "The dithering was abysmal. A year of dithering. The smart move would have been to end things sooner. The pain of losing him couldn't have been avoided, but the pain of holding on to what was already gone—that could've been. Live and learn."

"But you had to try," I say.

"Maybe," Matt says. "We went on date nights." He rolls his eyes. "We tried for a while. Then we each began to consider other possibilities."

I press him for details: blowouts, infidelities, even minor betrayals like staying out too late or squandering shared money. Nothing. He insists on it. He shrugs and says sometimes things are just done. Then he asks why this bothers me so much. "Last time, too," he says. "When we talked about this before. What do you think, Mike, that you find true love and things immediately click into happily-ever-after mode—decades and decades through a soft-focus filter, to hide the wrinkles?"

I want to tell Matt that the idea of actually starting a relationship seems difficult enough—unlikely enough—as it is, that if we throw in the possibility that it might simply run out of juice like a spent battery in a year or two, or even three or four, then I might as well throw in the towel now. That hearing him say this makes me feel utterly hopeless. But before I can say a word, the waiter comes over with the bill in a plastic tray, and Matt points him to me.

TWENTY MINUTES LATER we're walking the green, each holding a small cup of gelato. Matt has gotten a flavor called "Stracciatella," which has chocolate shavings in it. The name sounds like a song when he says it, so I ask him to say it again for me, and he does so a good six times, rolling the r and dragging out the l's. Then he insists I say it, which I cannot, and then that I try a spoonful, which I do, and it is particularly excellent. I return the favor, letting him sample my salted caramel.

"Not as good," he says. "But good."

"Well, sometimes you've got to be satisfied with not as good."

"Not with gelato," Matt says. "With gelato you should always get the best."

"What about with love?"

Matt informs me that love, even in its best incarnations, is never as good as dessert. But in both cases, he notes, all the best options are made by Italians.

Our walk doesn't last long. The stores along the green are closed, and there's no one else around. It's a Thursday night, and a bit too cold to be out without a coat. Definitely too cold for gelato. But come summer—Saturday afternoons in July and August—the town sets up a bandstand on the lawn. People bring blankets to watch the musicians. I tell Matt about it, tell him he would like it, even though it's generally country music or fiddle bands. He suggests we go.

"So you want to hang out with me again?" I ask.

"Why wouldn't I? Because you had a crush on some other guy? I give people second chances."

I wonder if Matt would ever give Javier a second chance.

"Besides," he continues, "we're just talking about an outdoor concert. And sex. It's likely we'll have sex, too. I'm not sure what you having a crush on another guy has to do with any of that."

"Okay," I say, a little wobbly on his logic. "We've got a date for July."

"And you don't have to buy dinner for that one. Well, maybe you do. We'll talk about it later."

The mention of sex makes me consider inviting Matt back to my place—for the company, to help fill the house. It feels easy being with him right now, even feeling attracted to him, since he knows about Dave. In fact, I'm surprised he doesn't suggest it himself. But he doesn't, not even with his body language. It's just as well. I haven't had sex with anyone since that misfire with the guy in gold briefs, and I don't think I could.

We finish our loop around the green and say goodbye in front of the restaurant where both of us parked. Before we go, Matt gives me a hug, and it feels good. He feels solid under his denim jacket.

16

THE NEXT DAY I visit my father in the hospital. He seems alert, comfortable. At first he's even animated, sitting up, going on about how he was awake for the whole procedure. How they injected dye into his bloodstream and he saw it all on the monitor: the guidewire going up through his heart, the metal mesh opening, widening the artery. Arteries. They did both, inserting multiple stents into one.

But after a few minutes, he starts to seem sullen, grumbling about feeling trapped, how he refuses to spend another night here. Then he lies back and pretty much stops talking. I ask about the food and where his roommate is—Jack, the *Jeopardy* guy—and he gives short, unengaged replies, not really turning his head away from the television. So I stop trying. I sit and watch with him—FOX News, of course—and head off when a woman comes to take his dinner order. He thanks me for coming, a quick "yeah, thanks," but it isn't clear to me that he was all that aware of my presence.

WHEN I RETURN on Saturday, I find him waiting downstairs in the rotunda. Beth is there, too. She's dressed more casually this time: hair clipped back, a sweatshirt, leggings. But again I'm struck by how put together she seems.

I am on time—my father said ten and it's ten—but he and Beth look settled in, seated at one of the small tables near the snack kiosk, each with a cup of coffee. There's an overnight bag by my father's feet, not one I recall seeing before. Beth must have brought it to help pack his things. It looks like she's talking as I start toward them.

My father stands when he sees me and raises an arm.

"I thought you'd be up in your room," I say. I don't sit. There are only two chairs at the table, and I don't think we're staying long.

My father remains standing. "No, I want to get the fuck out of here." His words are spoken half under his breath. He picks up the new bag, and Beth stands, too.

"It turns out the cancer brought on the heart attack," she says. "He'd had radiation treatment right here"—she runs a finger up and down her sternum—"and it damaged his heart or his heart lining. Something. So the cancer went into remission, and six months later he had a heart attack."

I look at my father, confused. "Who are we talking about?"

"Phillip," she says. "My husband. Former husband. I was telling your father that he's lucky. A small heart attack that doesn't cause any damage—it's a warning without consequences, like being pulled over and not receiving a citation. You thank your stars. Or better than that, since the stents reverse the damage. Your father had a ninety-seven percent blockage in one artery."

"Yes, very lucky," my father says flatly. "Can we go? Let's go."

The three of us migrate to the door and figure out who's parked where. It turns out that Beth is following us back to the house. She's going to take my father to the local Kroger, to shop for items the nutritionist suggested: whole wheat pasta, olive oil, avocados, and probably a few other things my father won't want to eat. He doesn't talk much on the way home, but he perks up when I say he must be glad to be out of there. He says that lying in bed all day long, you might as well be dead already.

And he does seem a little happier once we pull in the driveway. As we're getting out of the car, I tell him I washed and folded his laundry—my Friday-night activity. Maybe that helps.

Beth pulls in behind us, and we pause, waiting for her to get out of her car. Instead, she lowers her window and calls us over, asking if my father wants to head to the store right away. She's got her trunk stuffed with grocery bags. My father shakes his head, mumbling that he wants to go in, and turns toward the house. There's a massive wattage difference between them—at least at the moment. Beth turns off her car and gets out.

As soon as we're inside, my father takes off his shoes, heads for the living room, and sits on the couch, slouching far back into it. This leaves me in the foyer with Beth. She sits on one of the wicker chairs in there, untying her shoes.

"Would you like a cup of coffee?" I say.

"Already had one," she says, springing up. "Do you have green tea? You could make a cup for your father and I. It's good for the heart."

We settle on Sleepytime, the only herbal tea we've got, and Beth offers to help me make it. I don't need any help, but my father, flipping channels, seems largely unaware of our presence, so I agree.

"He's feeling a little mortal this morning," she says, standing beside me at the kitchen counter while I fill the electric kettle.

"Yeah, I imagine he's worn out," I say. "Maybe shopping isn't a great idea."

"Sometimes it's better to get people moving. Sometimes it's not. Your father might be one of the latter. This morning, anyway."

"You honestly think he's lucky?"

"We're all lucky," Beth says. "We're here. That makes us lucky. What are the odds of being born, that particular mix of genes and chromosomes? But he's especially lucky his ninety-seven percent blockage didn't get to a hundred percent. He could need a pacemaker right now. Or a headstone."

Beth thinks for a minute and then walks out of the kitchen, toward the living room. "What are you watching, Peter?" she calls from the hallway. "Do you want a cup of tea?"

My father doesn't answer. Beth comes back in.

"He may not feel lucky for a couple of days," I say.

As I'm pouring hot water into mugs—one for Beth and one for my father, who will almost certainly not drink it—Beth starts opening the cupboards. She asks first, "May I?" but doesn't quite wait for my assent before moving forward.

"A lot of macaroni and cheese." She takes down three boxes of it and puts them on the counter. There must be half a dozen more in there. "At least you've got bran cereal." Then she takes down a can of something. I look over and see it's Progresso soup, Beef Pot Roast. My favorite flavor. She starts reading the label.

"It's best to start small," she says. "Introduce a few new foods, cut out a few of the worst offenders. Your father isn't very good with change, is he?" She opens the fridge, takes out a container of sour cream, and puts it on the counter. "A good first step is to get rid of this."

Then my father comes into the kitchen. He drops the remote control on the kitchen table. The television is still on in the living room.

"I'm not up to going to the grocery store today, Beth," he says. He stands there. Maybe because I know my father, I can hear the shortness in his voice. It's both defensive and sharp, the kind of tone my sister and I knew growing up to step gingerly back from. The right answer is "okay." Just that one word.

"Maybe I will go through the cupboards with Mike to organize a few things," she says. She picks up the sour cream again—probably to show him or tell him something about it.

She's about to start speaking when my father swoops over.

I see the action happening a moment before it does. It's tiny compared to my father's rages when I was a kid, but it has the same suddenness, the same bite. For a moment, he's large and imposing again. He grabs the container right out of her hand, walks over to the fridge, and jabs it in. Then closes the fridge too hard.

"We're not cleaning any damn cupboards today," he says, shaking his head, and walks out of the room.

Beth is taken aback. Physically. He didn't touch her, but the swiftness of his action seemed to push her, as if the sharp movement of his body created an air current that swept her back. For a moment, I fear she's going to fall. But she steadies, looking after him, a little dazed. Then her expression hardens.

"No, I guess we're not."

I come over, closer to her, hesitating only a moment before I put my hand on her shoulder.

"What's gotten into him?" she asks. Then, "Your father is a bully."

"It's the heart surgery, Beth. It's just got him worried. That's how it is with my dad. Sometimes his worry comes out sideways."

"I've experienced a lot of worry in my life," she says. "But I've never bullied anyone."

It seems like Beth is making the decision to leave. I see it in her body language; she's squared her shoulders, picked her purse up off the table. And it seems important to me that she not leave like this, not just yet. "Please, have your tea, Beth," I say. I hurry back to the counter and bring both mugs to the table, setting one down in front of where she's standing and the other on the next place over.

I sit. After a moment, Beth sits, too.

"He'll apologize later," I say, though I'm not so sure he will. "Being in a hospital bed for three days has—"

"We'll see if he does." She takes a sip of tea. "Tell me something, Mike. Answer me honestly. Did your father beat your mother? He's an older man now, but he wasn't always. Abusers grow to be old men, too."

"Not even once," I say. "Honestly, not even once."

"But he screamed at her. Maybe he pushed her a few times."

He did. Of course he did.

I start to explain that all couples scream at each other now and then, but Beth isn't having it. She presses me again, so I say that he's calmed down as he's grown older, especially since my mother died. He's become more introspective, more aware, and that he will feel very bad about this later.

Beth nods. She tells me that she's no stranger to men hitting women. It's what she saw growing up—in her own family and in those of her friends. Big Catholic families in the upper Midwest. The fathers dispensed violence like that was their sole purpose on Earth. Generally the violence was meted out as punishment for some infraction, but not always. She describes an incident from her childhood, her father yelling for her, ordering her into the house because of some name she'd called her sister, and then a moment of decision. Instead of coming back, she ran far into their hayfield to hide. Beth says she lay out there, the grass above her, long after her father stopped shouting. Maybe for a couple of hours; she's not sure. When she came back, which seemed much later in the day, he'd simply forgotten about it.

"You can draw a number of lessons from that," she says. "About justice and punishment. About the statute of limitations. Maybe the experience of lying in that hayfield, my heart banging inside my chest, was punishment enough for whatever I had called my sister. Probably ugly and stupid, though she was neither, may she rest in peace. But mostly, that experience taught me a few things about men and their anger. Namely, that it's best to leave them to it, to let them circle the ring alone. I don't tiptoe around angry men. No point in tiptoeing around a house on fire, and wielding buckets will tire you out much quicker than it will douse the flames. It's better, always better, just to go."

Beth finishes her tea, and then she does just that. She goes. She does not knock on my father's door to say goodbye, and he doesn't come out. I don't knock on his door, either, to let him know she's leaving. At least she doesn't seem angry anymore, though it's not clear to me that she will ever come back.

My father stays in his room through midafternoon, when he comes out to make a sandwich. He doesn't mention Beth. I don't either.

THE NEXT DAY, Sunday, I mark research projects at the kitchen table. My father passes in and out of the room—as he heads to AutoZone; as he comes back with a few high-powered flashlights that may prove useful, he says, in a blackout; as he makes himself egg salad for lunch; and toward late afternoon, as I'm finishing up, to tell me he's going for a walk. The papers are fine. I give as many A's as possible. I'm not paid enough to split hairs, and definitely not enough to deal with students who want to litigate grades. But I haven't wholly given up standards. There are a few C's in there, too.

If my father feels any remorse, I can't detect it—at least not any more than in his usual manner, which is pretty somber. If he wants to talk, he gives no sign.

I do want to bring it up. I want to bring it up all day. What I want is to accuse him. To put him on trial. Some cross between "Why did you do that?" and "Why have you done that my whole goddamn life?" With a good measure of "apologize to her" mixed in. And maybe some compassion mixed in, too. Just a few drops of it, like what a witch squeezes into the cauldron at the very end, to make the whole thing belch smoke. Compassion because my father had made a friend. Because I'm not convinced he'll ever get the chance to make another.

MONDAY NIGHT, I'm at Matt's apartment assembling an IKEA couch. Matt is drinking a glass of wine in the wingback—which looks set to remain the only piece of real furniture in the place—and watching me tighten bolts.

"Maybe I'll take it back," he says. He's been mulling the purchase for the last half hour, ever since we got the components out of the box.

"It *is* a piece of shit," I note. I finish bolting the armrests in place and wave Matt over to help me flip the couch.

"No! It's not a piece of shit!"

We heave the couch over, and Matt pets the armrest like it's a cat, as if my comment might've hurt its feelings. "The fabric is a nice color; it's soft." The fabric is gray like a bland business suit.

"Any sofa that costs under $300 is going to be a piece of shit. Whoever heard of a sofa you assemble at home? But the assembly is pretty ingenious. Next step: screw the legs on."

There are four roughly rectangular black legs, and these simply screw into plastic plates at each corner. I slide two of them across to Matt.

"Do you think I should return it?" he asks.

"I think you should return it, yes. And get some real furniture."

"But it's cute."

The couch is reasonably cute. We get it lifted on its legs and attach the cushions with their Velcro strips. Then Matt goes back for his wine and sits on the couch. He lifts his legs and holds them up, as if there were a coffee table underneath them. "Do you want to help me assemble the coffee table?"

"Sure I do," I say. "I bet that's going to be a piece of shit, too."

"Sit down." He pats the cushion beside him. "You'll see, it's surprisingly comfy for a piece of shit."

I agree that it is comfortable, and then Matt spins himself so he's leaning against the armrest—sort of leaning, I'm not convinced the armrest could take an adult's full weight—and swings his legs up, onto my lap. "I'm going to keep it. Maybe I'll get a more expensive couch later." He takes another sip of wine and places his glass on the floor.

"What do you think of the proposition that it's better to have sex at the beginning of a date rather than at the end, so that you can just relax and enjoy each other's company during the date itself?" he says.

"How about the pleasure of delayed gratification?"

Matt suggests that this may be overrated. He puts his arms behind his head and closes his eyes. "Let me tell you what I've been thinking about. Going back to the beach. Tuscany. Lying on the sand, feeling the sun, hearing the sea. Really feeling like you are lying against the planet . . . an enormous ball and you are on top of it, your back pressing against the curve of the Earth."

"How do you know you're on top of the planet?" I ask. "Couldn't you be at the bottom of it? Or on one of the sides?"

Matt wiggles his feet in my lap. "Did you want to rub my feet?"

"Did I?"

"When's the last time you were at the beach, Mike?"

There are a few lakes in this part of the state. I start to tell Matt about Stone Lick down near Cincinnati, which I visited last summer. He cuts me off.

"Lakes don't count. It's got to be sea or ocean. The point is being on the edge of something unfathomable, something that suggests immensity of scale. Plus there has to be waves."

"There were waves on the lake."

"Ripples."

We debate the relative merits of lakes and seas. This particular lake has a sand beach, which knocks off a few of Matt's best arguments. I start rubbing his feet. Maybe because I want to, maybe because they're in my lap and there's nowhere else particularly convenient to put my hands.

"Come lie on top of me," Matt says.

I look over. He still has his hands behind his head, still has his eyes closed. "I'm not sure the couch would hold us if I took my feet off the floor," I say. Then I add "bathroom" and get up. I scoot off, and Matt's feet fall on the spot where I'd been sitting.

In the bathroom, I stand at the sink and take a minute to look closely at my face in the mirror. The overhead is florescent-bright, and nobody looks good in this kind of light. I turned fifty this year, and it shows in the texture of my skin, which is mottled, wrinkled. Bluish under my eyes. Red, roughened on my forehead and neck. The closer I look, the more I see it. I haven't had sex with anyone in over a month. Maybe that doesn't sound like a lot, but for me that translates into: haven't kissed anyone, haven't touched anyone's hand, haven't really touched anyone at all in over a month. Haven't really relaxed with another person. So why shouldn't I have sex with Matt? There's not infinite time left. Not infinite opportunity. I splash cold water on my face, then bend down to the tap to cup some in my mouth and spit it out.

Instead of going back to my place at the end of the couch, I settle in atop Matt, who slides down a little farther so his head is on the cushion. I'm 5'10, and my ankles are up on the opposite armrest. I point this out.

"It's an apartment-size couch," Matt says.

I kiss him, and right from the start, my heart isn't in it. As soon as I admit that to myself—as soon as Dave pops into my head—it gets harder and harder to stay in my body, to be in the moment. We keep at it for a few minutes. I sit up, half straddling him, and lift his shirt. Then run a palm slowly over Matt's lean, furry stomach. It's sexy, just what I'm attracted to. I lean over and kiss him there. "So sexy," I say, but even as I say it, I feel myself backing off, moving toward the end of the couch, to where I was sitting before. Then I sit back down, lifting his legs onto me, his ankles on my lap. His stomach is still exposed. I reach over, to continue running a palm across it. I feel like I'm trying to take off a Band-Aid slow.

"Remember I told you my father had a girlfriend?" I say.

"Yeah."

"I don't think he does anymore."

"What happened?" Matt doesn't seem to register that I've moved off of him. But I'm looking straight ahead, avoiding his face.

"He barked at her. My dad barks. Grabs, pushes. Just rage, I guess. Rage happened."

"He should apologize."

"Yeah," I say. "But apologies address infractions, right? Can you apologize when you've shown an ugly side of yourself? 'I'm sorry I *am* this' is a hell of a lot less convincing than 'I'm sorry I *did* this.'"

Matt reaches down with his right hand, lifts my palm off his stomach and brings it to his crotch. I jerk my hand away.

For a moment, we're silent.

"I'm just not feeling it, Matt," I say. "I'm sorry. You're damn sexy but—"

Matt sits up, pulling his shirt down. "Okay, we don't have to," he says, an edge in his voice. He reaches for his wine glass, which is empty, and stands.

"You're still hung up on this guy," he says.

"I don't know. Maybe I am."

"What's that about? He's hot, right?"

Matt says this from the kitchen area so I'm not sure he can see me shrug.

"Are you hooking up? On Scruff or Grindr or whatever."

"I chat with guys, but I'm not feeling that, either. One guy, his handle is 'The Jeweler,' invited me over to play around in his shed. He said he's got a space heater in there—"

"He asked me a couple of times, too," Matt says, coming back over, sipping from a full glass. "Seemed a little sketchy. People get murdered in sheds."

This guy has probably asked a third of the local gays to visit his shed. I wonder how many have done it.

"All the tools for burying a body are right there, on site," Matt continues. "Besides, I suspect he's got a wife and kids. They'd be in the house, sleeping or watching television while he's outside with you in the shed."

"I almost went. But I couldn't. I'm just not feeling up to it."

"You're stingy with your heart, Mike. Probably a little sexy time is just what you need. You can skip the kissing."

Matt could be right. But just now the idea sounds distasteful. "Well, if I'm not feeling it, there's no point in doing it, is there?"

"Did you text this guy again?" Matt asks.

"You mean Dave?"

"Yeah, Dave. Pornstache guy."

"No," I say. "I didn't text him. I put it all on the line, and he bailed. He knows what there is to know."

Matt takes another sip of wine. "Italians don't give up so easily."

"If I had one indication from him, anything, that he was even a little interested, I would try. But without it, it seems . . . I don't know. You know the first rule of being in a hole: stop digging? Otherwise, it feels like I'd just be digging. Adding 'pathetic' to his list of reasons for not being interested."

"Doing nothing is pretty pathetic, too," Matt says. "I mean it would be one thing to move on and go into the bedroom with me so we could make out, or even to go get hacked apart in some suburban closet case's shed. Either of those actions would be absolutely *not* pathetic. Especially the former. But on the pathetic hierarchy, doing nothing may be more pathetic than doing too much. Do you want a cookie? I took some home from the copy shop yesterday. One of the women who works there brought them for her birthday."

I agree to the cookies, and Matt goes back to the counter. I understand what he's saying. I do. But I have exposed too much of myself to Dave already. And I'm confused. Still confused. I know he was there with me—when we were doing the water heater, talking at the bonfire, having sex. It all felt connected. But he's gone now.

"I just need something, Matt, some sign." I'm not sure he hears me, so I repeat myself when he sits back down with some half dozen pinwheel cookies on a paper plate.

He holds them out so I can take one before setting the plate on the floor in front of us.

"If you get crumbs on my new couch, it's over," he says, leaning back against the armrest, cookie in one hand, wine in the other.

"So what would you do?"

"I'd get the fuck over it," he says. His tone is a little more gentle than his words. "There are a lot of guys in the world."

"There are a lot of guys in San Francisco. And in New York. And Atlanta. But Dayton—"

"Then I'd move, Mike. These are really good." He holds up the cookie.

They are good. I reach for another.

"Okay, but if you couldn't move or get over it?"

"I guess I'd serenade his window. Show up at his work. Go full stalker. Make him get a restraining order. Whatever you need to do to get past it. All less pathetic than pining." He makes eye contact with me when he says that last word.

"I could send him a text to let him—"

"That's not the kind of thing that wows the heart," Matt says. "But yes, better than nothing."

When I finish my cookie, Matt straightens his legs again, putting his feet back in my lap. I take the cue and start rubbing them. Then I tell him about my father and Beth, and there we agree that an intervention is definitely called for. And then I assemble his coffee table.

17

WEDNESDAY IS THE final day of class. The students sit in a circle, eat brownies, and talk about what they've learned this term—not just with me, but from their whole experience at school. It takes maybe forty minutes to go around, each student offering a few things, and sometimes—the best-case scenario—others chiming in, laughing. (They occasionally throw out funny stuff.) For me, the discussion can be a little dull; I do it every semester with every class, and the responses are all pretty much the same. But I remember also that it serves a purpose, this ritual of closure, this chance to express pent-up feeling. It clarifies, resolves. A couple of students voice thinly veiled frustrations with the class or with me, the usual stuff about too much writing or getting a low grade because I disagreed with their positions. I can see in those students, in their body language, that it was stuff they needed to say.

So that night, I decide to talk to my father about Beth. I still believe he needs to apologize to her. But I'm thinking about it differently now—that maybe I should have the conversation with him for *my* sake, so I can get closure on the event, not just for his.

I find him in the garage after dinner, the door open, the light on. I used to park in there before he moved in. Now it's filled with his boxes, as well as some of the furniture from the house he shared with my mother out in Uniontown. An old white couch, the cushions still individually wrapped in plastic sleeves, as they have been since I was a kid. A dresser. A black lacquer dining room hutch that screams 1980s. The idea is that my father will take this stuff with him when he gets his own place. A few years ago when he moved in, that plan was necessary to make us both comfortable with the present arrangement. Looking around at the boxes—and at my father sitting on one of them, bending over another—it seems clear that the plan is still necessary. Even if it is pretty baldly a fiction.

I stand in the garage door. "Hey, what are you looking for, Dad?"

"Ah, nothing," he says. "Nah, just my old yearbook. I wanted to check the name of this guy I knew in high school. Evan Reeferson. He was with me the day I met your mother. I was going to look him up online, but I'm not sure I have his name right."

He reaches into the box in front of him and pulls out a blender.

"Is there a box with books in it? It looks like that one's full of kitchen supplies."

"I remember putting it in this box. It was out on the counter when I was packing up the kitchen, so it ended up in this box." He lifts out something else—something not even vaguely book shaped—and unwraps the newspaper around it. A set of three ceramic mixing bowls.

"I remember Mom using those," I say.

"She made a lot of nice meals for us, your mother." He puts the bowls to the side, then reaches back into the box.

"Are you going to try to get in touch with this guy?"

"I thought I'd look him up on Facebook." My father joined last year. I didn't think he used it that much. He doesn't have a picture of himself up, or anything filled out or posted.

I come closer so I can look into the kitchen box, too. It's half empty now, and I can see books on the bottom. Likely cookbooks, but who knows.

"Hey Dad," I say. "I know this is none of my business, but I was curious if you've seen Beth at the Silver Sneakers center this week."

"I saw her," he says, bringing his face up from the box.

"Did you talk to her?"

"I apologized."

I do my best to hide any expression of surprise.

My father continues. "I'd just had a heart attack; I wasn't thinking right. I just wasn't thinking right." For a moment, a look of real pain flashes across his face. "I walked on the treadmill next to hers, and she asked me some hard questions. She spoke a lot about violence. She asked if I was violent. She said I needed to tell her about my temper."

"What did you tell her?"

"I told her I have a temper." He shrugs. "She was asking me about my father and telling me about hers. She thinks I'm angry because my father was angry. That's what she said. Do you think I'm angry?"

I pause. My father has never asked me a question like this before: a question about himself, not to win an argument or as part of an implied threat. Not rhetorical. But with an openness to hear what I really thought. "You've had a hell of a temper, Dad," I say slowly, watching him. He seems to be okay, but he can't be used to receiving much feedback about himself. "It's not so bad anymore."

"I guess I had some bad years."

"Yeah," I say, nodding. "There were some bad years. You could be pretty scary when I was growing up."

My father bends into the box again and pulls out one more newspaper-wrapped item and then a stack of half a dozen hardback books. The yearbook is on the bottom. He immediately starts leafing through it. It takes him a few minutes—finding the right year—but he eventually locates Evan Reeferson. Or Reiferson. He'd been spelling the name wrong.

He's staring at the picture. "What are the odds he's still around?"

I start to say that I'm sure he is but halt mid-sentence. Evan would be about eighty, too, so there's a good chance he might not be. Or if he is, that he's in no condition to respond to an email. For a moment, we are silent.

"Was I violent, Mike?" He lifts his face to look at me.

"You don't remember?"

"It was a long time ago," he says. "I remember my father was violent to me."

"But that was even longer ago."

Then my father tells me a couple of stories I've heard before. His father using a belt. His father hitting him backhand on his face. A few times. Once at a ballpark. Once in a department store after pushing him halfway down an escalator. And then, when he was fifteen, breaking his arm. "I didn't do that stuff, did I? Your mother really raised you and your sister. I was at work most of the time."

"Not that stuff, no, but you could be scary."

"I don't remember." His voice is low, heavy. He's shaking his head. Looking at him, listening now, it seems almost impossible that he could be the same person I remember from back then. He seems so much smaller, so much more tentative. Somehow it seems cruel to bring up details, to ask this man to account for the actions of that other one. Though they are the same, must still be the same, at least on some level. I saw that when he snatched the sour cream from Beth.

"Is there anything you'd like to ask your own father," I say. "I mean anything from your childhood that you'd want to know about?"

My father waves a hand in front of his face. "Nah, you couldn't talk to him."

"But if you could. You wouldn't ask him why he broke your arm?"

"He was a miserable sonofabitch, that's why he broke my arm."

"You don't want to know what was going through his head?"

My father shrugs again. "Why should anything have been going through his head?"

"Or if he felt bad afterwards?"

What do I want to ask about my childhood? That's the question, right? Because I can now. I've got as much of an opening as I'm ever going to get. I could ask about any of a hundred incidents where he shouted me and my sister down, where he brought out the belt, where he exploded for no reason I could understand. Did he realize we tiptoed around him, that his thunder came down on us sudden and unpredictable—that everything, everything was harder when he was around? Maybe I should ask something less confrontational, more general. Why were you at work most of the time? Why were you always so angry when you were at home?

But even that seems futile, the answers suddenly half-obvious and half-immaterial. *Because I had to work. No, I didn't realize it was like that. Yes, I did realize, but I couldn't help it. I was worried about money. I was trying. I don't know why I was so angry.*

Are there words that would change anything?

"So," I say, standing, forcing my voice to brighten, "things are all right between you and Beth now?"

"I don't think I'm invited to Tucson anymore." He sets the yearbook aside and begins putting the other items—first the cookbooks—back in the box.

"But you're still friends?"

"She said she accepted my apology."

"Follow up, Dad," I say. "Buy her dinner next week. Apologize some more."

A COUPLE OF days later, my father does follow up. With lunch—not dinner—at the Chinese buffet. He tells me about it that night. He and Beth discussed their childhoods, and she told him more about her father's temper. I want to ask him if men were just mean in the 1940s. Is that possible, that a whole class of people was mean? Violent and aggressive in a way that got passed down through generations. Maybe men are better now. I hear people at school talk about their kids, see them rush home to ferry their kids to one practice or another, or make major purchases based on their kids' hobbies, and it seems pretty indulgent to me: softball, chess tournament, dance, Soap Box Derby. But even if it is indulgent, it's got to be better than outright hostility or gross neglect. It makes me wonder if this is another strike against gay men of my generation: the pitiful role models we had for how men love, for how to love men. Listening to my father, it feels like a chain of damage, with my generation as the final banged-up link.

And what about gay men of my father's generation—what chance did they have? And then, when they were in their forties, AIDS hit.

I'm glad my father has made up with Beth. He says she helped him make heart healthy choices at lunch—nothing fried, not easy on a Chinese buffet—and it seems to please him that she did, that she was willing to help again despite what happened last time. I do wonder what's going on in Beth's head, how her view of my father has changed, has complicated, but I don't say anything.

ON THURSDAY, I'm back at Lowe's. The shift starts out well. I'm in at eight, and Rob doesn't get there until ten. As I'm punching in, I'm able to get in a few words with Kimi, the night manager, about picking up extra hours over the weekend. Kimi is in her mid-fifties, tough, solid, and kind. She slaps me on the shoulder and says, "Sure thing, Mike," when I tell her I have time now that the term is over. Even with double the hours, I'd still need to find additional work for the summer, but I've got a lead on that, too. A guy from out of state is looking to have someone mow his property west of town, a couple of acres. It seems like an easy gig—shed with a lawn tractor, an old farmhouse. He left me a message last night.

So things are humming along. Even Rob seems friendly enough when he comes in. He walks over when he sees me working with a customer and waits until I've finished helping the guy select a trowel. Then he asks if my father is out of the hospital. When I say he is, Rob nods. It's not much, but it's the friendliest interaction he and I have had in months. I thank him for checking in.

But just after I return from lunch, I see Dave.

At least I think it's Dave—at the other end of the store this time, near the back wall where we keep lawn chemicals and shovels. I see a guy in a white windbreaker lingering there, right by the rubber doors that take you out to Lawn & Garden, and in that moment I feel sure it's him. The guy's got his hands in his pockets, looking my way. Big nose, mustache, square jaw.

I raise my hand and call "Dave." Not too loudly. But louder than I should. People turn and look.

As soon as I do that—call out—the guy melts back into the aisle behind him. It's perpendicular to the one I'm in and a good hundred feet off, so I can't see anything down there.

I don't think; I just start running. I knock into the end cap as I take off, and I hear the metal shelving rattle, then something crashes to the floor. It doesn't matter. Customers clear out of my way. I run out of Flooring, past the kitchen displays, past Electrical, until I get to the aisle that this guy disappeared down, and stop. He's not here. The guy's not here. There's just a couple standing in front of the yard implements. The woman has a rake in her hand. She's bent over, pretending to rake the cement floor.

There are three short side aisles coming off the yard-implement aisle, perpendicular to it, so I dash toward those, too, glancing into each. No Dave. No guy in a white windbreaker who looks like Dave. No guy in a white windbreaker who doesn't look like Dave.

I don't understand it. He was here. Someone was. When I get to the end of the pesticides area—almost at the front of the store now—I rush to my right, through Lawn & Garden, and then out in front of the store, scanning the parking lot. From there I run farther and farther, until I am all the way to the parking-lot exit where cars are pulling out. I look into traffic, trying to make out the drivers. One of the cars is a small silver sedan; it could be Dave's old Civic. Who knows. I stand there a minute shaking my head, then finally walk back into the parking lot, slower now, looking around. It's pointless. He's not here. But for a couple of minutes, I can't give it up. I go back inside and walk the whole length of the store—from Lawn & Garden where I exited to the Lumber entrance on the opposite side. No Dave. I tell myself I must be seeing things, but I feel, underneath, certain that it was him.

I debate it in my head—was it or wasn't it?—as I make my way to the back of the store and then down the long aisle toward Flooring. As I approach, I can see a guy from Electrical, Phil, near the end cap where I started, sweeping up. When I get closer, I see shards lying around. The end cap is a mess. There had been a sign advertising brown tiles—Capri, they're called—for $2.19 a square foot. And some half dozen of the tiles propped upright like dinner plates in a China cabinet. Behind the upright tile were boxes of the Capri, the "limited supply" that the sign mentions. Now the sign is down—it's on the ground next to Phil. The upright tile is down, too. Large fragments of it are still on the floor.

I immediately kneel beside Phil and start picking up shards. I notice one has slid under the end cap and reach my fingers toward it. "What got into you, man?" Phil asks. He doesn't stop working.

I don't have a chance to answer. Rob comes over. I hear his heavy steps before I look up to see him. He's got a clipboard in his hand.

"That's enough, Breck," he says, towering over me. "Did you see you almost knocked over a kid by Electrical? Kid started crying. Did you even notice that? At least you made it easy for me to can your ass. That's one thing you did right today. I'm taking you off the schedule right now. That's what I'm doing." He shoves the clipboard forward so I can see that it contains next week's schedule. "I don't know why you're picking up those tiles. You sure as hell don't work here anymore."

I get up slowly, so I am standing face-to-face with Rob. Well, just about face-to-face. I'm guessing Rob has a good three inches and fifty pounds on me, beer gut, thick arms. He's a gross man in just about every sense of the word: big, loud, unappealing. The kind of guy a friend of mine back in school would have called "rapey," as in, "Don't go near that guy, he seems kind of rapey."

It would feel good to tell him to fuck off.

But I don't. I think of my father and his outburst at Beth. I think of my finances. And I take a breath. I try to explain. I say that I saw an old friend—someone I lost touch with a while back—and had to catch the guy. My one chance, a fluke thing.

Rob waits for me to finish talking, and he is silent for an additional moment, long enough to let his silence feel like an affront. "I'm going to see if I can get the cost of that tile deducted from your last check," he says, sneering. Then he walks away.

I exhale. I don't want to tell him to fuck off anymore. I don't want to storm off. I spend another few minutes with Phil, helping him pick up shards and getting the end cap to look the way it did before I knocked it. And then I go. I don't talk to anyone on my way out. What kind of explanation could I give for my behavior? I just walk out. I do stuff my Lowe's vest into the trash can outside the store, though, punching the folded wad to get it in there. I do allow myself that.

18

FOR THE REST of the week, I feel angry at myself and stupid. Matt's right. I am pining. If there's a pathetic hierarchy, I may well be near the top of it. Who hallucinates ex-boyfriends and gets fired from Lowe's? Not even ex-boyfriends, but guys they went on three dates with. Though in my defense, three dates isn't such a bad run for me.

And my life is careening toward a financial train wreck. Some years, I can pick up a summer class. I've already asked about that, but I decide to ask again. At least there's the mowing gig. The landowner and I connect on Saturday, and it looks like a go. Seventy-five dollars a week will help. What I'm trying to avoid is working at the local Kroger. Maybe it's not all that different from being an associate in Flooring, but I can bring some life experience to that job; I know a few things the customers want to know. That's something.

Plus, my neighbors don't come into Lowe's all the damn time. Still, I've bagged groceries before. It won't kill me.

I wait to tell my father about Lowe's. This is strategic. First, I want to let my embarrassment settle. Financial matters bring out the worst in him, and I want this to be a better conversation. If I'm triggered, too, it will be a mess. And second, I wait until I have the mowing job locked down, so I can bring that up if he starts getting anxious.

Sunday afternoon I'm feeling less angry at myself—though no less stupid—so it seems as good a time as any to broach the subject. After I finish mowing my own lawn, I find my father in the kitchen reading a newspaper—a real one, the large, folded sheets spilling across the table.

"You got the *Enquirer*," I say, surprised. "Why'd you bring all that dead tree in here?"

He raises his head, then takes off his glasses. "I wanted to look at the obituaries. A lot of people died this week."

"That's not very cheerful."

He puts down the pages and shrugs. "People die every week. It's not so bad as long as you're not one of them."

"Any of them interesting?"

"No, no. Mostly people in their seventies and eighties. Lost their battle. That phrase came up a few times. They lost their battle. How would you like that? When you die, having people say you lost your battle?"

"At least it makes a guy sound heroic—"

"Did you finish the lawn?" he asks, cutting me off.

"Hey Dad," I say. "I've been meaning to tell you, I'm not working at Lowe's anymore."

My father blinks at me. "Did you get another job?"

"Not yet, no."

"You quit without having another job?"

"Well, I did get a lawn-mowing job for the summer. So I do have another job." I remind myself that this is a casual conversation and step back a few feet. Then I turn to the counter, get a glass, and fill it from the tap.

"A lawn-mowing job?" he says. His voice is thick with skepticism.

A car pulls up the driveway. I glance out the window above the sink.

"Is someone coming?"

My father stands. "Someone is coming! Beth is dropping off a few things. She made me a casserole."

He's clearly pleased. He heads to the foyer and opens the door. Beth is getting out of her car and going around to the passenger's side. She bends into it and lifts out a glass dish covered in foil.

"Why don't you go give her a hand?" My father opens the screen door and calls to Beth. "Wait, wait, Mike is coming to help." Then he walks out himself, in his house slippers, getting to the edge of the patio and stopping there. I jam my feet into my sneakers and walk past him, out to Beth.

"There's a bag in the back seat," she says. "Can you get that and shut the door?"

Casserole held out in front of her, Beth makes her way to my father, who holds the screen door open. I walk up a few seconds later with the grocery sack in my hands, but he lets the door fall closed, following her inside.

My father clears the kitchen table at Beth's suggestion, at first trying to refold the paper carefully, then lifting the bundle half-folded and shoving it on the counter, crumpling the obituaries somewhere in the mix. Beth takes the groceries out one by one, explaining the function of each. There's flax seed to go on top of cereal and almond milk to go in it, replacing the 2% my father usually uses. Then walnuts for snacking. My father nods, taking it in. He almost balks a few times. The lentil pasta is going to be a hard sell, and he looks downright dismayed when Beth presents frozen bags of "riced" cauliflower. But after each explanation, she says "just try it," and eventually it becomes a kind of joke. For the last few items, my father anticipates her: "I'll just try it" he says, and then, "I'll just try that, too."

When Beth finishes, she removes the foil from her baking dish and cuts three slabs off the casserole, which she pops in the microwave one at a time. It's a kind of lasagna made with chickpea-flour noodles and imitation cheese. The three of us sit.

The lasagna isn't great. The flavor is okay, but the cheese doesn't melt right and the pasta is way too soft. My father eats it all, says it's good, and thanks her. I follow suit. Maybe you get used to it?

Then I offer to make Beth tea. There was a box of it in her grocery sack, "Lemon Ginger Detox," and she instructs me to make a cup for each of us. So I get up to do that, grabbing the box off the counter. I see the tea is organic.

"These groceries must have cost a lot of money, Beth," I say.

"Did you talk to Mike?" she says.

I turn. She's looking at my father.

"Beth has got a stopped-up drain in her bathtub. We thought you could help her with it."

I start filling the kettle.

"I already tried Drano and the plastic snake," Beth says. "It might need more extreme measures. There's also a wall switch in the bedroom that doesn't work anymore and an air filter that needs changing. I told Denise about it. Denise is a good woman; the rent is fair. But she's not in much of a hurry to take care of anything." Beth lives in a duplex, upstairs and downstairs apartments. She rents the downstairs.

"You can go over and help her out, can't you, kid?" my father asks. "You have time now since you left Lowe's."

I squelch annoyance. He's right; I do have time. "Okay, sure. I can probably go tomorrow." I start the electric kettle.

"Did you get a new job?" Beth asks.

"He doesn't have a new job. Right now, he doesn't have any job. He quit." My father hits that last word particularly hard. "All he's got is a lawn-mowing job, like a teenager. What were you thinking, quitting there, Mike? It's a lousy time to be out of work."

I turn. My father and Beth are looking up at me. I don't want to lie, but I also don't want to go into this. "I didn't really quit," I say.

"You got fired?" My father stands, picks up his plate, and brings it over to the sink, dropping it in. He turns to face me. "How the hell did you manage that?"

"Let's discuss this later, Dad. Beth doesn't need to hear about me screwing up at work." *And she sure as heck doesn't need to see you lose your temper again.*

"People get fired from jobs all the time, Mike," Beth says. "There's no shame in that. I've been fired from a couple, myself. When you speak your mind, people fire you."

"I knocked into an end cap," I say. "Tile got knocked over. A few cracked. It was a mess. The Flooring manager has had it out for me for a while so—"

Beth is indignant. "The manager fired you for that? For having an accident? What kind of a place is that? You can march back there and talk to the store manager. To the boss! Let the boss know what happened."

"Well, it was a little more than that," I say, shaking my head. "I saw someone, thought I saw someone. A guy named Dave—you met him, Dad, the guy who was here—and I wanted to talk to him. So I ran over, and that's when I knocked into the end cap. It was me being stupid, that's all." I'm trying to tread lightly, to save a little face. And since Beth thinks I'm straight, maybe the mention of Dave's name will scare my father off the topic, at least for now.

The kettle clicks. I start filling mugs.

"Dave, the guy who was here?" my father asks. He sits back down. I set a mug in front of him.

"Yes, the guy who was here." I set a mug in front of Beth, too. She looks over at my father.

Neither of them speaks. I go back to the counter for my own mug.

They are still silent when I sit down, though now it seems like they're having a kind of wordless conversation, studying each other's faces.

After a few moments Beth says, "That guy, right? The one with the mustache?"

My father glances at me. I look from Beth to him.

"Did you tell Beth about Dave?" This strikes me as highly improbable. Would my father have mentioned Dave's facial hair? Would he even have noticed it?

"No," my father says, drawing out the word. He doesn't seem to be answering me, so much as instructing Beth.

"No what?" I'm starting to feel disoriented.

"I promised I wouldn't mention it," my father says—maybe both to me and Beth now.

I glance at Beth. My father promised something?

"Well, I didn't," she says. "I didn't make any promises. The idea of not telling your son!" She turns to me. "I met him in the hospital, Mike. Dave. He came in and sat with us while your father was having dinner. He brought me a cup of coffee."

"Dave visited you in the hospital?" I turn back to my father.

"A couple of visits," my father says.

"Dave visited you twice?"

"Three times, three visits."

For a moment, we're all silent. Then my father continues. "He came in the first night I was there. Then after that, once each day. He stopped by to check on me."

"He sat with us for a while," Beth says. "He told us all about the facility, some of the things they're working on now, like these patches that get sewn right on the heart and actually cause new cells to grow, getting it almost back to normal."

"Why didn't you tell me?" I'm looking at my father.

"He asked how you were," Beth says.

"He did?" I turn to Beth.

"He asked me not to say anything," my father finally says. "He made me promise not to. You seemed so upset when he left that morning, Mike, I didn't want to bring it up."

Dave saw my father three times. I feel myself getting agitated, so I take a moment to breathe. It doesn't mean anything. That's what I tell myself. He was being kind. Anyone would have done that, any decent person.

"I told him you were upset. When he left. I told him that it upset you."

"You told him that?" My forehead sinks into my palm, and I shake my head. Does my father have any common sense?

"He said he was upset, too."

"This is the man you were dating?" asks Beth, picking up her mug. She takes a sip of tea. "He seemed kind."

I blush, keeping my head in my palm. Clearly my father has talked to Beth.

"You should call him," she says. "The heart has its reasons, I know, but even the heart needs a nudge now and then. The heart can find new reasons."

"What else did you talk about?" I say.

"I didn't want to upset you," my father says.

"Did you talk about anything else?"

"I told him about your mother."

"About Mom?" It all flashes through my head: Dave sitting there twiddling his thumbs as my father goes on and on about my mother. "What exactly did you tell him?"

My father looks pained.

"I'm not upset," I say. But my voice comes out higher, louder than I want it to.

I take a sip of tea, feeling the hot liquid in my mouth and throat. It has a bite, lemon ginger, but it calms me as it moves down my body.

My father and Beth begin going back and forth about whether he should have told me. My father says he gave his word to Dave and starts describing how upset I got the morning he left here—which is itself kind of upsetting. Beth insists that the greater loyalty has to be to family, always to family, and she starts telling a story about a girlfriend of hers—someone from way back—who she caught stealing novelty earrings from a drug store. I'm only half listening. Dave visited my father. Three times. He heard stories about my mother. And about how upset I was when he left.

Then my father speaks louder, directly to me. "I told him what it was like to be married. Your mother and I were married fifty-eight years. I told him I knew she would always be there, your mother, about how she was my life. And I told him about when she was in labor with you. You were underweight. Not early, but underweight, so you had to stay in the hospital a while."

My father goes into the details: neonatal care, my mother's heartbreak when she went home without me, the month before I was able to go home. He was working full-time, but he took a few hours off in the afternoons to ferry her and my sister to the hospital so they could sit with me. I've heard this story a million times, but I try hearing it as Dave would, wondering what he'd make of it. I fear it makes me look somehow weak. Sickly. Or—that word again—pathetic.

"What did he say about that?"

"Dave?"

"Yeah, Dave, Dad. Who else?"

Beth speaks up. "He said you were lucky to have such caring parents." Both she and my father are looking at me now.

This all seems unfair. Wrong. That they should have had a conversation with Dave that I wasn't privy to. A conversation about my mother, about me. I don't trust my father's rendition of it, and I certainly don't trust him to have any awareness of how Dave was experiencing it.

Three visits.

"Shit, Dad," I say. Beth jerks her head back. "I'm sorry. But you should've told me. You just should've told me."

I get up and start for the kitchen door.

"Mike," Beth says.

I turn. "It's okay. I'm not mad. I just need to think."

"Does everybody in your family walk off as soon as they start feeling an emotion?" I glance back. Beth is speaking to my father. She turns to me. "Mike. Mike, sit down. What happened with this guy?"

Then my father starts to stand. Beth puts her hand on his arm and says his name. They exchange a meaningful glance, and he settles back into the chair.

"We are old, Mike," Beth says. "What do you think you are going to say that we haven't heard before? Sit down."

Slowly, painfully, I return to the table. I sit. And tell Beth and my father about how Dave and I met, and the possibility I felt with him. That he seemed like me in some essential way—maybe just where he's at in life. That he felt like a last chance at something. It gets easier to talk as I go on. My father doesn't have a lot to say, but he manages to avoid changing the subject or leaving for the living room to flip on the television. And he seems to listen. Beth listens carefully, nodding, offering encouraging words, describing the visit with Dave in more detail. She even tries to gauge his level of interest from what she remembers of his words and gestures. She says that sometimes people need a couple of chances, that Dave may feel just as boxed in by what happened as I do. We spend forty minutes talking before I leave Beth and my father to whatever they have planned for the evening. When it's over, I feel embarrassed, certainly, but also grateful. At least if I consider them together, as a unit, they seem to have understood.

I SPEND THE remainder of the night in my bedroom, almost texting Dave. It turns out "almost texting" is an activity that can consume hours. I think of all the things I might say to him, from the minimalist "hey" to a full-on exegesis, including a thank you for helping my father and an apology for coming on so damn strong. Though I'm not sure that's something I want to, or ought to, apologize for.

Both extremes of response don't seem great, but the problem is that none of the options in the middle seem so great, either. *What did my father tell you? Why did you go back to see him? Do you want to see me again? Don't you want to see me again?* All seem insufficient, unclear, and a little whiny.

What I need is to exchange a few words with him, even just a look, in person, in real time. That would tell me everything I want to know. Maybe it would even help me let him go, if that's what needs to happen.

Finally, around eleven, just before bed, I do send a text. But not to Dave. I text Matt. He's the guy to help me figure this out. I tell him I want to contact Dave. I ask for advice. I almost beg for it.

Matt texts back immediately—the face with rolling-eyes emoji.

A FEW DAYS LATER, I'm at the door of Matt's apartment, toolbox in hand. We've arranged a quid pro quo. Maria has a showerhead for him—a handheld model with settings like "pulse" and "jet massage." I'm to install it in exchange for a session with The Love Doctor, as Matt briefly styles himself, drawing out the word "love." I show up at 7:00 p.m., as directed.

Maria opens the door, a glass of white wine in her hand.

"Maria," I say, stepping back. I'm startled; I didn't know she'd be here.

"It is the ghost," she calls over her shoulder. Then she looks me up and down, making a face. "Hello, ghost. Come in." She moves to the side, letting me enter. "Come on. Matteo is in the bathroom. Maybe wine after. First, you work."

I follow her through the apartment to the bathroom. Matt's in there, sitting on the toilet, seat down, a glass of red wine in one hand. He's holding the showerhead package in the other, reading the back.

"Did you already get started?" I see a few mismatched tools laid out in front of the tub: adjustable pliers, a flathead screwdriver, and one dinky hammer.

Matt hands me the package and explains why my services are required. The old showerhead is stuck. He asks if I've brought a hacksaw. I tell him that I have, but that there's going to be all kinds of trouble if we have to use it.

Then I inspect the showerhead. The problem is lime. Lots of it. I've brought Lime-A-Way, too. And steel wool. The water around here is full of lime; this always comes up when changing out fixtures. I spend the next half hour alternately scrubbing and chipping off mineral, while Matt and Maria discuss gardening. Maria has decided to install raised beds. I casually mention that I could build those at a great price, and she gives me the side-eye. "Maybe," she says. "Maybe. I am not sure it is good karma to hire a ghost."

Eventually the old fixture comes off. I clean the threads and screw on the new one. It's easy, quick, and it works. Matt is jubilant. Maria seems pleased, too. She goes to the kitchen and comes back with a glass of wine that she grudgingly thrusts at me, saying that I earned it.

In a few minutes, we're in the living room. Matt is lying on the couch, and Maria is sitting on the end of it, drinking her wine. Matt stretches his feet onto her lap, but she swats them away, telling him that is disgusting. I sit in the brocade wingback.

"Okay," Maria says, setting her glass on the coffee table I assembled last week. "Tell me about this romantic drama that you threw my brother over for."

I demur—try to—but Maria insists. I don't feel particularly comfortable discussing all of this in front of her, but I'm not sure I have much choice. So I quickly bring her up to speed, avoiding anything that might suggest that I was spending time with Matt while the "romantic drama" was going on. I end by telling them what I learned a few days ago, that Dave visited my father in the hospital, and asking what action is called for. If any.

"I thought about sending a text," I add. "To thank him."

Matt pretends to yawn.

Maria turns to him. "You dodged a bullet with this one," she says, hiking a thumb back toward me.

"A bullet?" I say.

"A bullet of boring," she says, turning back.

I shake my head. "Come on, will you guys give me a break? You said we could talk about this."

Maria sighs. "Okay. Okay, okay."

"It's not just that it's boring," Matt says. "It's that—whatever hesitations he had before—a text isn't going to overcome them."

"But I ought to text to thank him, right? For looking in on my father. To let him know that I know about it, that I appreciate it."

"If that's all you want to do, a text is fine," Matt says. "Should we have cheese? With the wine, I mean. Do you want cheese?" He stretches a foot to nudge Maria with his toe.

"You ought to thank him?" Maria says, mulling the question—at least for the moment putting aside her ire. "So you thank him, but saying thank you is also inquiring if he has any interest in spending time with you again? 'Thank you, I want you'? Yes, I think you can do this."

"I can?"

"No, no, you must. He visits your father, you call or send a card to thank him, and you let him know also that you are thinking of him. He will get the hint."

Matt nudges her again, this time with his whole foot. "No one sends cards. Besides, Mike wants to hook up with this guy. Cards don't suggest passionate love making."

She swats his foot again.

"Fine, fine, no card." Maria leans in, looking me right in the eye. "Bring him flowers," she says, her voice getting low, husky, drawing out the last word. "Men love to get flowers. They will not admit it, but it puts them in the mood."

"No flowers," Matt says. "That's a silly idea."

"I thought you were going to get cheese?" Maria turns sharply back to Matt.

He shrugs then takes a sip of wine.

"What do you think of just texting to thank him and ask if he'd like to get together again?"

"This is safe," Maria says, leaning back against the couch. "Easy to ignore, but safe. But who knows? It might work."

"What's your goal, Mike?" Matt asks. "A text is a good way to remind someone that you exist. It seems like this guy already remembers you exist but isn't motivated to do much about it."

"So what are my options?"

Maria asks where Dave works, and when I tell her, she suggests that I visit him at the hospital. "You walk up to the front desk and say you are having trouble with your heart. It is perfect because it is true."

Using The Center for Cardiovascular Medicine as the backdrop for a romantic interlude doesn't seem like a great idea. I try to explain this to Maria.

"All I'm saying," Matt says, interrupting me, "is that there's not much to lose here. You've heard of a high-risk, high-reward scenario? Well, this isn't one. There's no risk; you have nothing to lose with this guy. He can't be any less yours than he is right now."

Ouch. I exhale.

"So . . . what? . . . I send flowers and candy—that kind of thing? But I don't know where he lives. Would you go to the hospital?"

"No," Matt says. "Don't do that. That's creepy."

We go around half a dozen times imagining scenarios, most a little outlandish. Maria really wants me to fake a heart ailment. Matt eventually concedes that I may have to visit Dave at work, since that's the only place I can be sure of finding him. He suggests leaving something for him, like a dinner invitation, a romantic note, or—his favorite option—a cock ring in a velvet jewelry box. Whatever I think might tug at Dave's heart.

"The point," Matt says, "is not just to get his attention, but to get him to talk. To open up. To find out if he's got any feelings for you, and if so, what's running interference for them. You may have to back him into a corner. It's an interesting technical problem because that kind of conversation isn't exactly your strong suit, either. You're not a great communicator."

Matt's looking right at me. An accusation.

"Anyway, why do you like this guy—this Dave—why this guy and not my brother?" Maria asks. My glass is empty, has been for a while. It seems like a good time to go fill it.

Maria waves me back into my chair as soon as I start to rise. "No wine, no bathroom. No cheese," she says. She turns to glare at Matt. "No cheese! Now answer my question, why not Matteo?"

"Shush, Maria." Matt nudges her again.

"No, I will not 'shush.' This is an honest question. An important question. It has to be asked. Mike does not have to answer if he does not wish to."

Maria looks at me intently. Matt is shaking his head—at her, I think.

Okay.

"I don't know," I say. "Matt is sexy, fun, and smart, and I have a good time with him. I have a good time with you, Matt." I meet his eyes. "It would be easier if it could be you. If it felt like I had a choice, I would choose you." I pause. How could I not have a choice? But it feels true that I don't. "I guess there's a kind of connection I'm looking for that seems possible with this guy, or that I already feel with this guy, the sense that we're fighting the same fight—that we're doing it separately, but that we could be doing it together. That doing it together would be different, that it wouldn't feel like fighting, but instead like being on a team, being part of a team. This guy could be my teammate. I've never been on a team in my whole life, never felt like I was." Matt and Maria are both looking at me now. "I don't know if it's sexual or psychological or spiritual, or some combination. Or just nothing, just a fantasy. But whatever it is, it's there, in my head, in my body; I want this guy. He is what I want."

For the second time in three days, I feel like I've said too much. I look over at Matt, trying to gauge if he's upset. He's sipping his wine, his face calm, maybe more serious than I'm used to. I wonder if he's going to ask me to leave.

It feels like I'm holding my breath.

"Okay," Maria finally says. "Now you can go get more wine. Go, go get some."

I go up to the counter and grab the bottle of red. Before I sit down, I top off Matt's glass, then spill some into my own.

"It's cool, right?" I say. "It was okay to say all that?"

"Yes, it was okay," Maria says, exhaling. "I am not sure it shows you are a person of discernment to like some guy over my brother, but it is okay. I can forgive you for being a ghost."

"It's okay, Matt?"

"You're a bit of an ass, Mike, you know that, right?" He pauses. It's a long pause. "But it's okay."

I wonder if Matt is blushing. He doesn't look upset, but perhaps it's costing him some effort not to look that way. Again, I admire him. Maybe it's maturity or some kind of emotional control, I'm not sure. But Matt does seem capable of things that I am not.

"It really is okay. Now both of you stop looking at me." He raises his glass. "Friendship."

19

MOST OF THE next day, I puzzle over what I could leave at the hospital for Dave. Maybe one of those toasted-coconut starfish from the candy shop in the Oregon District. Even if he didn't recognize it—what it calls back to—it would still be better than sending a text. Sweeter, more substantial. And I bet Dave would really enjoy that kind of gesture. I doubt he's been on the receiving end of many of them in his life. I also think about leaving a note with a dinner-reservation time. I could say that I'm going to take him out to thank him for checking in on my father. Not ask him to come, but tell him that we're going. Would he show?

I picture us talking over dessert, really getting into it. My impulse is to prove to him that he feels a connection to me by bringing up examples from our dates—counting them out on my fingers. But that's not the point, I know. I need to see him, to hear him speak.

To learn if he doesn't want to spend time with me, if there was no real spark there, or if he just feels like he can't. I might be able to talk him through the latter. Or at least give him space to take a step forward. Even half a step.

The more I think about it, the more I think Matt's right. It's too easy to shrug off a note, even one containing a dinner invite. Why not try something he can't shrug off so easily? Like Matt said, this isn't a high-risk scenario. Or not exactly one. There is a risk related to opportunity. I probably can't try twice.

So I think bigger. Face-to-face. No way in hell I'm going to fake a heart ailment, but I could visit Dave at the hospital, wait around until he has a few minutes to talk. My father said Dave first visited him there on a Wednesday night, after his dinner. I could show up this Wednesday at 7:30.

But it's not a great idea to tax people at work. They've got co-workers around. Supervisors. They feel inhibited. So I think of other places I could find Dave. I consider intentionally damaging my car and bringing it back to MacAllister. A good scrape along the front passenger side would do the trick. I could measure distances to make sure only a single panel is involved and try to keep the damage light—something that could be buffed out. I'd have to shell out a couple of hundred bucks, but I could spend the whole day in Hansen's waiting area. No ride back. Hansen would tell Dave I was there. Wouldn't he? But he never did forward my email. . . . Anyway, the more I think about it, the bigger a lift it seems, intentionally scraping the Celica. I recall a news item about a climber out in Utah who got stuck in a crevice, and after a few days trapped, made a tourniquet and freed himself by sawing off his own hand at the wrist. Clearly I'm a lightweight.

As I pull into my driveway, another idea occurs to me. Also a little expensive—but I have credit cards. And it's significantly less painful than scraping my car.

Hansen's deck.

I said I'd fix it, didn't I? Or that I'd make sure it got fixed. Hansen didn't make a big deal out of it, but I lost a bet. I like to think I'm good for my debts.

I begin to game it out, how I'd do it. Reconnaissance: make sure it's possible. A trip to Lowe's. Then come back when Hansen is likely to be around. The project might take a couple of days, which is a feature. Time for Dave to get wind of it. The more I think about the idea, the more I like it. Fixing a deck is work I know how to do.

I KICK AROUND the idea for a week. As I drive to local retail stores, dropping off job applications, I picture unloading my tools out there. When I'm on the rider, mowing that guy's property, I imagine Dave watching through Hansen's kitchen window as I measure out boards. Just my presence—maybe the absurdity of it, maybe the dedication—winning him over. I know there are holes in the idea; I haven't lost touch with reality. Hansen not remembering who I am is one of them. But maybe he does remember and calls Dave to come help. Maybe Dave shows up and kneels down beside me where I'm working.

One afternoon, I even drive out to Hansen's place. It's not like I have anywhere else to be. I'm sitting at the kitchen table, eating cereal, and it occurs to me that Hansen is almost certainly at his shop at that hour. That I could do a feasibility study. So I bolt up, leaving the half-finished bowl. I dig out a clipboard and baseball cap, throw on slacks and a tan polo, and head out. I'm a guy from the electric company checking the meter. Or from All Gas inspecting the tank. Official business. That's what I'll say if anyone calls me out. My credentials are in the car. Wait here a minute, I'll go get them.

I park a good half-mile away, just on the edge of Laura, and walk along the road—no sidewalks out here—carrying my clipboard, trying to look official. There's almost no traffic on these rural roads, especially at midday. But when I get to Hansen's place, I continue past it a couple of hundred yards anyway, then circle around to the back, keeping a good distance. It feels safer, this oblique approach. I get deep into the cornfield where Dave and I rode the ATV, out of view of the street, before heading for the deck.

It rests against the house on two sides, along the main length and abutting the addition. I almost bail before stepping onto it. Maybe if Hansen does come out, I can say Dave agreed to meet me here. I glance around, take a few steps toward the slider doors, and look in. Kitchen table covered with bills, dishes mounding in the sink. A dark, empty house.

All right.

I exhale and get down on all fours to inspect the boards, jabbing a screwdriver into the wood here and there, testing for rot. I walk along the length to take rough measurements and make notes on my clipboard. Then I slide myself underneath with a flashlight, to check the supports. As I poke around, I imagine heavy footsteps coming out of the house onto the boards above me. Or Hansen yanking me out by my ankles. Or a neighbor running up, barking questions. Finally I decide I've seen enough and scramble out.

The deck's not in bad shape, not really, though there's a lot of rot under the section against the corner made by that addition. My guess: the problem is the gutters and downspout, pooling rainwater. It seems doable.

It would take a day and a half, tops. When Hansen comes out to find me working, I can tell him to call his brother, that his brother should be out here helping with this. Or maybe just ask him to let his brother know that I finally started the job. And Dave would come by. I know he would. He's the guy who waited around after he dinged a stranger's car. The guy who saw that I wanted to try out an ATV and hopped up to claim one for us. The guy who kept checking in when we were in bed together. He'd come talk face-to-face.

But would I have the guts to do it?

I hustle out to the cornfield to put some distance between me and the house before crossing over to the street. Soon, I'm back at the Celica.

THURSDAY NIGHT, I'm lying on my couch, television on, fretting about my life. Every time I've seen my father for the last week, he's told me what I need to do to find a job. His instructions range from the embarrassing ("Go back to Lowe's, your manager has had time to cool down!") to pure fantasy ("Go back for your PhD and become a professor!"). Maybe I do need to do something radically different like returning to school. But I can't seem to focus on that. My thoughts keep coming back to Dave, to how passing days are pulling him further away from me.

It all starts to seem pretty hopeless, so I pick up my phone to open Scruff, but as the grid is loading, it occurs to me that Matt might be lying on his couch, too—wine in hand, reading a novel in Italian or watching a miniseries. Whatever it is he does on his couch. Shopping for IKEA housewares on his phone, maybe. So I call him instead. It turns out that Matt's at the print shop, grading paper by color and weight, from newsprint to cardstock. Right: he's got a job. I listen as he rattles off ways that he's reorganized the copy center. Functional and elegant, he says, his goal in all things. He insists he'll be "commanding this ship soon enough." When I ask if that's a reward or punishment, he says that it's better to reign in hell. I imagine his face as he says it—that grin, like one of those purple devil emojis guys on the apps use to indicate a sexual subtext, as if one can't always be assumed there.

Then Matt says "customer" and disappears. As soon as he gets back on—I can't help myself—I start lamenting that I haven't tried to contact Dave yet.

"Are we going to talk about that again?" he says.

"Apparently."

I tell him about my plan, my reconnaissance trip to Hansen's place. I even describe how it could all play out: me working through sunset, Dave coming out with a couple of beers. Then he sits down on the edge beside me and slides one over.

"And then you start giving each other back rubs, right? I've had fantasies like that, too."

"No, Matt," I say. "Then we talk."

"How about the part where you get arrested—does that include back rubs?"

"Fixing a deck is not a crime."

"And getting thrown in jail will demonstrate your undying devotion?"

"Look," I say, "I lost a bet, right? I'm obligated to do this. And anyway, guys like Hansen have their own guns. They don't call the police. Especially not when someone's repairing their stuff. And we know he wants it fixed. He was trying to get his brother to do it."

I press Matt to tell me what he thinks of my idea, and I can almost hear him shrugging through the phone. "It's what comes of being a repressed romantic," he says. "A little opening, and it bursts out in ridiculous ways."

"Should I do it?"

"So we really are talking about this again."

This is hard enough for me as it is. "Hey, didn't you tell me I need to do something? And wasn't there a toast to friendship in there? I distinctly remember a toast. And I'm pretty sure you're the guy who made it. You know, there's no one else I can talk to about this. Please, Matt. I need a friend, okay?"

Matt begins talking, too, while I'm saying all that, so for a few moments we're talking over each other. He says, "Weren't you slouched in my armchair going on about losing the love of your life?" and I start to explain that that's not what I said. In the meantime, he says a few things I don't catch.

"Anyway, anyway," he continues, silencing me. "Yes, I made a toast, and I did say you can't just wait around for your life to happen to you. So go ahead, do it. Maybe if you release some of this pent-up energy, your romantic flights can express themselves with more sanity."

I pause. "I'm afraid. I don't even know of what."

Matt says, "Getting arrested," and then he's gone again. I hear him explaining where bubble mailers are located.

When he comes back on, he lets out a long sigh. "Okay, okay, it's a truly ridiculous plan, Mike. But we can talk about it; let's talk about it. First, tell me why you don't just call the brother to set it up."

"He might tell me not to come. Or worse, he'd talk to Dave, and they'd both tell me not to come. And I couldn't really do anything after that—not even leave something at his work or send an email. Whatever window I've got would be shut."

Then I tell Matt that I know it's risky. In fact, I describe, probably in too much detail, things that could go wrong. Maybe Hansen's out of town. Or just got a pair of Dobermans. Or someone does call the cops. And then there's Dave. Maybe I try to talk to him and get the same shut-down look in his eyes that he had the morning he left my house. I talk and talk and talk, and I can see that he's just waiting for me to finish up and go.

Matt says I should bring steaks for the dogs, that it always works in cartoons. But on the other score—Dave—that there's no easy way out. "If you're really going to try this, you have to be fearless, Mike. Or pretend to be. It amounts to the same thing. Do you remember our hike—I did a remarkably life-like Dolly, and you did a few bars by Otto Something-or-other?"

I tell him I do.

"It will be like that. Except your eyes will be open."

The thought floods me with a burst of panic and then despair. "How can I do it, Matt? I'm not that guy—"

I hear a sharp voice in the background, and then Matt telling a customer he'll be with her in a moment. "You can do it," he says.

"Listen to yourself, Mike. You have to do it. And once you accept that, and accept that you can't control the outcome, it might even become fun."

Matt puts down the phone to help the customer, but afterward, he stays on with me for another twenty minutes. We talk about fear. When I say he doesn't seem to be afraid of anything, he asks if I'm joking. Then he tells me about leaving Italy alone, about leaving Houston, and even about moving up here where the gay community seems—his words—"dishrag thin." But he says fear doesn't have to get you stuck. You can feel it and do what you need to do anyway. The way out is to try, he says, and to continue to try, and when in doubt, to try something different. Before we hang up, I let him know that he's got this friendship thing down.

THE NEXT MORNING, I make sketches. Lists, too—of what lumber I'll need, what fasteners. At least to get started. My father comes into the kitchen and looks over my shoulder. Soon he starts telling me about how posts should be anchored and what pitfalls to avoid. I let him talk. I listen, even as he leans over me and runs his forefinger across the sketch I'm doing, criticizing it.

And that afternoon, I go to Lowe's. I can at least buy supplies. Maybe I'll return them. Or use them on another job. But I will buy them.

I feel sheepish walking in there. Judy at the customer service counter asks if I'm on tonight. I smile and tell her that I've been permanently turned off, and then explain when she asks what the heck that means. I also run into one of the other guys from Flooring, an older guy named Jimmy. He heard I was fired, but not the circumstances. I give him a few details. "Shit happens," he says, shrugging. I clap him on the back. I'm relieved to see a couple of guys I know in the lumber department, too. When I tell them I was fired a few weeks back, they congratulate me. One of them, Martín, asks how I managed that, saying he'd like to get fired, too. I like these guys and want to tell them the story, the whole story, because I think they'd find it funny—so I do, glossing over Dave's gender. The guys either don't notice or don't much care. They laugh at the story, and it's a good lead in for the favor I'm about to ask of them.

I tell them I'm fixing a deck for that person, "my ex." To win them back. But money is an issue. First, can I root through the cull bin? That's where we store warped or damaged wood.

The guys are great. I show them the clipboard page on which I've written out what I need, and they take me in back. I find a few useful pieces in the bin, and Martín brings back four 12-foot two-by-sixes and slashes his orange marker over the UPC code. "These are culled, too. They're warped. Check out with Ditsy Linda. She doesn't look too close."

My second favor is to ask if one of those guys can make the purchase for me, so I can get the employee discount. I've got cash; I just need one of them to come up front and do the transaction. Another guy, Sam, agrees to help out on his break at 4:00, which is only about fifteen minutes away. So I go gather up the last few things I'll need. Additional boards—I'll pay full price for those—decking screws, post brackets, gutter hangers, nails. It all costs more than $150. I wince as I count out the bills to Sam. But I *am* going to do this. Maybe it's right there I actually decide.

As I drive away, I realize I'll need stain, too, but figure that can wait. The project might not get that far.

By the time I'm nearing home, I start to feel jazzed, even a little confident—or maybe reckless. I roll down the windows, turn up the radio, and look around. It's a beautiful late-spring day, low seventies, sunny, everything vibrant. The Stones' "Honky Tonk Women" comes on, and I turn it up and sing along—the chorus and the scattered words I know: "She blew my nose . . . then she blew my mind." I can't say what it is, exactly—spending money I don't have, the risk of working on Hansen's property without checking in first, or maybe the possibility of seeing Dave again, finally seeing him—but I feel alive, really alive.

LATER THAT NIGHT, just before heading to bed, I get a text—a few texts—from Josh. Josh as in Josh-and-Gary, who I haven't heard from in months. That in itself isn't unusual; months do sometimes go by between contacts. But after our conversation at Starbucks, I wasn't sure I'd hear from him again.

The first text reads, *For u.*

The second is a video less than a minute long. It's Josh in what must be his garage. He's naked, his back and backside to the camera and his palms on the hood of a black car which is, I'm assuming, his TLX. You can't make out his face, but he's rocking his pelvis forward and backward, so you can see his glutes and the muscles on the back of his legs tense and relax. It's sexy. Also corny and pretty vulgar. I watch it a few times.

And the last text: *Gary said I can do anything I want now.*

I lay the phone face down beside me on the couch.

I remember Gary's face at Starbucks, how wounded he seemed, a lanky guy hunched over his latte. Maybe Gary did say Josh can do anything he wants. Maybe he said it in a fit of anger. Maybe it was said in sarcasm or bitterness. Maybe he didn't say it at all.

What are the options? To be single, sure. Or to be Gary, trying to hold tight to a guy who has one foot out the door. Or to be Josh, constantly pushing against constraint. I remember a Looney Toons cartoon from the '70s. An abominable snowman character who chases Bugs and Daffy, eventually gathering each of them into a smothering embrace, saying, "I will love him and hug him and kiss him and call him George." Bugs and Daffy try desperately to wriggle free.

I guess I could be both. I could chase after Dave like the abominable snowman. Clutch him, call him George. Is that what I already did? But there's got to be a way to talk honestly to a guy without it being read as smothering. That said, if a man had grabbed onto me, told me what possibility he saw for us, wouldn't I have reacted the same way Dave did, wriggling out, Bugs-and-Daffy style? I definitely would've felt the impulse.

Maybe a better approach is to be like Matt and Javier. To hold loosely. Whether that's trust or lowered expectations, I'm not sure. In my heart, I believe—even fear—that model may be the best. The best, but not something I can do. Love without the security, the safety, of a tighter fit.

I pick up the phone and reread Josh's text. What he says about himself really is true for me. I can do anything I want. No commitment, no connection constrains my behavior. But in another way, it's not true at all. It's like I've been locked in a groove for years, unable to do anything but continue along the path I've been on.

I text Josh back. I say I'm not up for it. That I liked Gary—that Gary seems like a good guy, and that I don't want to be part of anything that might hurt him. Then I go further. I say he's lucky to have Gary, that Gary seems to love him, and that he should be grateful. That if I had someone like that, I hope I'd be kind to him. And that he shouldn't contact me again.

I can at least try to do something different.

20

THINGS DON'T GO wrong immediately.

In fact, they start off well. Around noon the next day, I start loading the truck. Lumber, sawhorses, a few power tools, along with the toolbox that contains my hammers and the like. My father comes out, asking if I'm off to do that deck job and what I'm getting paid for it. I tell him that it's just helping out a friend, and he looks dismayed. He says I need to help out myself, too.

I decide I'm not going to lie to him.

"It's Dave, Dad," I say. "I'm heading over to fix the deck at his brother's place. I'm going to make him talk to me."

My father asks what that has to do with fixing a deck. I sputter, eventually saying something that borders on incoherent, but he doesn't seem too concerned about it. He falls in beside me, helping load the last few tools.

"Good, kid," he says, bending into the truck bed. "Good luck. I'm glad you're going. I want this for you. Your mother was there for me my whole life. I want you to have that, too." I look over. He's affixing a bungee cord.

If my father and I were different people, we might hug. As it is, we don't even make eye contact. But it feels good, hearing him say that. I want to hug him.

NERVES HIT ONCE I get in the truck. Next to me, I've got my clipboard with the list of supplies and tools. The last page has notes on it, sketches of the deck and a few cues for myself, including reminders for my conversation with Hansen. Keep things light, talk about the bet, make him get Dave out there—that's the biggest thing. One item I haven't planned out: what I'll say to Dave if—when—he shows up. Be fearless. Sing with eyes open. Make him talk. All of that. I'll start with "Hello."

I go back in to use the bathroom. I check over my notes three or four more times. Then I hit the bathroom again. It's nearly two by the time I pull out of the driveway.

I almost turn back once I get off the interstate near Laura.

But I decide I can still back out—can delay the final decision—until I turn onto Hansen's street. So I push myself a few more miles.

The street arrives quicker than it did the last few times I drove here.

Finally, I sit parked in Hansen's driveway, telling myself that I can just unpack my tools and see what happens. Hansen shouldn't be home. Not yet. No harm in getting things set up.

Then I close my eyes and say aloud, "Fuck it, I'm fearless," and get out.

I SPEND A good two hours working. Setting up my tools and then carefully taking things apart. I'm nervous at first, but it's quiet, and I just concentrate on what I'm doing. I remove half the boards from the top of the deck. A couple of the rotten ones splinter apart in my hands, the ends cracking off. But mostly it goes okay. I keep things organized. Less shock for Hansen.

I'm actually in there, inside the framing at the corner against the house, when he shows up. That part of the ledger—the support beam bolted onto the house foundation—is also rotten. It's coming apart as I'm unscrewing it. I've decided it's the first thing to replace.

I hear Hansen before I see him. He comes around from the side of the house shouting. "What's going on here?" or "Who are you?" Something like that. It's hard to tell because the words come fast. More than a few expletives mixed in there, too. He stops when he gets to the edge of the deck. Maybe he recognizes me. I hope he does. I've got my speech all planned out.

Fearless, right?

I don't feel fearless.

I inhale deeply. I've actually written on my clipboard to do this: "Before speaking to Hansen, take full breath." Then I step up out of the framing, onto the extant boards, and approach, extending my hand.

"Hey Hansen, Mike." I point at myself. "I was at your bonfire a few months back."

His face is red. "Mike. Right. We did your car. What the fuck are you doing here, Mike? What are you doing to my deck?"

I shrug as if it's obvious. "I told you I'd come by and fix it, remember? We were playing cards. I lost the bet. I've been planning on taking care of this for a while. Finally ended up having time this week, so I thought I'd swing by. It shouldn't take me more than a day or two." I smile broadly. "I'm good for my debts."

Hansen doesn't respond. It takes everything I have to continue smiling. I must sound like a lunatic.

"You probably thought I was going to stiff you. No. Just took a little longer than I planned. Hey, you want to give Dave a call, see if you can get him to come out here and help? The two of us could knock this out tonight. . . ."

Hansen's glaring, his face hard. After a moment, he says, "You talk to Dave about this?"

I pause. I have no idea how to respond. There's real anger just beneath the surface of Hansen's voice. If I say no, he might explode. And yes seems like a lie that's too easy to catch. After a few seconds of silence, I half-smile and shrug.

"Shit," Hansen says, shaking his head. "Dave didn't say a goddamn thing about this." He narrows his eyes. "I have people coming in an hour. I can't believe Dave would be stupid enough to schedule this for today. I got people coming. Forget about the debt. Just get all this shit back together."

I let out a nervous chuckle. "Okay. Okay I can do that." Then I look around, trying to calculate if that's possible. The corner of the deck wasn't usable before, so Hansen can't expect it to be usable now. At least a few of those boards are never going back up.

"I mean right now," he says.

"Okay." I force a smile.

"The tools, too. I want everything back in your truck. It better look like you've never been here." He takes out his phone and starts poking at the screen. The next thing I hear him say is, "Dave?" It's more an accusation than a greeting. "Dave, what the fuck—" He starts walking away, back around the house, but he turns to call out, "You better get started" before disappearing from sight.

TWENTY MINUTES LATER, Hansen is back.

I've got the ledger jerry-rigged. I put the bolts back in, and I'm sistering a new board onto it. That's as far as I've gotten.

Hansen has showered, put on fresh clothes. Slacks, a button-down. His shaggy hair is neatly parted in the middle and combed behind his ears. He opens the slider doors and peers out. Earlier I removed a few boards that ended in front of the sliders, leaving a gap there. He doesn't try to jump it.

"Shit," he says, shaking his head. Then he says it again. "Dave doesn't know what the fuck you're doing here. That dumbass. He's going to be here in a few. You can work this out with him." He exhales. "Get up here."

I hesitate.

"I'm going to hand things out to you. Put that down and get up here." He's got a cooler in his hands, and he gestures with his head to the far side of the deck, away from where I'm working. "By the grill."

A WOMAN IN her late thirties and a teenage girl show up first. Hansen doesn't introduce me, but by the way he greets the woman—a kiss on the mouth and a palm run around her lower back—I gather this is Eileen. She puts on music—some station playing Kenny G—and helps Hansen set the picnic table. Soon more than half a dozen other people arrive including an older couple and a middle-aged couple with kids. All related, I think: brown hair, olive skin. All dressed a little formally, too, in slacks and polos. Hansen passes out drinks—nothing alcoholic—and he and Eileen step around me as they bring things over from the grill. No one speaks to me. I do hear Hansen explain that there was a scheduling mix up. I'm a contractor who got the date wrong. They have a laugh about me. I avoid making eye contact with any of them, keeping my face down toward the deck.

I will myself to be invisible.

I'm not sure how long this goes on. It feels like hours.

Then Dave shows up. I hear his voice from across the yard. The older woman sitting at the picnic table—no bonfire today—calls out, "Hello, David!" and I hear his gruff, cheerful greeting. It's all I can do not to turn around. I'm inside the framing, on my knees, trying to bolt a screw lower down on one of the decking boards where the wood is still good, without using the drill. The thought of power tools drowning out the conversation makes me wince. I don't turn around—not even once—but I pick up every word Dave says as he approaches the picnic table. He's been busy at the hospital; he's working hard; no, no, he hasn't lost weight, maybe even put on a few pounds, ha ha ha; then he asks how her flowers are doing.

A moment later, I feel his eyes on my back.

I put more pressure on the screwdriver, trying to force a screw to bite into the wood. This isn't going to happen without pilot holes. The damn screwdriver keeps slipping.

The old woman goes on about her daylilies. Apparently they're orange doubles. But they won't bloom for a couple of months yet. She's sure they're going to be glorious.

I grind my teeth. The screwdriver slips.

As I'm listening for Dave's response, it slips again, this time scraping down over the knuckles of my left hand. I mutter "shit" and bring my knuckles up to my mouth. Then I hear footsteps coming up behind me.

They stop.

"Mike."

I don't look up. I'm too embarrassed. Embarrassed to be here, to be exposed like this.

"Hey, Mike."

He can't be more than a couple of feet from me.

A moment passes. I'm literally trapped in the framing. Another moment passes. And another.

"Come on, Mike."

There's no avoiding it. I slowly turn to face him. Dave is standing above me on the deck, looking down. Slacks, a white polo shirt. Head freshly buzzed, bright blue eyes. I feel the pull of him. Every bit as desirable as I remember.

"What are you doing here, man?" His voice is low. He's clearly not angry. It's worse than that; there's compassion, maybe pity there.

I set my jaw, meet his eyes. "I don't know," I say. Or mumble. I'm not sure he hears me. Even with his buzzed head and big nose, Dave can look gentle, like the kind of guy who would cup a wounded bird. That's how he looks now. It feels like a worst-case scenario.

For a moment, I just look at his face.

I am not a wounded animal. I repeat that to myself. Not wounded. If anything, he's the wounded one. He ran away; that's something a wounded animal would do. I remind myself that I'm here for a reason. And that this is my one shot to be here.

"Look," I say, gathering myself, "I can't get this back together without making a few cuts. Can you give me a hand? Just bringing stuff around front. I don't want to disturb things any more than I already have." I glance behind me.

Eileen—she must be Eileen—is over at the grill. She's got a Diet Coke in hand, facing the yard. A little boy is trying to do a handstand. The people at the table are watching, too. He does half a handstand—sort of—and tumbles over. The older woman starts clapping and saying "Bravo." Dave watches for a moment, too.

"Give me a second. Let me sort out a few of these boards. We'll do everything at once."

Dave nods. I take a few moments to decide what needs to be cut and drilled—and to think. We'll do it up front, while I'm cutting wood. We'll talk. About why he visited my father. About what's in his heart. We'll cut wood and figure out what's going on here.

Dave doesn't hesitate to pick up a couple of fresh boards and the sawhorses, bundling them against his white polo. I quickly grab a few of the old boards and the two power tools closest to me: the drill, still in its storage bag, and the Sawzall I was using to cut out rot.

"Family barbecue?" I say as we're walking around front.

"On its way there. Hansen and Eileen are announcing their engagement over dessert. There's a hell of a strawberry shortcake in the fridge."

Great day to spring my plan. But I'm here now. There's no going back.

Dave points out an outlet behind a scraggly boxwood near the front door. Then he starts in again. "What's going on, Mike? What are you doing here? Hansen's going to have a fit once the Bible thumpers go home."

"You know why I'm here, Dave," I say. It comes out more aggressive than I mean it to, so I take a minute. I set up the saw horses and lay a board across them, the one I've been trying to get screws into, and then begin again more slowly.

"I'm here because I want you to talk to me. You just left. You said nothing. I get it. I've been hanging out with guys for decades. I know the rules. But I'm fifty now, and the rules haven't gotten me much other than laid."

Dave looks at me, his face pained. "Now's just not a great time to do this," he says.

Again, I take a moment to breathe. I kneel by the DeWalt bag and fumble through it for my safety glasses and a drill bit. I didn't bring over the decking screws, so I err on the side of something too small.

I don't glance up at Dave. Just start tightening the bit. "Ten minutes," I say calmly. "Give me ten minutes. You can't spare ten minutes from talking about daylilies? I'm not a stalker. It took everything I had to come out here and talk to you today. Common decency, you've got to give me ten minutes. . . . Shit, Dave, just own it. Whatever it is you were feeling, tell me." I stand now, drill in hand. It feels like I'm holding something powerful, a kind of gun, and it stiffens my spine. "Just tell me, all right? I think you liked it. Liked me. Liked hanging out. Liked the sex. Maybe even liked the possibility of being with me. I think you thought about it . . . tried to imagine what it would be like. I saw it on your face. I felt it from you."

Dave glances behind him then around the yard. There's nobody in the front but us. Not even passing cars. He exhales.

"Yeah," he says slowly. "Maybe I liked it. I thought about it, Mike. I thought about trying to do it with you. Trying to—"

He goes silent.

"Is it so hard even to say it?"

"Trying to get to know you, okay? Hanging out, whatever. Feeling myself get attached. But it's just not the life I've got. I work, hit the gym. Get laid. It's what I know how to do. I don't have other kinds of connections. It was so good being out here with you the night of that bonfire. Being with you and my brother and his friends. I was feeling proud, so much more . . . real . . . or alive to them. Something like that. It was a whole different experience, doing it with you. But you want to know what I did after that night? I worried, Mike. About texting you. About what you expected, what you thought it meant. When I should've been sleeping, I was going over it again and again in my head. I even tried talking to Hansen about what it was like dating someone, if he felt nervous all the time. Or tied down. Or scared. I like the idea of it. Of being with someone. Of being with you. I like you a lot. But maybe it's just not something I can do."

I start drilling. It feels satisfying, the drill whirring in my hand. I bore a hole into the board.

"But you went to visit my father," I say.

I line up the drill, press down. The bottom hole now, the motor screaming again.

"You went to visit my father because maybe it is something you can do. Or maybe because you *are* still considering whether or not you want to try it." I'm drilling as I say this, so my voice gets louder. But the work is helping. I feel vehement, increasingly sure of what I'm saying.

"I sat with your father because I remembered him, and because he was a sad sack, like any guy after a heart attack."

"That's why you went to see him three times?" I turn to Dave, raising the drill. "Spent an hour or two with him. Talked about me?"

"I wanted to see how you were doing, yeah, that was part of it, too." Dave starts to come closer, toward the sawhorses, but when I take the board off and swing it around, he backs off.

"How about this, Dave," I say, placing a new board, one of the fresh ones. I lay a rotten one alongside it to measure out the length. "How about you went to see my father because you can't let this go, either. Because part of you wants to try, and you're scared of that. Balancing your fear of doing it, is your fear of *not* doing it. How about if after the years of not being with anybody, you want to try with me. Or are just wondering if you could. If it's a question that keeps coming back to you."

I pause to line up the boards. Then I glance over. Dave is staring at me, his lips tight, brow wrinkled. He doesn't look so sure.

"It's been twelve years for me," I say, steadying my voice. "Twelve years since I even seemed to be starting something that could be called a relationship. Something that wasn't just fucking. Since before I was forty. I think about that, a decade, and it makes me nauseous. Was the window of opportunity so damn brief? How come no one told me it would be? Am I so different than other people who do manage to do this, who manage not to spend their lives alone? Don't you ever ask yourself questions like that?"

Now he looks stricken.

We lock eyes for a moment, then I turn away, kneeling to poke around behind the boxwood so I can plug in the Sawzall.

"Come on," I say, standing again. "Be honest with me. That's all I'm asking. Just take a minute, put the fear and anxiety, all the bullshit, aside, and experience what you're feeling. I think you've got some emotions for me." Do I really think that? I recall him lying in bed with me, our breaths mingling in the dark, and decide that I do.

"I don't know," he says. "I don't know." For a minute, he looks like he might cry.

I raise the Sawzall and press the trigger, to make sure it's powered. The blade grinds into the air.

"Just be honest with me—and with yourself. Why were you there with my dad? Why are you still out here with me now? What do you feel when you see me? Look at me, Dave. Does any part of you want to try this with me—is there anything here? What do you think would happen if you did try? What's the worst that could happen?" I pause, looking at him. "We can deal with the nervousness and anxiety together, day by day."

When I see Hansen coming around the side of the house, I realize we are being loud. Or I am. Between the drill and the Sawzall and my voice carrying, maybe very loud. Hansen marches toward us, his finger poking forward.

"Dave, what the hell are you doing out here? We're looking for you. I'm saying I'm going to introduce you to Eileen's brother, and you're nowhere to be found. Get your ass back to the barbecue. And you," he says, turning to me, "got five minutes to finish, get this shit cleaned up, and get out of here. You know we can hear this, all this."

Dave doesn't say anything. Hansen looks from me back to Dave again, then says "asshats" under his breath and storms off. Dave looks down at his feet. Once Hansen is gone, I turn back to the sawhorses and start making the cut.

Dave begins to speak as I'm cutting. Quietly at first. I can barely hear him over the Sawzall, but I don't want to stop, don't want to do anything that might keep him from going on. I listen close.

"Maybe. Things seem so complicated when I try to reason it out, Mike. When I pull back a little bit, it's like a fantasy. Checking in with you during the day, watching a show together after work, getting breakfast on a Sunday. But when I really try to put myself there, all these fears come. . . . You know, I tried to get in touch with you a couple of times. But I chickened out, I just couldn't. I came to talk to you at Lowe's. I asked one of checkers when you worked and—"

When Dave says that, I glance up. It was him. I *knew* it was.

He's looking at me now, arms hanging loose at his sides. Almost defeated. In that moment, all I want to do is touch him, and maybe that would be the right thing—maybe that's what he needs. Not words, but a hand on his arm or his cheek, or even a kiss. Something to break up the jam inside him. But then my balance seems to falter, and I feel the support under the Sawzall give way, the board just melting apart at the cut. The momentum of the tool swings my hand down with it, and the next thing I feel is a sharp gash into my leg, even as my grip loosens and the motor cuts out.

For a moment, I don't understand what's happened.

Then I look down and see the blade partially embedded in my thigh. The top of my right quad. A good chunk of muscle lifted. It looks like a turkey breast half-sliced with an electric carving knife. My hand opens and the Sawzall falls. My stomach flips, and pain floods me. I fall onto my left knee, and maybe I scream because very quickly Dave is on me. Maybe he's screaming, too. He lays me down on my back and takes off his shirt to bind my leg, pressing the loose chunk of skin down onto the wound. His polo instantly colors.

"Can you keep pressure on that?" He puts my right hand on the wadded shirt and presses down, his hand atop mine. "Mike. Mike, put some pressure, Mike."

I do.

"Good." He lifts his hand away. "I'm gonna get you to the hospital." For a minute as he hovers over me, it's like he's holding me in his arms, his face right over mine as if he's about to kiss me. "Hold on, buddy, I'm going to get you to the hospital right now."

Then I hear other voices and see Hansen running into the front yard, followed by the other middle-aged guy and one of the kids.

"We got this," Dave says. Maybe not to me. Soon Hansen is there with us, and Dave is directing him to help carry me over and lift me into his car.

"Call Miami Valley and tell them we're coming in with a deep wound to the anterior thigh. About four inches long. Power tool, serrated blade. Losing a lot of blood. We're twenty minutes out."

Hansen says "What?" and Dave barks, "Call Miami Valley. Thigh. Serrated blade. Four inches long and deep."

I feel lightheaded. I'm in the passenger seat of Dave's Civic, and there's a commotion around the vehicle. I hear a lot of voices now, including the old woman with the daylilies. "My God." She says that over and over. "My God, my God. Will he be all right?"

I also hear Hansen thanking Dave, his voice dripping with sarcasm. That sticks out. And Dave's response: "Save a piece of that strawberry shortcake for us, bro."

I glance over and see Hansen shaking his head like this is the sorriest shit he's ever seen. Dave gently presses the passenger door closed. "Keep applying pressure," he says. Then he gets in on the driver's side, shifts the Civic into gear, and we're moving. I feel his hand rest on my left leg—the one that's not wounded. The pain from my right is almost blinding, but there's also Dave squeezing my thigh, the warmth of his calloused palm. For a moment, the sensations balance. Then the pain swells again. I try to say Dave's name, but all that comes out is a moan.

"Just listen," he says. "Just keep applying pressure and listen. You're right, okay. What you said is right, Mike. I want to tell you something."

He pauses. I keep my eyes closed. It feels like the car is flying.

Then Dave starts talking. It's hard for me to follow what he's saying. His voice is fast, urgent. Something about Lauren, the woman he was with for a while. I open my eyes and see him facing forward, talking at the windshield.

"Hey," I say. It comes out quiet. I want to tell him to speak slower, that I'm not following.

He glances over. "Are you still applying pressure?"

The polo under my hand feels wet. I'm dizzy, but I nod. Dave reaches over and briefly puts his hand on top of mine again, pressing down on the wound.

"More pressure, buddy, okay?"

The back of his hand brushes my face, then he brings it up to the wheel.

It's quiet for a few moments, just road sounds, and then he starts speaking again. I hear the heaviness in his voice but catch only a few words here and there. I do note one thing he says, though. About losing heart, that he "left part of himself back there." I stick on that phrase, even as he continues on.

Every few minutes his hand comes down over mine, pressing on my leg.

Time passes. Ten minutes, half an hour. It's hard to tell.

Then the vehicle comes to an abrupt stop, and I hear the emergency brake ratchet up. Before I know it, Dave is outside, opening the passenger door. "Hey," he says, his voice suddenly loud. "Hey, we need a gurney over here." I feel his hand on the top of my head, and I open my eyes again. He's looking down at me, his face right above mine.

"This is what a boyfriend would do, right?" He smiles gently. "Bring you to the hospital? I can handle this part."

I try to smile back. I want to kiss him, to lean forward for that. But when I try, a funny thing happens. The sunlight behind Dave starts to get brighter as if it were a spotlight and someone was slowly turning up the wattage, his face becoming more and more bleached out or overexposed. I say his name—I think I do—and it occurs to me that I'm forgetting to put pressure on my leg, so I try to do that, too. And then the brightness behind him suddenly gets much brighter, and for a moment all I can see is light.

THE NEXT TIME I open my eyes, a nurse is shaking my shoulder. "Mr. Breck, stay with us. Mr. Breck." I'm in an emergency bay. An IV is in my arm. A doctor is there, a stern older woman with glasses and hair pulled tightly back. I come to clarity with a sharp jag of pain as she inspects my thigh. She's saying something about a "complicated wound," that they will be taking me up to surgery shortly. Then she instructs the nurse that I am to be prepped. While the doctor is talking, I see Dave behind her in the bay, his arms folded, face tight. When our eyes meet, his face relaxes, and he gives me a private smile.

I WAKE UP in a hospital bed. My father is sitting beside me. When I try to sit up, he puts down his magazine, asks what happened, and before I can answer, starts lecturing about safety protocols. I let him talk. What could I say? *I know all this, Dad.* Apparently, I don't.

He does take a break to pour me a glass of water and ask how I'm doing. Then he starts to fret about the "unconscionable" charges for an emergency room visit—that's his word, "unconscionable." He says it so many times that I want to find my phone, to see if it's even in the dictionary. When he pauses again, I manage to eke out, "Thank God for Obamacare." Even in my woozy state, I get a little pleasure from watching him try to swallow that.

Eventually he gets around to telling me that he's glad I'm all right. He says I've got eighteen stitches in my thigh and that they're keeping me overnight for observation.

I ask if Dave is here.

My father says it was Dave who called him. "He's working a night shift. He'll be back tomorrow. With your truck. He's going to bring you home."

AND THAT'S WHAT HAPPENS. Dave shows up in scrubs at 7:30 a.m. and sits with me for an hour until they discharge me. He helps me from my bed into a wheelchair, and then we sit in the lobby, sipping watery coffee out of paper cups. We don't say much. It's not that I'm in pain. I feel reasonably clear-headed and alert, and the throbbing in my leg is manageable. But the lobby feels too public, too exposed, for the conversation we need to have, and it doesn't seem like we can start any other conversation until we've had that one. Dave gets a kick out of wheeling me through the halls, though. As we're heading to the parking lot, he asks if I want to race, and I look up to see him grinning. That lightens the mood a little.

Then we're in my truck, crutches stowed in the bed, and we're driving. Part of me wants to start apologizing—for just showing up to work on the deck (it seems pretty embarrassing now), for spoiling Hansen's big announcement—but as I lay in the hospital bed this morning, I decided I wasn't going to. There were good reasons to do what I did. But I do want to continue yesterday's conversation where we left off. And to tell Dave that whatever part of himself he thinks he left behind can be found again. That there's still time.

He says I must be looking forward to getting home, and I make a crack about my father waiting to take care of me Kathy-Bates style, now that I can't get around so easily. Dave says my dad's not really a bad guy, and I nod. Then we're silent. I instinctively reach out to turn on the radio but bring my hand back down. If I put on music, we'll never talk. I remind myself that I already did this yesterday; I started this conversation. It's just continuing what I already started.

"Hey," I say. "What were you saying last night . . . when we were driving to Emergency? I didn't catch a lot of it. It seemed important."

Dave doesn't look over. I can see in his face that he's thinking. I wait.

"You know, it's easier to talk to a guy who's bleeding out," he finally says. He smiles but still doesn't look over.

"That's a pretty high bar for conversation. I am hopped up on oxycodone, if that helps."

He exhales. "It would help more if I could have some too."

"Just say what you said yesterday." I smile and shrug as if that will be the easiest thing in the world. "Just tell me what you already said."

Another minute or two passes before Dave speaks. But then he does. "I told you about the morning after I left your place. I said that I thought about texting you all day. . . . Most of the night, too. That I thought about the weight of you sleeping against me, how good that felt, and how I wanted to tell you that. Like it would be some kind of apology. Like I was thinking we could still hang out, that as long as you knew it wasn't going anywhere, maybe we could still do it."

I don't interrupt. I want to because it feels so good to hear him say that, to hear him confirm some of what I felt and admit that he felt something, too. But I don't.

"And then I talked about something you said when we were downtown. You suggested looking for Lauren. Do you remember that? Facebook and LinkedIn, you said. It had occurred to me before but . . . I don't know, when you said it, it clicked, how easy it would be. So I did it. Maybe I wanted to check if she was still in the world. Or to see if it really happened, if that life with her had really existed."

I reach over and put my hand on his knee. Maybe this is harder—repeating what he said without the adrenaline that charged it the first time. And then a little of the conversation comes back to me. "I remember you saying something about that. You talked about pictures."

"Yeah," Dave says. "Pictures. It took a few hours. She's got a new last name. She's a Realtor up in Spokane now. I found a picture of her in a blue pants suit, with a SOLD sign behind her. Cheesy-ass smile. Hair cut short, pink blouse open at the neck. But still her. I could see her face in the face I was looking at.

"Then I looked her up on Facebook. It wasn't tough once I had her last name. I spent hours going through her feed. All her pics. Ten years of them. Pics of Thanksgiving dinners and houses she was listing and all these cats. And lots of pictures of her husband and kids. That was the point. Lots of them. He's older. A fat guy with a goatee. A biker. Not the kind of dude I would've pictured her with." Dave chuckles.

We pull up to my house now, and he's quiet, parking the truck, taking it out of gear. I don't say anything either. But neither of us makes a move to get out.

After a moment, he goes on.

"She's got three kids. Lots of pictures of them, too, starting from when they were around ten. They look just like them. Like her and Paul. That's the biker. Grade school, high school. A pic from last May: the girl graduating from Washington State. They look just like her—and like him. The boy does. No other kids I could see. Nothing of me in her life at all, Mike. She went ahead and made herself a whole new life."

There's a thickness in Dave's voice, an edge of grief. He is bowed forward, head bent toward the steering wheel.

"All I could think was how I hadn't done that. Hadn't built any kind of life at all. Not for twenty-five years. You remember how when you used to get photographs developed, you'd get little strips of negatives in the pouch? Those kids were like the negatives of my life. What my life would look like in reverse. All the life I ended up not living.

"I lost heart. I just couldn't contact you after that. I was ashamed to contact her. I couldn't talk to anyone. It was easier to chat online and hook up and not think about it. I almost texted you, Mike. I kept almost texting you. And then it started to seem too long, like too much time had passed, and what would I even say—"

Dave takes his hand off the clutch, reaches over, and takes hold of my hand without turning to look at me. "I was ashamed. I guess that's it. I'm sorry I bailed. I don't know what I was thinking. If I was. It just felt like something I didn't know how to deal with, or couldn't deal with. I won't do it again. I don't think the worry is going to stop, but maybe it won't be so bad if I don't have to pretend I'm not feeling it. I mean, if we hang out again, if you want to do that—no promises or expectations, just to see what happens."

Dave stops talking, and he only turns to look at me when I say that yeah, I'd like that, and then he nods. That's all. Neither of us says anything after that. It feels like enough words have been said for now, and those words need a little space, like any more would only detract from them. Like the moment has taken on all the intimacy it can bear—or that he and I can bear, at least for now.

After a moment, Dave gets out of the truck, retrieves my crutches, and comes around to my side to help me down. There's dull pain as I steady myself on the gravel, but once I start moving it's not so bad. Dave walks me to the step, and my father is there, waiting at the screen door for a hand off. Then Dave calls for an Uber, refusing my father's offer to give him a ride back, and we make small talk as we wait. Dave and I don't kiss before he leaves, but we hug deep.

IN THE WEEKS that follow, Dave comes by every couple of days. He surprises me at first, just a few days later. He shows up with medical tape, surgical scissors, bacitracin, and a spool of gauze. He announces that he's come to change my bandage, that he's chomping at the bit to do it since they don't let him near blood at the hospital. He and I sit in the foyer. My father sticks his head in to greet Dave and offer us iced tea, but he leaves us alone after that. At first, Dave and I don't talk much. He unwraps my dressing, cleans the wound, and then carefully wraps it with fresh gauze. I watch, trying not to grimace as he dabs at it—but I love that he's doing it, that he's come by to do this for me. He doesn't stay long on these visits—an hour or so—but they start to feel easy and good. We chat about what he did at the hospital that day, what I plan to do for work once I'm 100% well again. Nothing momentous. On Dave's fifth visit, almost two weeks later, I ask to kiss him before he goes. While we kiss, he squeezes my hand.

We return to the Oregon District for a real date—our fourth—once I can get around comfortably again. It's a Friday night in late June. This time, we skip the coffee shop and head right to the steakhouse. And, of course, all we can talk about over dinner is the Supreme Court decision handed down that day. Obergefell v. Hodges. We keep coming back to it. How many gay guys will actually get married, whether they'll be able to swing it. How the ruling will go down in different parts of the country. And how it will go down where we live, north of Dayton. We make a lot of jokes, from gay divorce to gay divorcées, to couples getting Grindr notifications at the altar. But underneath our joking, there's something else: a kind of awe. Neither of us thought it would happen in our lifetimes.

EPILOGUE

I DON'T BELIEVE anyone can tell the future, so I won't pretend that I can.

But I can tell a future. One in which my father, Beth, Dave, and I are having Thanksgiving dinner. It's five months later, and my father is in a lather about the Republican primaries and Hillary Rodham Clinton, who he understands to be one of the Four Horsemen of the Apocalypse. When my father asks Beth what she thinks of Clinton, Beth jabs her pointer finger forward and says, "I'm with her," which only sets him off again, and Dave lets out a big laugh. And maybe after dinner, while we're eating Beth's pumpkin pie—heart-healthy, a coconut oil and whole wheat crust—my father brings up money and starts asking how I plan to work things out and then suggests that Dave should move in here, which would save money all around. Dave and I laugh it off, but now that the idea is out there, it never quite goes away. Maybe that night, Dave stays over, as he does once a week or so by then, and though I only sleep intermittently on those nights, I love them. Love seeing him there first thing in the morning, the warmth of his body, his mouth on mine, the immediate arousal of it.

Maybe for Thanksgiving the following year, my father does, finally, accompany Beth to Tucson to visit her son. Maybe I drive them to the airport, to see them off through the double doors, each rolling luggage behind them, and then come home to find Dave napping on the couch, still in his scrubs. By then he's got a house key, a set of fresh scrubs hanging in my closet, a drawer in my dresser with jeans and a few T-shirts, and his dandruff shampoo in a caddy hanging from the showerhead. And he brings it up that night in bed, that he could give up his apartment and try moving in here. His roommate is still, he notes, a dick. "It's a good idea for purely financial reasons," I say, his head on my chest, my hand on his shoulder. He repeats the phrase back to me, "purely financial reasons," before we both fall asleep—which is something I can do more easily now, with him here. In fact, I often sleep better with his body beside me. The solidity of it. And the next morning, he picks up the conversation upon opening his eyes, as if it hadn't been interrupted by hours of sleep, telling me that it really would be good to get out of his current place. As we're fumbling around, readying an apple pie for the oven—to bring to Matt's holiday pot luck, where he will be debuting, so he says, a new boyfriend—Dave and I agree to a probationary period of three months, after which we'll assess how it's going. It's an idea we never revisit. Three months turns into a year, then into years.

And maybe those years aren't easy. And not always great. When my father has a much more serious heart attack and comes home from the hospital, suddenly a very old man. The year I spend bagging groceries at Kroger, feeling embarrassed to be an adult man doing it, until I get a new job running a tutoring lab at my school, the forty-hours-a-week I'd spent my life avoiding. And find that it's not so bad. When an x-ray shows a tumor in Dave's chest, large, the size of a ham sandwich, and specialist appointments become the focus of our lives—not to mention the months of chemo. And maybe just talking isn't always easy, either. Sharing vulnerabilities, insecurities. Trying to be open. But there are lots of good times, too, like when the oncologist puts a hand on Dave's shoulder and tells him that they'll stay vigilant, but that he's going to be okay. And how we celebrate by taking a drive—a long drive from western Ohio out into the Great Plains and north to see the Badlands.

But beyond the question of good or bad times is the feeling of being connected, of being anchored, that fullness, the sense of belonging to another person, and, in that belonging, feeling affixed to the world. For example: to sit next to someone at Thanksgiving—six years on, now—with the family of Eileen, Hansen's wife, most of them half-pretending that Dave and I are not gay. Even without speaking, I feel Dave beside me, eating too much, and admire his ease and warmth, his ability to shrug it off. To know that, on the car ride home, he and I will laugh about all the stupid shit Eileen's brother said, cheerleading for some right-wing radio host, and the way her mother kept referring to me as "David's friend," her tone putting the phrase in scare quotes.

And not long after that: just a form, a ritual, but one with undeniable power. Dave and I standing side-by-side in front of a local judge to make our declaration of intent.

Maybe a person has to be alone for a long time to feel the specialness of that kind of anchor, the gentle remarkableness of it, of not driving home alone, of having someone in your bedroom as you undress for bed, of being comfortable enough to fall asleep easily against another body. And never questioning that that person will be in the house in the morning—possibly in the kitchen feeding the dog and the cat, both three-legged, that he brought home one day from a shelter. No announcement, no preparation, just the initial tumult of them both loosed in the house, all the hissing and scrambling.

Probably, that person will be putting on a pot of coffee, too, for you.

Maybe, if you've been alone for a long time, being connected in that way supersedes the idea of good and bad years, happy or unhappy ones, creating an embeddedness that you never really take for granted, that can feel, perennially, a little astonishing.

Even starting in your fifties, if everything goes right, you can get twenty years of it. If things go really well, you can get thirty.

ACKNOWLEDGMENTS

I'M DEEPLY GRATEFUL to friends who lent their support: Bruce Cohen, Steve Green, Lukas Lesnewski, Clare Rossini, Paul Simmons, Steven R. Young, and especially Julien Strong, who provided invaluable encouragement and insight. Thanks also to the University of Hartford for the release time that made this book possible, to Wally Lamb for his generous words, and to Courtney Ochsner and the rest of the folks at the University of Nebraska Press. My biggest thanks to Percival Everett, who made this daydream a reality. And lastly, a hat tip to the late Toni Morrison for words that spurred me forward: *If there's a book that you want to read, but it hasn't been written yet, then you must write it.*

JAMES ALAN MCPHERSON PRIZE FOR THE NOVEL

2022 Parul Kapur, *Inside the Mirror: A Novel*
2023 Ben Grossberg, *The Spring before Obergefell: A Novel*

Printed in the USA
CPSIA information can be obtained
at www.ICGtesting.com
CBHW020043120824
12933CB00006B/8